To the ama[zing...] Dreams come true.

The Gentleman Tramp

Toby Glover

T. Glover

Illustrations by Amy Koch Johnson

Future Classics

FUTURE CLASSICS
The Gentleman Tramp
Toby Glover

Published in the United Kingdom by Future Classics.

Copyright © 2014 by Toby Glover
All Rights Reserved

All rights reserved. This book was published by Toby Glover under Future Classics. No part of this book may be reproduced in any form, by any means, without express permission of the author. This includes reprints, excerpts, photocopying, recording, or any future means of reproducing text.
The right of Toby Glover to be identified as the author of this work has been asserted by him in accordance with the Copyright, Designs and Patents Act 1988.
Published in the United Kingdom by Future Classics.

This is a work of fiction. Names, characters, places and incidents either are products of the author's imagination or are used fictitiously. Any resemblance to actual events or locales or persons, living or dead, is entirely coincidental.

To Dad.

To those of you who dare to dream.

And to Charlie Chaplin.

I dedicate this book.

Enjoy.

Part One
1. A Dog's Life
2. A Spot of Bother
3. My Psychologist
4. The Talkies
5. Bewitched
6. The Great Escape
7. The Himalayas of Nepal
8. The Big Fight
9. Welcome to The Jungle
10. Party, Party, Party
11. Magic Mushroom Milkshake
12. Awakening
13. The Witch Doctor
14. Rio de Janeiro
15. The Gentleman Tramp
16. Scraps
17. The Police

Part Two
1. Hospital
2. The Search for a Happy Ending
3. New York City
4. Life of Luxury
5. The Damsel in Distress
6. The Gold Rush
7. Romance and Adventure
8. Home Sweet Home

Part One

'A real gentleman, even if he loses everything he owns, must show no emotion. Money must be so far beneath a gentleman that it is hardly worth troubling about.'
Fyodor Dostoevsky

A Dog's Life

Don't you just hate it when people decide to have a carnival on the street where you're trying to sleep?

I do, I really do.

I'd learnt to always have some food with me for when my ravenous hunger peaked and I could no longer entertain any other thought than the deliciousness of food. So, when I awoke from a brief spell of shut-eye one night, holding my belly and suffering from a nasty, nightmare-induced sweat, I was extremely grateful that I'd left treats in my bag. A few slices of chicken, half a bag of potato crisps, half a bar of chocolate and a fizzy drink was just what I fancied – fortunately that's just what I had. However, as I began digging through my belongings with sticky eyes and a fuzzy head, blindly feeling for my late-night supper, my heart began to pump harder and my muscles tightened in a panicked hunger. I quickly got a feel for the can of drink, but where was the food? It didn't take long to get my answer.

A few feet from where my head had been, I saw Scraps licking his lips, the empty chocolate and crisps packs by his feet.

'You greedy, selfish son-of-a-bitch,' I said – low blow indeed, but I was furious.

'Woof,' he said.

'Don't you woof at me you utter bastard. That was my food, you just went into my bag, my private bag, and took my supper.'

'Woof.'

'Don't talk to me like that.' I stood up to shoo him away. 'Leave me alone you vile beast.'

'Woof, woof, woof,' said Scraps as he got up and started to leave. He growled as well – can you believe the cheek of him? He actually growled.

I'd been on the streets for several weeks and had been sleeping at the same spot for a couple of very pleasant nights, but I was not anticipating that this quiet little part of the Cantagalo favela was to be over run by the Rio carnival.

At first I just heard a few murmurs as I lay down to rest, but then it got louder and closer as a small group gathered nearby to drink beer, talk and giggle. As more people arrived on the scene, I realised they weren't just drinking beer but selling it and my private sleeping quarters had become most chaotic and unpleasant. Blocking my ears, rolling over to face the other way and sighing loudly, were all ineffective as I tried to ignore the merriment and doze off into sweet dreams. Relaxation became even more challenging when music began to blast into my head, and the gathering started to get closer. My next plan was to inch slowly away from the party. Shuffling further and further with quick small movements while dragging my belongings seemed to be working, until I ended up with my face pressed against a cold wall. Some moments later, I rolled over to see that I'd been followed and the party was now right in my face.

The real encroachment of my territory came from a tall, drunk male in a red football shirt who nudged me with the back of his foot as he danced around, singing!

*'Gosto de cantar e dançar, pois é festa no Brasil
há cerveja e mulheres com lindo bumbum.'*

He was moving with great glee as women giggled, clapping to his moves. I peaked out from my pillow (my neatly folded shorts and shirt) to see his dirty toes in a pair of cheap sandals: surrounding this were prettier feet with colourful nails, all moving to a very wonderful rhythm.

'*Gosto de dançar com você,*' said one of the women.

'*Você deve dançar com ele,*' said the man.

The laughter that followed was maybe at my expense, and there was some pushing and shoving going on amongst these people.

The minutes had ticked by to a full hour and the party was now in full swing, there were people everywhere. I really didn't like the idea of attracting the attention that I would undoubtedly get by getting up and leaving. To top off my discomfort, they were beginning to set off fireworks nearby. It sounded like gunshots and made me twitch like a cornered badger.

Bang, flash, wallop, kaboom they went, followed by everyone's cheers. Surely nobody could believe I was actually asleep, and yet I was too terrified to move, or even open my eyes all the way.

Eventually, I overcame my fear, encouraged into life by the cold beer being poured on my face by the Brazilian entertainer. I reached down to my battered, filthy tramp shoes and put them on before tying the raggedy laces.

'Wow a free beer,' I said. 'How very kind of you.'

I put on my coat and hat, grabbed my things, straightened my back and prepared to leave. The party was wild, but everyone moved back as I stood up and there was a pause in the music and a gasp from the crowd, as if I had arisen from the dead.

'*Dançar com ele,*' said the man to the women around him. He wanted one of them to dance with me.

There was a long pause before I sprang to life singing, '*Gostoso ma dancar es muito muito bonita,*' in a bad imitation of the showman who had woken me. One of the women grabbed me and did me the honour of the most wonderful dance. I tried to pretend it wasn't for the amusement of her friends as I smiled and we looked into each other's eyes. I moved my feet to a comfortable position, she moved her hips closer to me and shook her round bottom, bending her knees and jiggling her boobs, which were trying to struggle their way out of her sequined, blue top. She was a charming girl, a great dancer. I was mesmerised. She put her arms around my neck for another shake of her body, and I was lost in her magic as she spun around to show me her wiggling bum from another angle – it was just as fantastic.

When it was over, the man took her hand and she gave me a farewell wave before leaving me, to dance with him. He didn't look such an accomplished dancer as me, I'm a great dancer – I really am. He spun her around and she Samba'd before giving him a kiss. I was jealous, but relieved that everyone looked happy as it gave me the chance to depart safely.

'*Obrigado,*' I said to these people before shaking hands with them and moving off down the street, momentarily abandoning my customary Chaplin walk in favour of a pathetic attempt at Samba. Don't you just hate parties when you don't feel a part of them? I do, I really do! The revelry continued, as did the terrifying fireworks.

Why was I so miserable in a place where so much fun was being had? I felt like the ultimate outsider, a good-for-nothing. Searching my pockets, I had enough money for breakfast and lunch tomorrow. I considered trading this for three beers now, so I could join in the fun of the city. Yet beer was just not possible; it was a luxury I could not afford. I would need food tomorrow and, because of Scraps, I was already starving.

I was suddenly struck by an idea of genius. I was living close to one of the best beaches on the planet, on which I spent most of my days, so why not spend the night there as well. Not just near the beach but on the beach itself. It would be marvellous to end this horrible evening with the pleasant sound of waves crashing, and that wonderful smell of the sea, while I lay in a bed of sand.

Carnival was marching through the city and the colour and noise was breathtaking. Men in pure white suits led a procession of green peacock Oompa Loompa looking people who all moved in unison as a single organism. Fireworks lit up the sky as if it were the end of the world, and confetti rained down on me and the other bystanders. The beating of the drums, the sights of the sexy samba and the huge floats made me run up for a closer look and sway my body to the rhythm. I picked up a Brazilian flag from the floor and began waving it with great enthusiasm.

I've never been impressed by modern celebrities too much, but I really wanted to get closer to these carnival performers. One lady in particular was the queen bee on a gigantic float that also carried dancers and sadistically grinning animatronics. She was swaying from side to side in rhythm with the drums on a platform ten metres above the other dancers. She seemed to lead the dance, and I was imitating her movements from my lowly position in the crowd. Her long dress flapped and shook with reds and blues. Her eyes and smile radiated a pure joy of which I have yet to experience. I could see how she would make a good celebrity, mysterious as she was. I was definitely a fan.

Following this float came all the vivid colour of the Amazon rainforest. Colours I just don't normally see, the noise, the costumes and the dancing told a story of sexual competition, community and love. The spectators were as much a part of the show as the floats, and the festival of flamboyance was a relentless party of energy and self-expression. I was awaiting a crescendo, but it just went on and on.

What a night of rattling great fun. I chose to leave early as it was way past bedtime and I wanted to get my sleep. Bad things happen when you don't get your sleep. That's what I've always thought anyway. Sleep is very important to a young man, so I battled my way through this procession of loudness and joy. By the time I got away from it all and walked across the vast street that led me to the ocean, I was a very relieved gentleman I can tell you. There is only so much the senses can take before it's time for a sit down.

I prepared my bed with great diligence, sleeping outside is no excuse for not having a comfy bed. I unrolled the blanket that I borrowed from a hostel, and laid it out in a tight rectangular fashion with no creases. I'm not a fan of creases. Then I took out one pair of shorts and a shirt that folded carefully to make a pillow. I wedged my other belongings between me and a nearby wall. It's always good to do this, as there are thieves in the city that can cause you problems. I took off my hat, coat and shoes and unbuttoned the top of my shirt. I sat down and pulled my jacket up to my chest and dipped my toes into my shoes in case I should need to make a hasty retreat. Normally I would then lay down and sleep if I could, but on this particular night I decided to open a present I was given a few weeks before. I'd been waiting for an appropriate moment and this seemed like a nice time. Tearing the packaging apart, I found a box with a stuffed penguin in it. 'How very thoughtful and odd,' I thought before lying down and letting the refreshing sea breeze wash over me as I drifted off into a moments sleep.

Then those goddam Samba drums turned up on the beach.
'Son-of-a-bitch, bloody bastard,' I thought. 'Is there no peace for the wicked?'

A Spot of Bother

Delicious treats were all I could think about as I yawned and stretched, rubbing my eyes to catch a glance at the new day and trying to find enough saliva to swallow.

I awoke to the faint glow of sunrise, and I sat bolt upright as I realised that I was not alone. There were a wide variety of dogs sleeping across the beach. One of them, a wretched mutt, was sleeping right next to me. It was Scraps. He had a terrible knack of finding me. I never understood how he knew where I'd be but, in truth, I was usually terribly glad to see him. Today, however, I was still fuming about our argument. I could see a man rooting through the beach bins searching for any food he could find.

'I would like to treat this gentleman to a slap up meal,' I thought to myself. 'But not today, I only have enough money for myself.'

I got up and gathered my possessions. The dog sniffed, he looked and he listened as I fumbled around desperate to get my breakfast money. I would describe Scraps as extremely reliable in most instances, but also one of those chaps that you can't trust when food is involved. You know the type I'm sure. You want to trust them, you really do, but you also know full well that the will of their stomach is very capable of overcoming their sense of decency. He turned around to bark at one of the other dogs, which was wandering over.

Back on concrete, I was in the mood for further alone time and private meditation. However, Scraps was following me, so I tried to shoo him away. Perhaps the pesky dog thought I had more food for him to steal. I wished! Or maybe he was just lonely. No, he was definitely after food – the bugger.

I tried to push him away, feeling he did not deserve anymore of my kindness and that I needed to stop with the niceties. I gave him another shove with my leg and he grabbed a hold of my trouser with his teeth. I was in public now and I didn't want to make a scene, but that bloody Scraps wouldn't let go, so I had to drag him along with me. I eventually put a stop to this nonsense with my sternest look, to which he replied with his dopiest expression. I wanted to shout at him to leave me alone, but there were enough people around to have made a full-blown argument between man and dog most embarrassing.

I relaxed when I got to the café. Scraps was not allowed in; that would teach him to steal my supper. I was greeted by the loveliest of waitresses. A magnificent example of feminine wonder and beauty was she. Her face was warm and endearing, her smile glistened and her eyes twinkled. She reminded me a little of Mariana – but nobody is that beautiful.
'Ola, tu du bem?' she said.
I simply smiled and pointed at the things I wanted on the menu. The first thing to arrive was the juice, which I drank down fast. I was seriously dehydrated, so next I moved onto the coffee. Then the food arrived – fresh fruits, breads, bacon and egg. My appetite was no longer as strong as my thirst, and I was busy trying to impress the waitress with my best smile ever. Over the wall that separated the cafe from the street, I saw Scraps giving me sad, pathetic eyes and making a low-pitched sob. When nobody was looking, I threw him some of the salad that garnished the plate. He looked down at the salad and then at me. After a few moments, I couldn't take his pleading eyes anymore and I tossed him some bacon, which he wolfed down. This was a mistake and was probably the reason Scraps kept finding me all these weeks. I forced down the rest of my breakfast. I would need the strength. The bill left me with nothing but coins.

Soon after, I passed an internet café and could not resist going in. This meant I would have to sacrifice my dreams of a fast-food burger lunch in favour of the cheaper Brazilian rice and beans in order to pay for this opportunity to catch up on my correspondence. I opened my social media page to see no new messages. At the top of the page was a picture of my brother, Bruce, with an elderly couple amidst the Himalayan landscape. Bruce was making a fortune leading tourists on adventure holidays. He had started this in Papua New Guinea, after contacts in the army recommended him to a retired Colonel. The word spread that he was great at it, and now he was working for several families that were keen to see more of the world. There is no way Bruce's adventures are as exciting as mine though. Just no way!

When we were kids, Bruce liked to sleep out in a tent in the garden. I joined him a couple of times, but hated it. It was too cold and wet for me. Not my kind of adventure, thank you very much. Bruce would go on long bicycle rides in the great city of London (anyone can do that). He would practise sports in the garden, he played a lot of sports, both team and individual, and would come home with cups and trophies (I suppose that must have felt nice). He was six years older than me and always seemed to want to take care of me. He often tried to teach me things anyway, but he took great pleasure in my embarrassing failures, did old Bruce, the swine. Like when I first joined him on a bicycle ride and I fell in a wet ditch and stood up covered in mud. Or when he taught me to catch a rugby ball, and I missed his javelin-like spinning throw and it hit me in the gentleman's region and crippled me to the floor. My brother's raucous laugh echoed for miles. I never laughed much at all, apart from a stifled chuckle when thinking about what good old Charlie Chaplin had been up to in his movies.

I wasn't really interested in Bruce's picture, because underneath was a picture of my great love, Mariana. She was right here in Rio, so close. But in this picture she was holding hands with her boyfriend. They looked so happy. I logged off immediately and walked off feeling upset and sickened.
'Seis reais,' said the internet girl.
'Oh, Desculpa,' I fumbled in my pockets and all my change fell on the floor. Growing red, I had to get on my hands and knees to pick it up. I put the six on her desk, grabbed the rest and walked out barging through the door and off into the street with sweat dripping down my face and horrible images in my head.

I hadn't talked for an awful long time before I met Mariana, back when I was a troubled teen in London. All a bit strange I gather, but I sort of became a mute for a while. As soon as I saw Mariana I wanted to talk, she was one of those people that you just want to talk too. Actually, I wanted to listen to her more than anything else. She was kind of mysterious I thought, and I wanted to know if she was the same as everybody else. I always got the impression she knew things. Things I can't even imagine with my little brain. I often wonder what she knows that I don't.

What's next in the day of The Gentleman Tramp, after a hearty breakfast? A good old scrub and wash of course. I returned to the beach where there were showers and began to strip off for a clean. Scraps had, of course, followed me.

It was day on Rio de Janeiro's world famous Ipanema beach. It's the home of the sexiest people on earth, you know. No other nation can pull off speedos and thong bikinis. It had been the main location for my funny business for some time. Tourists are fairly generous to my Chaplin routines, but it is the locals who are more amused and willing to help me out with a little spare change. I guess, to them, I am totally different, a freak, a wonderful distraction from the intense boredom that life can be.

In my vagrancy I took for granted how amazing it was to be there among so much vitality, but that day I decided joining the lovely locals for a brisk swim in that inviting water would be most pleasant.

A morning swim, the romance of it was fantastic. The water froze my foot, but how refreshing. Bruce would be so jealous of this.

I approached the ocean relieved to see Scraps had his uses; he was sitting by my belongings and guarding them. Now I could really enjoy myself. The soapy backwash slapped my legs with icy venom before receding and pulling me deeper into its embrace as my toes squelched into the wet sand.

The water was building up for a big crash, and this time it reached my waist and pushed me onto the beach before sucking me back in. I took my opportunity to venture deeper as the sea retreated, so I lifted my knees high and bounded further and further forwards. I was still gallivanting on when a wave slapped me across the face and chest so hard that I was knocked down. I felt utterly invigorated and although my face hurt it still wore a giant smile. I got up again and ran even deeper in excited anticipation of my next battle with this salty foe. My body had adjusted to the temperature, so I plunged down into the murky depths and resurfaced to a forceful surge of water that I surfed into shore. Terrific fun! Beyond the mighty swells it looked serene and peaceful, so I threw myself forward battling past the waves to the calm still waters.

'Incredible,' I thought to myself, soldiering on. I had noticed several signs warning about the dangerous current, but I thought it would be just fine as soon as I got past where these waves were breaking – and, of course, these warnings were for ordinary members of the public. It would be OK for The Gentleman Tramp.

I fought my way past several waves that cast an impending shadow over me, like a blue whale falling from a skyscraper, until eventually it calmed and I could float. No more massive waves breaking. So I lay back, relaxed and enjoyed the soothing, nurturing ocean that surrounded me.

'Fantastic, what could be better?' I said in my best Bruce voice.

When I turned around, Scraps was nowhere to be seen and nor were my belongings.

'That double crossing mutt has stolen my things,' I thought. 'Bloody hell, I will have to go back.' It really looked a long way and the rough sea was breaking hard again. I was submerged by a couple of waves, but it was OK because they were taking me closer to shore, I thought!

I began swimming harder until I was picked up by an almighty wave that spun me around 540 degrees before dumping me unceremoniously on my head. The thud of skull on sand was deafening, the pain billowed through my entire being. Quite the bang on the noggin, I can tell you.

Aware that another mighty crack on the cranium would be most troublesome, I was very careful to land on my feet when the next huge rush sent me twisting and turning. Submerged, I struggled for air but inhaled sea. When I did get air, it was with a splutter and a cough. I began swimming for my life, but would you believe it, another wave soon arrived.

Crash! I spun and flew along the ocean. The under current was so powerful that it tugged at my swimwear and before I knew what was happening my trunks had been yanked down to my knees. I managed to catch them and pull them up. For a person such as my self, emerging naked from the water, clenching things, is even worse than drowning. I waited patiently to resurface, but I could see I wasn't getting any closer to land, so a fierce and resolute determination to get back as soon as possible overcame me. Digging in and flailing my arms frantically towards the far-off beach, I was furious that the waves were giving me such a dam good thrashing.
'Come on, keep swimming,' I pleaded to myself.
Reaching down with my toes, I felt no sand. Exhaustion began to kick in and I wondered how long I could continue this exertion. My body was reaching its limits and so was my mind. 'Please get me out of this mess,' I begged the universe.

As I resurfaced from another smashing there was some hope – two other swimmers not far away. They didn't seem to be struggling, so maybe I was getting close to safety. I scraped the floor with my big toe before being battered by another big wave and losing that feeling of ground. These two men were closer. I must be getting nearer.
'Are you a gringo?'
'Yes,' I replied.
I swam away from them, but they waved and shouted to follow. It dawned on me that they were lifeguards and within thirty seconds we were back in the shallow water and I could stand – all a big fuss over nothing, but the stars were aligning to ruin my day.
'Thank you, thanks so much,' I said shaking their hands ferociously.
'No problem,' they replied.

On land I was unexpectedly greeted by an excited Scraps, who was barking enthusiastically. I didn't really care that he didn't have my things, collapsing fully in the sand for about fifteen minutes was more important.

Eventually, I mustered the desire to start dragging myself along Ipanema beach searching for my clothes. Hoping we were heading in the right direction, I followed Scraps like a disciple. I trusted in his superior sense of smell and direction. My vision was blurry and I felt like I might vomit as the dog quickened his pace.

'He's found it,' I said out loud.

Then I saw why Scraps was running. He hadn't found my things. He was running towards a large stall on the top of the beach that was selling hotdogs. He looked back at me with pleading eyes. My gentleman act completely fell apart.

'Oh, just fuck off!' I shouted turning my back in fury and walking the other way. I clutched my head and continued my search.

I came across a water fountain and I drunk greedily, then ran my head under the spout, before walking to the other end of the beach in total desperation.

'Please, sorry to bother you, have you seen a black bag and a suit?' I asked a respectable looking couple. They did not speak English.

Now that I had broken my silence, it became easier to ask. I find that a lot. I can be so shy, but once I've spoken to one person, suddenly it's easy. I had that when I finally spoke to Mariana, suddenly I could speak to lots of people.

One woman understood me and had a long think before looking around and asking another guy in Portuguese. He thought hard and then asked a young guy. This continued until there was quite a crowd. The attention was soothing. Another woman joined the crowd and asked me exactly what had happened.

She recounted my words back to the crowd, and I noticed the universal noises of sympathy. This cascade of care eased my tense mind and limbs. The adrenaline was dispersing from my aching tired body, but with this relaxation came a bigger problem. I have epilepsy you see. Actually, I often forget I have it, but then I'll be reminded of it at the worst possible time.

My first fit was on an awful grey, thundery and muggy Wednesday back at school, in a maths class, when some kids were throwing things at my head and calling me names. I was so angry that my brain over-fired and my nervous disposition electrified to cause what would be the first of these epileptic fits. The feeling was horrible and my mind became a vile place. I used it as an excuse to take days off from school, where I could just study Chaplin and read – so it wasn't all bad.

To have this happen now, on the beach, was dreadful. Everything became very surreal; my hearing went, I tried to speak but nothing came out. I crashed hard to the floor in violent spasms.

I don't know how long I was unconscious, but I remember drifting out of my body, floating up and seeing a pathetic wretch convulsing on the floor. When I awoke, I tried to stand, but had no strength. The paramedics were urging me not to move.
'*Fique onde está,*' said the man.
'Where am I? What day is it?' I replied.
A huge crowd had gathered and there was cheering and clapping. At the front of the crowd was Scraps, sitting patiently so as not to annoy anyone and be chased off. Nobody was answering my question.
'Him, that dog,' I said pointing at Scraps 'he's my friend.' I tried to pat his head. 'What day is it?'
They attached an oxygen mask to my face. 'Ah get off me,' I protested. They issued reassuring statements that reminded me I was not a dying animal, and I was taken in an ambulance to hospital where I was put in a bed. A real bed! My first real bed in weeks! Luxury!

'What are you doing here in Rio de Janeiro?' asked a pleasant looking doctor with a smart side parting and black-rimmed spectacles. I knew he was a doctor because of the white coat, stethoscope and clipboard. Also he introduced himself as Dr Santos, but I was in a big blur.

'Searching for romance and adventure,' I replied.

'Your passport has been found with your bag, we also found your suit, hat and furry toy penguin,' the doctor said, reading from his chart and tapping it with a pen.

'I don't think the penguin is mine.' I had enough problems to worry about without becoming the thief of a child's toy penguin.

'It's not a problem,' continued the doctor. 'Why were you wearing these clothes? The temperature is 37 degrees in Rio today,' he asked.

'It's just what I wear.'

It's really because I like to dress like my hero.

'Where are you staying?'

Scratching my head, trying to find the answer to every question – the answers were buried somewhere. I really thought hard and long before telling him, 'I can't remember, sorry.'

'Do you have any travel insurance?' he asked.

I could not remember this either. 'I think maybe I live here, maybe I do, yes!'

'Get some rest, I will come back later,' he said patting me on the arm.

As he departed, a middle-aged nurse came into the room and started to take my pulse and heart rate. She also gave me some cold water to sip.

'*Tu du bem?*' she asked.

'Yes,' I replied.

I didn't really understand anything else she said. I said yes a lot. As she lent over me to fluff my pillows I, embarrassingly, started to get a twitchy erection. Why do these things always happen to me at the worst time? It's most un-gentlemanly. My brain had suffered considerable trauma and my body was exhausted and aching, but apparently my penis had no idea. She wrote some things on another chart and I said, '*Obrigado,*' as she filled up my water before leaving.

I am alone in my hospital bedroom now, trying to piece together how I ended up like this.

I am The Gentleman Tramp. Or, at least, I think I am. This is my story. Or, at least, I think it is.

My Psychologist

I came to be living on the streets like my hero Charlie Chaplin's comedy character, The Gentleman Tramp, because I love Charlie Chaplin, he's so funny. There was that wonderful film where he falls in love with a blind girl and she thought he was a rich guy? *City Lights* it's called. I love that one the best. He has to be a boxer in one bit and he keeps hiding behind the referee, so funny.

When I was at school, my parents used to worry that I loved Charlie Chaplin too much. Maybe it was because I stopped talking to everyone. There was this psychologist I had to go and see, he was a funny old chap. Anyway, he seemed to have some ideas about why I loved The Little Tramp so much. I think I liked him because he was so funny, but this psychologist guy got very deep about it. People like to get deep about things. They never think anything can just be simple.

I've always wanted to be a gentleman. It can be hard though, it really can. Sometimes, I've not been a gentleman at all. Sometimes I'm kind of an idiot. I don't like to admit that, but it's the truth. 'We can only do our best,' is what my dad says. I don't want to talk about parents though, except to say that mine are very nice indeed. They do their best, and I think too many people blame their parents for their own shortcomings. 'My parents did this' or 'my parents said that', people say.

I think we need to take responsibility for ourselves, because parents have parents too and their parents have parents. If we blamed them for everything, where would it all end?
'I can't control my temper because my ancestor, living back in the caves, was a bit of a tyrant when it came to dinnertime. He wouldn't let anyone have any woolly mammoth until he was full, the scoundrel. It's left me with a lot of resentment,' is what some of these awful people would say, if they got the chance.

I really don't think a gentleman would embarrass his parents by discussing them, but I will say that they worried about me a lot. I didn't really like that, so I tried not to tell them things that would make them worry. The problem was that most things I would've had to say would have made them worry, so I kind of stopped talking altogether. This worried them. You can't win, you really can't.

When I got home on my fifteenth birthday, they told me that I wasn't getting a normal present that year, instead they were paying for me to have someone to talk too.
Three days later, I had my first meeting with Dr Jove, the psychologist.
'Hey there buddy, great to meet you. Why don't you take a seat? It's a great sofa, really good for chilling. We're just going to chill out in these sessions, like a couple of cool guys,' said Dr Jove, when I first went into his sterile office.

I would have preferred to have stood to attention, or sat on a hard plastic chair, like the ones they had at school. It was eerily quiet in that office, and I felt like I was entering a dark world as he greeted me and went to shake my hand. As had become my custom, I shook his hand warmly, offering the Chaplin smile that I had by now perfected, but I could not say hello. He asked me some questions about my date of birth, address and full name. When I wouldn't answer, he gave me the form to fill out myself.

Dr Jove gave me the creeps; I didn't like the way his beady eyes peered over his low hung glasses. His voice was soft and deep, but seemed totally unnatural. It was also strange how, after we sat down, his voice shifted from this groovy, hippy type of voice to a softer and deeper resonating hypnotic drone. They both seemed like a performance.

Dr Jove talked about what we would be doing and the aims of these sessions, I sat and smiled. It appeared he wanted me to be doing most of the talking. 'No way,' I thought as I smiled and nodded and tipped my Derbyshire hat. I wasn't emotionally against the idea of talking, but I hadn't spoken more than a few words in years.

We would sit for those hour-long sessions, with me being there in body but not in mind. I nervously smiled and nodded at the questions that would be rephrased in different ways.

'When did you stop talking?'

'How does blah blah blah make you feel?'

'What is it about this Charlie Chaplin character that you feel so connected too?'

'Are you taking any kind of drugs?'

I always answered with an innocent shrug of the shoulders and a smile, although I did shake my head about the drugs. I know I was only a boy, but I still think old Jove was a bit of a cheeky so and so with some of those questions. I mean it's just not polite is it?

Of course I was not capable of telling him this. I had gone too deeply into my mind at that point in my life, and this strange man was the last person I wanted to talk too. However, I did make some noises. I had an embarrassing problem in these sessions. The dusty silence and awkwardness, mixed with the time of day, made my belly rumble terribly from hunger. It was impossible to stop these gurgles and groans once they'd started, and when Dr Jove would run out of questions my loud stomach would echo throughout the room. It seemed to happen every week, and I would dread it. With the first rumbles I would curse myself and think 'not again'. He took to getting me a glass of water, but this never helped. I needed food and he always had biscuits on his desk and never offered me one. On a couple of terrible occasions his stomach started rumbling too and our guts made a distasteful symphony for the full hour. I was so relieved by the end of the sessions that I would practically run out.

After a few weeks of smarmy politeness and caring, Dr Jove seemed to be getting frustrated by my lack of co-operation. 'Come on, answer the question,' he said one day while I sat smiling, with lovely manners. I shrugged after a few seconds.

'Your mother and father are paying good money. Don't you think you should talk? Why can't you talk? Why won't you talk? What's the matter with you?' His face looked red and sweaty.

'Most un-gentlemanly,' I thought. How the devil did this man become a doctor? Surely this kind of doctoring should not be compared to real doctors. You know those ladies and gentleman who stop people dying.

He must have told my parents that I was not co-operating, for they asked me most kindly to please answer his questions.

'Well if you really can't talk, at least write down the answers to the questions, to give to him. Can you do that for me?' asked my mother.

Of course I would do that. I was well aware that a gentleman always follows the requests of his parents. I wouldn't have gone to these sessions at all if I didn't believe that. So I eased the minds of my parents by communicating this using body language and facial expressions.

During my daydream escapes from school and reality, I studied the facial expressions and non-verbal performance of Charlie Chaplin so much that I began using them to replace my communications. Instead of talking to people, I would respond with Chaplin's free and sweet smile, or a nod of the head or a body gesture. I thought I was very good at doing this. However, it quickly began to irritate people, especially my family. They finally lost their patience with me when they asked me what I wanted for dinner and I wrote down on a piece of card, with a magic marker

I will be very happy to receive whatever you can give me

I could see why they were upset; it must have seemed quite rude. I said sorry.

Although I never did this again with my parents, I began carrying card around with me everywhere, to write on with a big black pen. This was my plan so I wouldn't have to talk. I got in trouble for doing this at school, and of course the other kids made fun, but it didn't stop me. I pictured the cards as being like subtitles in the movie of my life. However, I only wanted to do this when absolutely necessary, as I was intent on being able to communicate non-verbally, like Chaplin.

So the next week, I turned up at Dr Jove's office armed with my subtitles. The normal introductions were done and he sat down looking resigned to another week of monotony. His plate of biscuits sat just out of my reach as usual.

'Did anything interesting happen to you this week?' he asked.

I pulled out my pen and started writing. I noticed him sit up straight and pay greater attention.

I turned the card over to reveal.

Not really

'Can you tell me anything that has happened this week?' he asked looking excited that some sort of communication was taking place.

I again started writing.

I watched *Modern Times* again.

Pretty much since starting school, or at least by the age of nine or ten, I'd have this routine – I would get home from school and go straight to my room, where I'd lose myself through books and movies. I would take great delight in recording things from the television or renting movies. One night, I had recorded an action movie starring Bruce Willis and was watching it back. The tape had continued to record after the movie ended, so I looked to see what else was on the cassette, I came across a film called *Modern Times*. The credits rolled at the start.

Modern Times **starring Charlie Chaplin**
Modern Times **written by Charlie Chaplin**
Modern Times **directed by Charlie Chaplin**
Modern Times **produced by Charlie Chaplin**
Modern Times **music composed by Charlie Chaplin**

I couldn't believe he'd done all this. Nowadays the credits go on for about ten minutes, with hundreds of names. Later I found out that he only hired actors that could mimic him perfectly. As the film started, I realised I was watching Charlie Chaplin's mind unfold. Enthralled by his art I watched the movie about three more times that week.

They were showing another one of his movies, *The Circus,* later in the week, late at night, so I set my recorder. I ran home from school the next day excited to watch it, and I absolutely loved it.

What a great man, a homeless tramp who behaves like a gentleman even in the most undignified circumstances.

This reminds me of my own constant attempts to be dignified. Like when I was five or six at this summer birthday party, where I met a lot of new kids, everyone was swimming in a large, inflatable swimming pool. I accidentally exploded stomach rubble out of my bottom while sitting in this pool. I quickly grabbed hold of the humiliating evidence before running out and tossing it into a nearby bush, then rushing to the toilet. I was accompanied all the way by the sounds of disgust and laughter from the other kids. Children appear so wonderful, innocent and free, when you're an adult, but when you're one of them they can be cruel little bastards. I spent the rest of the day hiding behind a sofa.

'Come on, let me help you dear, it's nothing to worry about,' said somebody's mother.

'Thank you,' I said, but I didn't move. I think she went to put a hand on my back and I brushed it away.

She went away, but seemed to come back every now and then. One of the kids came to see me too.

'Are you OK?' she asked.

'Yes, thank you,' I replied. What a sweet girl she was. I don't even remember her name. I think females must have a higher tolerance for these awful things in life. They are always the first to respond to bad things.

Eventually, I was picked up by Mum, who apologised to the other adults as I ran out the door, barging my way past people in desperation to be somewhere else. The shame of this lasted a very long time. It was not gentlemanly behaviour. So I learnt from this that going out and socialising with other children was a mistake. 'Yes,' I had thought, 'home is good, out is bad.'

I was fascinated with this Chaplin character, so every night I watched *The Circus* and *Modern Times* until the next week, when I saw *City Lights*. Everyone must see it, they really must. It's Albert Einstein and Winston Churchill's favourite movie, not just mine. I stood in my bedroom copying Chaplin's hilarious boxing skills and the way he shakes peoples' hands to offset them wanting to beat him too a pulp.

The following week was *The Kid*, where he becomes a father to an orphan baby who later grows to be a young boy. The acting was superb. The final week was *The Gold Rush*. In this film, he goes searching for gold in the mountains and gets stuck in a cabin with two terrifying characters twice his size. I took notes on the way Chaplin behaved. Maybe I could use his comedy to tame some of my own bullies.

From becoming a fan, I began to grow obsessed. I would rewind scenes over and over again, copying what Chaplin was doing. The dancing potatoes from *The Gold Rush* I worked on for hours. I worked on facial expressions and mannerisms. I borrowed my father's spanners and pretended to be the factory worker from *Modern Times* who was having a nervous breakdown. I would move like a robotic fairground exhibit from *The Circus*.

The world is a magical and terrifying place from a child's eyes, new, curious and intriguing. I just existed in exploration and play. I was innocent, excitable, easily impressed and vulnerable. There were only good people and bad people in my world. It was all black and white. Chaplin opened up a whole other universe, full of motives, emotions, desires and hardship. Most of all, I learnt I was not alone. There was someone else who had the same feelings and thoughts as me. Only this man was a genius.

I watched these films so much that I started to behave like Chaplin. I developed his penguin walk and I would be seen moving around everywhere like this, with my toes pointed out as I shuffled.

I'm not sure my family understood my fascination with these films, but they were just glad something could make me smile.

'Is this a film?' asked old Jove.

Yes with Charlie Chaplin.

'Well, I can see by what you're wearing that you are a big fan of his (I was dressed in the cheap fancy dress Chaplin outfit that I liked to wear). This is something that worries your parents, I think. So we want to get away from that and talk about you.'

I had no idea what he meant by this.

'Can you tell me what is your earliest memory?'

Bruce

'And who is Bruce?'

He's my brother

'What can you tell me about Bruce?'

He's my brother

These were ridiculous questions.

'Anything else?' he asked.

He has a good laugh. It sounds like an adventure.

'Do you laugh with him?'

I used too, when I was younger.

'Why did you stop?'

He joined the army. He left. I don't see him much anymore.

'And you miss him?'

I thought hard and long about this, before writing

Yes

'Do you like adventure?' asked old Jove.

Yes, like The Little Tramp I'm always searching for romance and adventure.

'Right, let's try and stay away from Chaplin for now. Let's come back to Bruce. Do you think him joining the army has damaged your relationship?'

Well there was a little incident just before he left

'Can you tell me about this?'

Oh for goodness sakes, I thought. What does he want, my life story? I puffed a sigh of air as I continued writing with my big pen.

I punched him in the face for being rude at the dinner table.

What did he do?' asked Dr Jove. I sat motionless. This was none of Dr Jove's business.

When I was about ten, my father lost his job and there was a lot of stress about us moving to a smaller house. I wasn't going to be attending the same public school that Bruce went too as it was too expensive. The other children from little school were all going there, but I didn't mind. There was also mention that Bruce should get a job now he was sixteen. Bruce had a very beautiful girlfriend and he wanted to carry on studying and to spend all his time with her. Dad was filling out application forms for new jobs and he asked me to run down the road and post them. I made the most terrible mistake of posting them in one of those bins for doggy doo-doos, very silly of me. During dinner Dad asked me which letterbox I went too and I told him. Realising my mistake, he was a little cross but then he laughed. He made some jokes about it and I laughed too. Bruce heard this and shouted at me, cruel words they were. He'd never shouted at me before. Then he shouted at Dad too, saying he would be disciplined if he did that, and that I should be disciplined. They started arguing, and Bruce was really shouting saying he was joining the army and that somebody had to make money for the family. I think he sounded proud that he was joining the army. I think he was showing off. Bruce was so rude, saying Dad shouldn't have lost his job. He also asked if he had any idea what happens to wimps like me in the school I was going too. Mum was getting very upset. I got very angry indeed, so while he was in the middle of his shouting I got up and thumped him as hard as I could across the face – scowling at him. I don't think it hurt him, but it shut him up. He looked shocked. Everyone went quiet and finished their dinner. Bruce left a couple of weeks later.

'Do you speak with him now when you see him?' asked Dr Jove after finally realising that I wouldn't be answering his last question.

He does the talking. He takes me to the park and kicks and throws balls at me.

'Do you enjoy that?'

Yes

'Do you like sports? Do you like to play sports at school?'

No, they don't let me.

'Who doesn't let you, the students or the teachers?'

Neither

'Why is that?'
They hate me
'Why do you think that?'
They tell me
'The teachers tell you they hate you?'
Yes with their eyes. The pupils use their mouths.
'I see. Do they say any other unkind things to you?'
Yes
'Do you feel bullied?'
Yes

I spent a long time in my bedroom as a teenager, metamorphosing into something tragic.

I wanted to protect my family from what was happening to me in that horrible school. They were better hearing about how Bruce was acing army life, or winning more sports competition, or dating beautiful girls. I was happy that this took the focus off me.

It's all a blur of incidents now. Like when the school football team decided it would be 'fucking funny' to pull my trousers down to my ankles, lift me fully off the ground, carry me to the girls' changing rooms, kick the door open and throw me in. I can still hear the deafening screams as I thudded onto the cold floor. I could barely hear my own voice as I repeated, 'I'm terribly sorry, it won't happen again.'

Then there was the time I was punched in the face by a boy with a terminal illness. I could hardly fight back under the circumstances, and everyone cheered him like he was Mohammad Ali. Or when someone told the teacher I was masturbating in class and the teacher actually believed them and gave me a whole week of detention. There were a few boys who always drew erect penises on my bag, or books, or pencil case. It's very hard to be a gentleman when someone does that. Everyday they would come up with a new form of torture.

'I see,' said Dr Jove taking along time to consider what I wrote. Have you told anyone this before? That you don't like school?'
No
I suddenly panicked! Hating school was top-secret information and I'd been tricked into telling the wicked, little man. He'd

obviously used some sort of hypnotherapy or Jedi mind trick on me. How could I have been so foolish? My stomach started rumbling again.

'You must tell your parents about this.'

No, I want them to think I like school

'I think I must tell them, so that they can discuss it with you.'

I suddenly got very angry. I got angry occasionally, but I was very good at controlling it. If Jove told on me though, I thought I might lose my temper. I hadn't lost my temper since I punched Bruce, I didn't think. I always felt so guilty about doing that.

I gave Dr Jove a dirty look, walked to the door hurriedly and left.

When I got to Mum's car, I got in and buried my head in my arms avoiding questions. Mum went inside to talk to that scoundrel Dr Jove. I never learned what they discussed.

This small incident broke the tiny amount of trust I had with Dr Jove, and the following week I only wrote down one answer. It wasn't about me. It was about Chaplin. He'd grown tired of my silence and was trying another tactic.

'What do you think Charlie Chaplin would do if he was being bullied?'

I don't know

But this question grew to fascinate me, and made all that time with Dr Jove worthwhile. I'd nearly finished school, but I began to explore possible Chaplin responses in later years. At first I just did this in my mind, but later in reality as well.

Fortuitously, my sessions did not go on for too many weeks, as when my mother would pick me up I would take to making sad faces with my bottom lip stuck out and my eyes wide open and blinking sadly. She had too much compassion to allow me to look like this and cancelled my sessions with Dr Jove. He wrote on my final report, that I snuck a look at....

He suffers from a state of low spirits caused by loss of hope and courage. Because of this he has immersed himself in a fantasy world in which he is a protagonist of tragedy. This is why he dresses and acts like his hero Charlie Chaplin. This fantasy realm of black and white movies is a world he thinks he understands. Outside of this world he feels helpless and at the mercy of his own emotions. By emulating Chaplin's tramp he is able to stifle and control his feelings. If he is to ever lead a normal life, I strongly recommend further counselling for him. Dr Jove.

Regardless of this, Mum and Dad were now more worried about my epilepsy than my strange behaviours. I had several fits in short succession towards the end of those awful school days. Boy did I hate the feeling it gave me. It felt like I was on another planet. They took me to several real doctors, and I was prescribed with medication that I had to take morning and night. These helped a lot. I had six or seven fits in the one year, leading up to getting this prescription. Now I have only one or two a year, and they are often my own fault for ignoring the medication or getting too stressed.

Walking out of those school gates for the final time was the best moment of my life up until then. My parents took me to college where I signed up for English, maths and history classes. I would sit quietly in lessons and appreciated that the people didn't want to be so nasty to me there. So I started dressing as The Little Tramp for college. It took several trips to Camden and various suit and fancy dress shops but, eventually, I had the perfect outfit. I have added too it over the years, changing bits and pieces.

I would walk around London at weekends with my feet stuck out and behave in an eccentric way, especially in my mannerisms. Away from school I could finally be myself. People stared at me, but that was because I was the most successful comedy actor of all time. In fact, I was the man who had turned the movies into an art form. I was the man who came from poverty in London to become Hollywood's biggest star. Of course everyone would be staring at Charlie Chaplin, I was happy with that.

I would go to college in the day, before going home to study more and watch my Chaplin movies and practice his moves. I had grown especially fond of the scenes where he is inebriated by alcohol and a scene in *Modern Times* where, unbeknownst to him, The Tramp ingests a massive, huge amount of cocaine. I guess my parents were pleased that I was practicing these comedy routines in my room and not drinking or snorting cocaine for real. They still worried about my lack of friends.

About a year into this more relaxing period of life, away from that awful institution of learning, I did begin to interact with the world again. It wasn't a psychologist, or an epiphany, or pets, or the love of my family that got me talking again though.
It was a beautiful girl. Her name was Mariana. I love Mariana.

The Talkies

I was eighteen years old and still living with my parents in London. I had my own name and identity, but I thought about this with as little psychological attachment as I have to my DNA sequencing. It was an irrelevant fact about who I was – in my mind I was The Gentleman Tramp.

I would spend most of the day at the library rather than in class. I liked it there, it was peaceful and serene. In the evenings I would watch my movies, read and I'd begun to write my own sketches, imagining what trouble and funny business Chaplin could get up to in modern London. My parents were still worried about me. Bruce was still thriving with his army career, which was now taking him on outdoor pursuits and peacekeeping missions around the world. He was only twenty-four and already an officer.

I would sleep well at night in a bed provided by my parents, after eating food cooked for me by my mother. I would use my parent's electricity and gas, sleep under their roof and yet could not even bring myself to speak with them. I was not lacking in manners and I was grateful, but something in my mind would not allow me to express this verbally. I knew the hurt I was causing and felt terrible about it, but I had reached the stage where I really just couldn't talk. I hadn't spoken properly in years and I didn't know how to do it anymore.

I used to frequent this charming little café on the south-bank of the river Thames to listen to other people talking, and I'd imagine things I might say in order to join in their conversations. I liked the waitress there, Mez. She served me the first time I went to the café. I was reading *The BFG* by Roald Dahl. I was a bit old for it, but I just liked it, is all. I'd read it a lot.
  'I love *The BFG*,' Mez said. 'But my favourite one is *The Twits*.'
  I smiled when she said this and lifted my hat in politeness.
  'Have you got *The Twits*? I can lend it to you if you want? My boyfriend's a teacher so we've got all those books.'

I continued smiling.

'What can I get you?' she asked after I smiled some more.

I had pointed down at the mug of tea on the menu, so she scribbled that down on her notebook, and then I pointed at this delicious chocolate cake, which she wrote down too.

'Good choice. I love chocolate and that cake is so nice,' she said.

I liked this cake and I always felt comfortable going back, but I always wanted to be served by Mez.

'You're the best customer, you never complain and you're never rude,' she said to me once, patting me on the arm before she went off to another table where a kid wiped his ice cream spoon on her and the dad made some lewd comment.

'Don't talk to me like that, who do you think you are?' she said to him. 'You need to learn some manners,' she said to the child. They sort of shut up, but they also seemed to find it funny. I gave the man and his boy a bit of a scowl.

They looked over at me and started pointing and laughing at me. I took this as an opportunity to use some Chaplin funny business. I stared at them looking mildly disgusted, and pointed to the side of my face suggesting they had something there. They looked away and I noticed moments later they were both wiping and checking each other's faces. They left soon after asking each other what was on them – the foolish devils.

On one winter's afternoon, as I sat down at my usual seat by the window, I noticed a new waitress working in the café.

I glanced at her from behind my copy of *Twenty Thousand Leagues Under the Sea* by Jules Verne. She was dressed in the waitress red that I suppose they all had to wear. It was very tight around her back I noticed. Her hair was dark and rich – it looked very soft and cute. Her legs were very gorgeous indeed and she was leaning over to take an order from somebody. I really couldn't stop staring. A gentleman should never stare, but I really couldn't help it. I was hoping she would turn around so that I could see her face.

Eventually, she did turn around. I don't want to sound too cheesy but her hair swung around like in one of those shampoo commercials to reveal the most beautiful of faces. Oh dear, that sounded very cheesy didn't it? I can't help it, I really thought she was lovely. I glanced up and down nervously from Captain Nemo's adventures. This book had enthralled me, but now it didn't interest me in the slightest. This fascinating new waitress was moving towards me. 'Oh dear!' I thought quickly turning my head back down towards the book. 'Oh dear! Oh dear!' I could feel her walking towards my table. My stomach tightened with the most fearful knots I'd ever experienced, Oh my goodness what a funny feeling.

'Hello, everything OK?' she asked in a thick and rich sensual South American accent that sent shingles of delicious excitement down my spine. I glanced up and momentarily caught a glimpse of her eyes. They were mahogany coloured, mysterious rivers of wonder and excitement. I could have stared at them like a puppy forever. I smiled pathetically with my customary Chaplin grin and nodded more vigorously than necessary.

'OK, well let me know when you're ready to order,' she said smiling the most gorgeous smile as I nodded more.

Terrified still, I waited until she wasn't looking and tried to leave without being noticed. These feelings were too intense and I couldn't handle it, so I tried to get out gracefully and inconspicuously.

Unfortunately, in my haste, I kicked a chair, making the most precise connection. Bruce would have been proud had it been a football or rugby ball but, alas, it was a chair and it went hurtling across the room. It landed with a loud, never-ending bang that startled everyone in the café. I ran over to pick it up and glanced around the room smiling apologetically. I lifted my Derbyshire hat to everyone displaying my bright red face and left.

Once on the street, tears began to well up in my eyes, this was most odd and unusual. I stifled them with a shout of frustration; it was the first noise I'd made for ages. I controlled my emotions with a skip, a jump and a fist pump.

I walked until I got to a public bench, and I sat down and stared into space with all kinds of magical imagery flashing through my mind. I'd not had any kind of emotional response to anything real in years. I'd hated emotions so I bottled them up. Now I wanted to sing, dance, shout, laugh and cry. This was alien and strange. The school bullies had been totally incapable of making me cry or get angry, but here I was ready to start sobbing over a small embarrassment.

My wall had been crumbled in an instant. These feelings had started in the pit of my stomach and spread up towards my brain, where they solidified from feeling to thought. Suddenly I realised I didn't want to hide behind Chaplin anymore. I didn't want to be a performance anymore. I wanted to be free. My imagination ignited into fresh visions of myself as a happy person with this mysterious girl. It had happened in seconds, and it triggered events that would change my life.

That night, I put away the Chaplin films and watched a Tom Cruise movie. Women loved Tom Cruise, or so I was told. So I started trying to stand like Cruise, walk like Cruise and smile like Cruise. I knew I was doing the same thing again, hiding behind a persona that wasn't me. I sat down and relaxed. I needed to be myself. I had a new goal, I was going to talk to the new waitress.

I tried on some of Bruce's 'cool' clothes, but it felt weird and I started sweating. I thought this would make me more relaxed, more normal, but it felt too strange so I got into my long johns for bed.

In the morning, I dressed as Chaplin again. I stayed at home all day, as I had to prepare for my meeting with a princess. I took a more fashionable book this time, *The Beach* by Alex Garland, and went on my way.

I walked fairly fast, trying not to walk like The Tramp for a change. The sickness began returning, I felt so nervous and weak legged that I slowed down when I got to the door. I glanced around and the new lovely waitress was not there, so I took a seat and was served by Mez, who brought my cake and tea.

However, one strange thing did happen when I paid and prepared to leave, Mez was collecting my money and I said two words, 'Thank you.'
She looked shocked and gave me the biggest smile I'd ever seen.
'Oh my God, you spoke! You're very welcome,' she said giving me a friendly hug.
Perhaps she would also tell the new waitress about this.

On my way home, instead of crying I grinned until my face hurt, and I jumped in the air throwing my arms around wildly. People stared at me, but I was used to that. Who cared, I felt so alive!

That night, I couldn't wait to return to the café. I dreamed of all the things I might say to people.

Yet, when I woke up, the sickness was back and during my tortoise-paced walk to the café I felt even more unwell. I was then thrown into total crisis when the beautiful princess that had consumed my dreams opened the café door for me.
'Hello, how are you?' she asked with her hands on her hips. The gorgeous exotic brown of her skin was tantalising and fresh, the whites of her eyes were angelic and the posture of her body was dignified and elegant. I paused like a startled rabbit trying to smile, but looking down at my feet feeling unworthy of gazing for more than a split second at such beauty.
'I love your outfit,' she said, 'it's so unusual. I like it.'
I continued to smile and edge nervously and anxiously towards my normal seat. I was making yet another bad impression. She followed me to the table, thinking me terribly rude no doubt. Then she put down a menu and asked me what I would like.
Mez had noticed this awkward exchange and was headed over to help.
'Mariana, he doesn't like to talk,' said Mez before turning to me and asking if I wanted my usual.
'Mariana,' I said quickly grasping my hands to my mouth in panic and shock at my own behaviour. I'd been wondering what her name was and, on finding out, I had this reflex to say it back to myself.

Mez and Mariana laughed at my reaction to my own words.

'See he does talk,' said Mariana. 'What is your name?' she asked.

One word was enough, I simply smiled and shrugged.

'I will get your usual,' said Mez.

'I would like to talk to you again some time,' said Mariana as Mez hurried off. 'I am learning to speak English also.'

Then she smiled the most hypnotic and wonderful smile and her eyes squeezed together so sweetly that I melted completely, smiling back at her with adoration. She went to serve another table as I drank my tea and nibbled on my cake. Later, I heard Mez giving Mariana a briefing about the local pubs, saying which places were good and which to definitely avoid due to unpleasant clientele or overpriced beer. Mariana was very interested as she said that she wanted to experience London parties. They noticed me looking over and I smiled.

'Do you know anywhere good?' asked Mariana.

'The library,' I said. 'I like the library.'

'Great, I must study, it's very important for me. You must show me this library.' Then she had to serve someone, an elderly couple who I noticed still looked happy and in love with each other.

As I left the café, I summoned up every ounce of courage in my being and called out, 'Bye Mariana, bye Mez, thanks for the cake.'

'Goodbye, see you,' said Mariana in that rich and luxurious voice of hers.

I was aglow with merriment. I drifted home on a cloud of happiness, dreaming of Mariana.

She was like an angel come to rescue me. You know what it's like, when you find someone you think is just perfect. Of course nobody is perfect, but when you think they are, you just go a little bit silly. You can't think straight or be very logical. I've had that a few times in my life, but it's always Mariana who does it to me. Nobody else, just her.

Over the next week, I said several new words. I actually began interacting with my parents and I told them I hoped I would see Bruce soon. I also asked them if they had a good day and thanked them for dinner, using fully formed and enunciated words. I went to some more college classes and actually said hello to some real people.

The person I spoke to most was Mariana. After a few awkward exchanges I was able to ask her about her family, her interests and why she was in England. I fell totally in love.

Bewitched

Mariana was from Niteroi, near Rio de Janeiro. She had lived there all her life.

'How wonderful,' I said. 'A beautiful country, I imagine.'

'Yes, Brazil is very beautiful, but there are many problems in the country. The government is crupt – is this the right word?'

'Corrupt, yes.'

'Corrupt, yes, and the people are not cared for properly. Everything is for the rich and everyone else must struggle.'

It was quiet in the café and Mariana had come to sit with me for her break. She usually had to have her break by herself.

'How did you end up in London?' I asked sitting on my hands to stop myself knocking anything off the table, which I did frequently.

'My parents thought it would be good for me,' she replied looking off into the distance.

'You are not here with your family?'

'No, my sister has school in Rio and my mother and father have work. I am stay here with my Aunt,' said Mariana refocusing on me and giving her fantastic wide smile that lit up the room,

'Is she also Brazilian?' I asked now thumbing through the pages of a brochure someone had left behind.

'Yes of course, but she is unusual for a Brazilian woman. In Brazil beauty is very important – too important. I don't like this. My aunt does not care for beauty. Actually she is very beautiful. But I think she wants to be ugly.'

'She wants to be ugly? What makes you think that?' I asked staring deeply into Mariana's eyes and getting lost.

'Her clothes, she is wearing this black clothes always and she hides her face. She sits in the dark. The whole house is dark. Kind of spooky. But it's OK for me because she let me decorate my room. I make the walls white and put up pictures and posters, and I got some sparkly lights,' she said laughing. 'Yes I like my room here and the bed is so nice.'

'It sounds lovely, maybe your auntie is a witch.'

'Yes, she likes to study a lot about witches,' said Mariana no longer smiling, but nodding her head in agreement to my joke.

'She does?'

'Yes, she doesn't like men too much. Her husband, he cheated on her and leaves. I remember this when I was little. She was so beautiful then. I didn't realise she was so different now, until I got to London.'

'I've never met a witch before.'

'Well maybe you have and you just don't know it. Maybe I'm a witch. I would like to maybe be a witch, but not like her. A good witch, a beautiful witch.'

I found this very funny because she had bewitched me. Mariana laughed with me.

'Well you are very beautiful,' I said nervously.

'Oh thank you. But my ex-boyfriend, he was not saying this. I come to London because my parents think he was very bad for me.'

'Oh, I see.'

'He was older than me, like eight years older. I was very in love with him. I am not studying so hard with him. He tells me all these things about our future. Now I know it was all lies. Now he says this to other girls and I am happy to be in London away from him.'

'I understand.'

'You do?'

I paused. I didn't understand at all. I had never had a girlfriend. A few days previously, I wasn't even able to talk.

'So are you studying now?' I asked changing the subject.

'No I have taken a year away from study. But I love to learn, so you must show me the library.'

'Yes of course, I would love too,' I replied with great enthusiasm.

Later that evening, I returned to the café as Mariana was finishing and we went to the library. I learnt more about this delightful Brazilian girl. She had taken a job at the cafe so that she would have some spending money and something to do while in England. She really wanted to make some friends here, but had found it difficult. The other waitresses already had friends and lives going on. She said that Mez had been very kind to her though, but she was with her boyfriend a lot.

Mariana would ask me questions too. At first I could only answer yes or no. I was to shy to talk about myself. However, with time my confidence grew and we would sit together when the café was quiet.

The first thing I managed to tell her about was my brother, Bruce. I used words like strong, handsome, brave, confident and adventurous. She said she thought that I was those things too and I began to open up more and more. Later, I told her about Chaplin and how he'd inspired me with his achievements, comedy and political beliefs.

She told me about her love of French cinema, and she would explain the stories for me and, enchanted, I would go home and watch these movies.

One day she asked me if I wanted to meet for a real drink. She wanted to try some of the places Mez had told her about. We went to the pub and drank beer. It felt so exciting and grown up, and I became the epitome of humour and charm, until I threw up in front of her on the way home. She thought it was hilarious. A week later we went to an amusement park together. We went on a spinning ride and I threw up again. This time she didn't find it so funny. But still she would meet with me. We went to the cinema and to parks and to London tourist attractions. Other times she would drag me around shopping or we would watch sports on the television. My parents were so pleased that I had a friend.

Mariana soon became the best friend I ever had. She would tell me about her friends at home in Brazil, her dreams to study further and work in fashion or media, and about her family.

I loved Mariana, but I was the perfect gentleman at this time. I'm not always a gentleman. I can be a terrible guy, but for a long time I really was a good gent. However, I started to curse myself for this. I thought perhaps I should attempt to be her boyfriend. I thought I would make a very good boyfriend. But it was complicated; maybe she was dating someone and hadn't told me. It was very possible. I never asked. I never made any suggestion towards the romantic, but boy did I want too.

I had my best chance to make a romantic move when we went away for two nights to a music festival in the countryside. I never had any kind of interest in anything like that, but Mariana's enthusiasm could get me interested in anything.

'They play all types of music on different stages,' she said. 'I've even heard of this festival in Brazil, we must go. It will be so fun.'

I didn't need this much convincing, but I enjoyed hearing her happy voice. We slept in separate tents for the two nights, of course, but we spent a lot of time together. It was cold and wet, and one time I put my arm around her for warmth. It was a magical sensation. It really was a great moment.

On the first day at the festival, I was in line for a tuna sandwich when out of the blue I was approached by a pair of guys who I quickly recognised as two of my childhood tormentors. They had seen I was with Mariana and wanted to be introduced. I was not happy that they were coming over to talk to me.

'Hi mate, long time no see, last place I'd expect to see you is at a festival. Thought you wouldn't like this sort of thing,' the large one said.

'I like it,' I replied.

'Who's that girl you're with? She's fit,' said the small one.

They were being unusually friendly towards me, but I wasn't foolish enough to assume they'd matured. I could sense their falseness. When Mariana came over she seemed to sense this too.

'We're heading over to the dance stage. Do you two want to come?' the large one said standing closer to Mariana and positioning his body to exclude me from the conversation.

'We're going to the big stage. Are you not going to the big stage?' asked Mariana.

'No Radiohead are playing, they're shit, let Chaplin go see Radiohead. You can come with us darlin'. We have beer and some joints. You'll love it,' said the small one with a wink while moving in to invade her personal space.

'No I would really like to see Radiohead,' said Mariana trying to edge closer to me.

'Well I suppose we could see them. It might be all right. What do you reckon Chaplin? Let's all go and get a beer at Radiohead,' said the big oaf whacking me with the back of his hand.

'We were already going to do that,' I said.

'Well now we're coming too,' said the small one. 'Can't keep a gorgeous thing like this all to your self Chaplin.'

'Actually we'd prefer to go alone,' said Mariana. 'We would feel uncomfortable hanging around while you two are kissing each other.'

'What did you say?' asked the big one.

'We ain't gay, ya cheeky bitch,' declared his friend as they began to move away. 'You don't even speak English properly, shouldn't be in our fuckin' country. Have fun hanging around with this stupid Chaplin twat,' continued the little idiot turning back in disgust. He was far more loud, obnoxious and infuriating than his larger friend.

At this point I got a rush of anger and I no longer felt like holding it back.

'Don't swear at her,' I said standing up to my full height and taking a step after them.

'Or what Chaplin?' said the little bastard from behind his big friend as they stopped to hear my answer.

'Or I'll punch your fucking face,' I said.

They began laughing at this, but when we made eye contact I could see they recognised my venomous hate.

'Come on, lets leave these geeks too it,' said the larger one encouraging his friend, who looked more in the mood for fighting, to walk off as well.

We went off to Radiohead laughing and mimicking these two chaps with their foul language and ridiculous walks. We imagined them sharing a tent together and waking up in a romantic cuddle. We had a magical evening, but in the morning things went downhill. There was a large group of people our age in the tents surrounding us and they were friendly. They offered us drinks and food and asked us questions about ourselves. I wanted to turn down all their offers, but Mariana accepted and soon we were spending a lot of time with them. I hated it. A lot of the guys were handsome, rugged and charming. I was jealous, but they did not seem to have the requisite skills to charm Princess Mariana. There were other pretty girls, but I only cared for Mariana. All in all, it was a wonderful weekend. I shall always remember it.

A few weeks later it was Mariana's birthday. I took her to London Zoo and then for a nice dinner. I insisted on paying for everything that day, despite her protests.

However, I really didn't have enough money, so this was very much on my mind the whole day, and I almost didn't notice when she said she would be returning to Rio de Janeiro.

'I am really missing my family. My friends are all getting ahead of me in their studies. I feel very left behind,' she said.

'I understand,' I said in a bit of a daze. Later I would be much more upset, but at the time I was really more worried about how I was going to pay for dinner. I couldn't ask her to help now. What a foolish thing to do. I was terrified of the humiliation that could ensue.

She was meeting her aunt to go to the cinema in the evening, so I waited until it was time for her to go.

'I'm going to stay,' I said. 'I'm still hungry and I really fancy the ice cream.'

'OK, do you want me to stay?'

'No, you go to the cinema, Mariana. Your aunt would be sad otherwise, and she might cast spells on me for making you late.'

'Thank you so much for this dinner, it was so sweet of you to do this.'

She kissed me on the cheek. I should never wash my face again. I sat smiling as Mariana left the restaurant.

I waited there for a few minutes considering my next move. Eventually, I asked for the bill and at the same time asked the waiter where the toilet was.

Once I was inside the bathroom, I stared in the mirror for a while, I knew what I had to do and, after a few deep breaths, I did it. I walked out of the toilet to the door. The waiter saw me and called out. That's when I started running. I'm a pretty good runner you know, quick as a cat, I ran for a long time until confident I'd escaped, but I didn't feel I'd fully got away with it. I knew I would be punished sooner or later.

So that night I lay awake, an outlaw. I didn't know I was capable of breaking the law. What was worse was that I was losing Mariana, she was returning to Brazil. I cursed my lack of courage. I had heard my father say many times that 'feint heart never won fair maiden'. Yet she never flirted with me and I thought any declarations of feelings would have been totally inappropriate. This turned out to be an accurate assessment of the situation because it came as quite the shock to her (and me as well actually) when I blurted out that I loved her while walking across the embankment of the river Thames one Sunday morning about a week after my crime spree.

We'd been chatting about travel, and she'd said, 'There are so many places I would love to visit.'
'Travel does broaden the mind,' I replied. I read that somewhere. I'd never been anywhere and wasn't planning too go. I got nervous when thinking about going to Liverpool.
'I think so too. It's such a good thing for the mind to travel,' continued Mariana.
'Where would you most like to go?'
'So many places, when I return to Brazil I will continue my study, but I would love to see more of my own country and one day travel all of South America.'
'It's very dangerous isn't it?' I asked.
'Maybe a little, but we can not live our lives in fear.'
'Very true.' I had no idea what she was talking about, to me life was fear.

'I would also love to see Australia and America. And when I have the wisdom I wish to see new cultures like Japan and China.'

'That's a lot of places.'

'We are so young, and we have our whole lives to do this. Do you not feel this way?' she asked.

I could feel what was about to come out of me and I knew it would be bad, but I felt powerless to stop it. I definitely didn't decide to say these words.

'I would go anywhere with you because, I love you.'

There was a long and uncomfortable silence. It could have been hours. I really don't know, but it was very long that's for sure.

'I think you are so special too,' Mariana said.

'Thanks,' I said feeling my heart shatter and an urge to vomit in my hat.

'I have experience with love. It has hurt me a lot. I am finally feeling OK.'

'I would like to be your boyfriend,' I continued.

'But I am returning to Brazil. This is impossible,' replied Mariana. 'We are so young, we must have time to explore ourselves and understand the world before we have such feelings, I believe.'

She seemed logical and convincing, but I still didn't know what she was talking about. As we continued along the river, we passed a policeman. I was already in an uncomfortable state and seeing this authoritarian enhanced my feeling of displeasure. I was a broken-hearted criminal.

'I understand,' I said.

'Good,' continued Mariana. 'I do not want you to feel sad, you are very special to me.'

I felt very sad indeed.

Despite this conversation, over the next few days I managed to convince myself that Mariana must love me too. It's funny how the mind responds to disappointment. All sorts of clichés like 'where there's a will there's a way' pop up. They're all lies. That's what I think anyway, because these ideas led me to behave in the most terrible way.

A few days after my initial declaration, I went back to the café while Mariana was working and told her again that I loved her and that I wanted to see her that evening. She told me she would see me as a friend. This is an unsatisfactory response for a man consumed by love.

'I can't be your friend anymore. We must be able to admit our love or I can never see you again,' I announced.

Mariana looked mortified.

The situation was only resolved when Mez got me to leave by taking my arm and leading me outside with soothing words and advice. I had made quite the scene. Mez said everything would be OK and that there are lots of girls, but that I shouldn't do anymore shouting, or talking about love like this.

After this ridiculously dramatic announcement, I did not know how to talk to Mariana. Sweet as she was, she still wanted us to be friends.

By telling her of my feelings I destroyed our dynamic. She was happy to act like this hadn't happened, but I felt so ashamed, embarrassed and pathetic that I hid away. I couldn't stand to be around her anymore. It made me feel horrible. So I would miss phone calls and I found a new café to go too. I could not think of anything to say to her that would not make me appear absurd and ridiculous in my own mind. I didn't even say goodbye when she left for Brazil.

Soon after, I saw on the internet that Mariana was back in Rio. There were pictures of her at parties with her friends in unimaginably exciting locations. In some pictures it looked like she was flirting with guys. It killed me.

When she left I became withdrawn, bitter and angry. I lost my romantic soul and got lost in a degraded fantasy. The TV, the internet and the people at college got me to thinking everyone was having sex all the time and I wanted to get involved in the only way I could. I began watching a lot of porn. I imagined myself as a sexual charmer, meeting gorgeous women and having great sex with them.

During one solo session too many, I was flogging a dead horse so desperately that I collapsed into an epileptic seizure. I fell off my bed onto the floor and gave my head and shoulder a mighty crack. My parents heard the smack and came to see what was wrong. They found me convulsing, face down with my pyjama bottoms round my ankles and called for paramedics who arrived before I woke up. With this humiliation, I again drifted away from my family.

This is the point in my life when I should have taken the new-found confidence gifted to me by Mariana and progressed upwards into greater happiness. Alas, I did not recognise this for the opportunity it was, and now I feel this is when things went wrong. This is when I became a person I didn't want to be. I lost Mariana, I lost Chaplin and I lost my soul. I am not proud of anything that happened for the next few years.

Mariana tried to stay in touch, but I didn't want to talk about my life anymore, compared with hers it was so boring. She sent me an email.

Hi, I miss you. It is so nice to be back in Rio de Janeiro, but here it is so hot. I love seeing my friends, but they don't understand my adventure in England. I meant to write to you sooner, but I was worried you would not reply. I really want to still hear from you. I have been so busy also with study and parties.
So how are you?
Mariana
P.S. The other day I walk past a Charlie Chaplin poster in Rio. Do you still dress like this sometimes?

I replied
Hi Mariana, Glad you are happy back in Brazil. I don't wear those clothes anymore. I must grow up. I now have a job and a

girlfriend. Are you enjoying the studies and the parties? Miss you too.

This was all lies, of course. I did warn you I'm not always a gentleman. I just really try to be a lot. But God, I can be a terrible man. This lying is the tip of the iceberg. It really is. She replied to me though.

Oh great for you. Is your girlfriend nice? How is your job? Yes, I go back to study. I am angry that I miss so much because now I have to work so hard. But the parties here is so amazing. Maybe one day you can visit Brazil.

I didn't reply to this for years. I just didn't know what to say. I was spending most of my time in a dark room feeling sad. I didn't want her to know this, and my imagination seemed incapable of coming up with anything else.

This lasted a long time, too long. I did eventually get a job and I got a girlfriend too. Sophie, her name was.

I'm getting to how I wound up in Brazil, living on the streets. It was all because of Sophie and this job of mine. They drove me mad, you see. I had to get away. I went travelling like a lot of people do. But I'm not the type to go off travelling. It was just that Sophie and this job drove me so crazy; they ruined my mind.

The Great Escape

It came as a relief when I finally got a job – I was an office assistant. It sounded quite exciting and grown up at the time, but I find myself cringing at the words office and assistant now. It was very boring – type this, answer the phone, take notes on that, do a report for so and so. What's worse is that at times I was actually interested in what was going on in that bloody office. I worked so hard to start with, determined as I was to do better as a grown up than I did as a kid. That's the problem with jobs, you sort of fall into them not knowing that they will become your universe. I'm so glad I'm free of it all now. I would rather be in this hospital with no money than in that office with a million pounds, I really would.

I've spoken to Bruce on the telephone and he's on his way to Brazil to help me out. I was beginning to worry, but he told me not too. I'm very surprised he's coming all this way, it must be quite a pain for him. I don't know what he's going to say when he gets here. Actually, I'm a little worried about it.

When I started my job I met Sophie. She was different to Mariana. She had a dry sarcastic humour that I found funny, but she didn't have the same passion for life. I never got those same electric thunderbolt feelings, but I thought that was a good thing after the torture of my previous emotions. One day, I asked Sophie out for a drink and I couldn't believe it when she said yes. Even more remarkably, it went well and I felt comfortable.

So, on our third date when Sophie kissed me, I knew I wanted to kiss her so much more. It was amazing holding each other and joining our lips together. This wonderful tingle of warmth overcame me and made me feel like a real person. Nobody had ever kissed me on the mouth before, and, as I had no reason to believe anybody ever would again, I felt such tremendous gratitude towards Sophie and I would've done absolutely anything to ensure her kisses kept coming. In time our relationship grew even more physical and I was disgustingly smug about what was going on between us after dark. When the day came that Sophie told me we were boyfriend and girlfriend I felt like a king, and although I was very confused by the whole sex thing. I knew I liked it a lot and I was keen to get better at it.

My life with Sophie over those next few years is not really something I wish to describe in detail, for during this time I was not The Gentleman Tramp; I was a shadowy cockroach. I continued my soul-destroying job part time while I studied at King's College London, where I never attended lectures but still managed to gain a lower second degree in English. My parents were so proud, but I was too set in my ways to even apply for a better job, so my qualifications remained meaningless. The fear of change and stepping out of my zone of comfort had followed me from childhood like a parasitic insect. So I went back to fulltime work as the office assistant, but my salary did go up a bit.

It was a shock to everyone, not least of all my self, when I moved out of my parent's house and got a flat with Sophie. We'd even gotten engaged despite me not liking her much anymore. I proposed at the pub where we had our first date. That may sound romantic, but I can't take the plaudits, it was all Sophie's idea. She suggested it several times in a very scary tone of voice that made me feel like if I didn't she would make my life a waking nightmare. I didn't truly realise at the time to what an impressive extent she had already done this.

On a typical morning, I would wake up and look at her back. It was so familiar and cold. I would reach over to stroke her hair. Hoping a morning cuddle would reignite some romance. She usually pushed my hand away. I was supposed to marry her and she wouldn't even give me a morning cuddle. It had been dawning on me for quite some time, but eventually I came to realise that Sophie was a bitch – at least that's what I think anyway. The idea of marrying her terrified me. I doubted she really wanted to marry me either, she spoke to me like I was a dung beetle and she looked at me with disdain. We were not treating each other well and the relationship was getting even worse – it was seriously unhealthy.

She had become the ball and chain wife depicted in much of Chaplin's early work.
She was the wife character that he would try not to disturb when he would sneak home in a drunken state. She was the soul-crushing witch, the ball breaker, the controlling, manipulative beast. She was my archenemy, disguised as my soul mate.
I couldn't remember the last time I smiled. I couldn't remember the last time I laughed. I couldn't remember the last time I cried, or the last time I felt any emotion that might have reminded me I was human. My emotions were grey, my life was grey and I was grey.

I didn't always feel this way about Sophie, and it wasn't just kissing that got me so deeply entrenched in the predicament. On the contrary, I really admired her before. She made me laugh, she was friendly to my parents, she was keen to do things and she was athletic and sporty. She had gone out with tall, athletic types before; three serious boyfriends, all tall and sporty – all broke up with her. When we first began dating we would be kissing and I would tell her I would never break up with her and I would do anything for our relationship. It's amazing what you'll say if you think you might get sex out of it. That's the problem with sex. It can be very hard to be a gentleman when you have sex on the brain.

My morning routines were predictable. I always took a long shower and didn't ever want to get out. Leaving the shower meant having to go to work. I would eventually dry off and get into my grey, itchy clothes. Then pour myself a black coffee. What a horrible way to start the day, drinking that foul thick nasty liquid, just to feel more alert and to snap out of the lethargic zombie like state.

Work was the most demented kind of purgatory. The despair in the eyes of my colleagues was intensely upsetting, so I tried not to look at them. They were doomed to a life of looking forward to their pub and sport weekends, while they survived the week by taking part in a feast of cruel banter and gossip. Something inside them made them settle for this office madness. Like the schoolyard the social hierarchy was crystal clear with people constantly battling and bitching in their attempts to climb some fictitious ladder of power and popularity, from which I dangled pathetic and vulnerable from a very low rung. Content to remain a fish in a very small pond, they soldiered on relentlessly while I pretended I wasn't really a part of it all. The idea of leaving the agonising security terrified and appalled my colleagues, and I suppose that fear is also what kept me trudging through the depressing surroundings and routine for so long.

The highlights of my day, the things that kept me sane, were sitting on the toilet and reading. I could usually drag this out to nearly sixteen minutes; lunchtime, I would make myself a cheese and pickle sandwich with crisps and an orange drink and look forward to going home. I spent a lot of time playing computer games on my work PC – I would minimise the window if colleagues came too near.

Most mornings, Duke would be throwing around his weight as usual. I tried to avoid getting involved in the 'banter'.
Banter = humourless boasting and abuse of friends and co-workers.
My favourite Duke monologue came one random Tuesday morning.
'I was down at McCluskey's last night. Must have had about fifteen pints when this sexy little blonde comes over and sits on my lap, sticks her tongue down my throat and presses her boobs against me. I took her into the toilets, gave her what for then had another three pints. Later, I went home and treated the Mrs to some prime loving. Woke up this morning and she's cooked me a fried breakfast as a thank you. I downed a glass of water and four ibuprofen, and here I am at the office, still more effective and dynamic than any of you wankers.'
'That's amazing,' replied Dave, Duke's main henchman, in awe of his hero's story.
'Well maybe one day you will grow balls as big as mine and you can stop bloody playing with yourself so much and get someone to do it for you,' replied Duke to the sound of laughter from the men of the office.

Dave actually laughed too. Not a genuine laugh, but a pathetic nervous, frightened laugh in desperation to move up Duke's social ladder. I should point out at this stage that I never called him Duke to his face. This is what all those spineless friends of his called him. It sort of caught on with most of the office, but I knew his name was Bryan. I didn't really call him Bryan either, like Beelzebub its best not to say the name out loud at all.

Most of the women pretended to hate Duke, but most had slept with him and he was working on the ones who hadn't. After all he was the King of banter.

He would often refer to me as the quiet twat, or the short twat, or the ugly twat. If I heard the word twat I assumed he was talking to me, but I didn't have a lot to do with him. He knew I wasn't a fan of his banter and he didn't see me as a threat, so I was mostly left in peace. He also knew that I was involved with Sophie, he liked Sophie. He liked all the women at work.

I had also taken a second job working night shifts at a call centre to save for the wedding and help pay the mortgage on a house. I would answer random calls from people struggling with their satellite, cable or internet, and I would try and talk them through fixing it. Again, when there was no work to be done, I read. I found it enjoyable and I liked to improve my mind.

I can fully understand how this lack of achievement and energy in my life was a big reason why Sophie wouldn't kiss me so often anymore. She was probably disappointed I hadn't made more of myself. I was lacking in passion, ambition and drive. My spirit was crushed so I actually didn't blame her for her lack of attraction, but surely she should have appreciated my sacrifices and how much time I was spending to save up for a wedding I didn't want.

Sophie was in charge of planning the wedding, I just had to smile and nod. Fortunately these were two of my greatest skills.

Duke was the kind of guy I knew Sophie really wanted. He was the alpha male, the centre of attention, the King of Banter. I saw them talking a few times and she would find his crude jokes funny and act all angry, but it just encouraged him. I sometimes wondered if they knew I was there, and it crossed my mind once or twice that they might start having sex in front of me. I raised the issue with her once and she said, 'Don't be so stupid. I love you. Jesus can't I even be friends with people now?'

They had a lot in common, Duke and Sophie. Things like golf and nightclubs and quizzes. Things I couldn't stand. Sophie had gone out with men like Duke before though, and she was fed up with them, she'd told me that so many times.

While living this hectic lifestyle of working two inactive jobs and making agreements to wedding plans and preparations, I didn't get much sleep, which was starting to drive me a little crazy. I never had any energy. I would have about three hours after my first job where I could lie down, if Sophie wasn't bothering me, and then after my second job I would get about three and a half hours before Sophie and I both had to wake up. I felt horrible all the time. There wasn't enough coffee in the world and I always wanted another shower.

One night I left my second job early; I was so tired that I couldn't take it anymore. It was making me feel terribly unwell, so I decided to go home. As I pulled up to the driveway I noticed a car next to Sophie's. The license plate read **DUKE 007**. I thought about going in, but I didn't quite know what I would do if I were to walk in on them committing unspeakable sweaty acts. I decided to call Sophie's mobile phone, but she didn't answer. I stood in shocked disbelief staring up at our window. There was light but the blinds were closed. Minutes later my phone buzzed, it was her.
'Hello,' I answered.
'Hi, I just got your call, what's wrong darling?' She never normally called me darling.
'I was just thinking of you and thought I'd call for a chat.'
'That's sweet but I'm really tired. Can't we talk in the morning?' Normally she would have shouted at me for waking her up.
'Yeah, I guess so,' I replied.
'Are you OK?' she asked.

'Yes I'm fine.' As I said that I heard a deep cough on the phone. 'What was that?' I asked.

'Oh, I just coughed. Think I might be coming down with something. Maybe that's why I'm so tired.'

She replied quickly, but it definitely wasn't her coughing. I knew the sound of her cough very well.

'OK, well bye.'

'Bye, see you in the morning,' said Sophie and she hung up.

I stood around a few more minutes not knowing what I was feeling or what I should do. I suppose I should have been angry, but I really wasn't. I was shocked that's for sure, but I must admit a sense of relief. I decided on going to stay at my parents'. I still had a key and they'd always said I could come over. So I drove to the house and let myself in.

Dad heard the door and came to investigate. I called out that it was just me and that I was feeling unwell, so he told me to go to bed and I'd see him in the morning. I lay in my bed staring at the ceiling. All I could think about was the embarrassment that my girlfriend had slept with Duke. I knew this was weird. When I used to lie in that same bed as a younger person, I dreamed of great consuming romances and of deep loves that were more important than anything, but there I was, my relationship destroyed, and I didn't care. In fact I really was starting to feel sort of happy about it.

The next day I called in sick and stayed in bed most of the day thinking about how my life had gone stupendously wrong. I didn't tell my parents the problem, just told them I was feeling sick. I also left a text message for Sophie saying I was at my parents' because Bruce was home. She'd left me several messages, which arrived like an avalanche when I turned on my phone. She wanted to know when I was coming home, so after the text I switched it off again for fear of more phone calls.

Later that day, Bruce arrived back from seeing friends with a hearty face-busting grin and a warm glow. He'd long since left the army and it was noticeable. He said he didn't like being told what to do.

'My man, how's it going? Come on where's that famous smile of yours?' he said. Bruce now had a job leading adventure-expeditions in different parts of the world. Tourists would pay big money for someone like Bruce to take them places. He made every trip fun and safe, and he would organise everything so that the customers could just sit back and enjoy the journey – which they felt was enhanced by Bruce's motivational enthusiasm. He'd been working for a company, but had now built up a big enough network of tourists to become self-employed. The rich contacts he made recommended him to other wealthy travellers with long retirements or holidays to fill.
They paid generously and tipped bigger – especially on his most recent trip to East Africa. He was briefly home to stay with Mum and Dad before he went off exploring again. This was the first time I'd seen him in months.

My parents were as pleased to see him as I was. They would have liked to have him around more often, but he made everything he did sound so exciting that they would sit in awe of his tales just like everyone else did. Over dinner, Bruce told us that he was leaving for Nepal the next day to trek the Himalayas. He was doing the first part alone, but would be joined by some tourists in three weeks. He had never been there before so he wanted to have an idea of the culture and conditions before he was paid to lead the trip. The Himalaya's was one of his greatest ambitions.

He asked me about the date of the wedding and I said I hoped it wouldn't be for a while, but avoided further questioning until after dinner when we had a couple of beers in the kitchen. After a little coaxing, I told him how much I hated work, dreaded marriage and despised my life. He suggested we went to the pub to talk over the matter in more detail and I thought it was a fantastic idea.

After a few pints, I started to relax and told Bruce about work and Sophie and Duke. We played darts and pool before deciding it would be a great idea to phone my two bosses and quit. Bruce made the first call in which he explained that I had just discovered that I was distantly related to the King of Swaziland and no longer required their employment.

Then I called my main job, where I made a series of unusual noises before stating categorically that I could not work for a company that did not allow me more than twenty minute toilet breaks or provide a bonus during Ramadan. Afterwards, we got more beer and I downed mine in one go. Bruce did the same before saying he was hungry again and going up to the bar to order two pork pies. It soaked up a bit of the beer, but I was feeling totally smashed.

'Well you seem to be taking everything very well bro. A lot of people would be crumbling. But you didn't like your job, so now you've quit. You don't like your cheating girlfriend so get rid of her, time to start again. Why don't you go and ask out the cute barmaid?' Bruce said.

'Why not, she seems very lovely indeed,' I said standing up and marching off to the bar to impress the young lady with my charms. As I walked over I panicked and turned back.

'Just do it,' cried Bruce, so I tried again.

'Hello, yes I think you are very, very, very beautiful and I wanted you to know that I believe you to be a special lady,' I announced.

'So does my boyfriend,' she replied. So I did the walk of shame back to my brother, who was laughing his head off.

'Very nice, smooth, I didn't know you were such a Casanova.'

'It's not my fault, its Sophie, because I was still thinking of Sophie,' I slurred. 'I need to tell her it's over then I shall romance the barmaid again.'

So I telephoned Sophie, it was the most horrible phone call I'd ever made, so it was a good job I was drunk.

'Hello. Where are you? You haven't been home all day and you didn't go to work!' she hollered.

'I had some beers with Bruce. I can't drive now so I'm going to stay here for another night.'

'Why are you drinking beer? You said you were sick. I could have gone out with work people. You never tell me anything.'

'Sorry.'

'Tomorrow we are going to look at the menus for the wedding, so you better be here at 9am sharp.'

'I'm going to Nepal.'
'What?'
'I'm going to Nepal with Bruce tomorrow. I've been feeling very stressed. I need a break and I want to go to Nepal.'
She started shouting.
'You better be joking!'
'No, I really need a holiday.'
'Well you can't. You're not allowed. We need the money for the wedding. How can you think something so stupid?'
'Yeah, I'm definitely going.'
She hung up the phone.
I tried to call her back but it went to voicemail, so I left a message.
'I know you were with The Duke. His real name is Bryan; you were sleeping with Bryan. Bryan, Bryan, Bran, I think we should split up. Going to Nepal tomorrow. OK then, take care, see ya later. Bye.'

Then I turned my phone off and went back in the pub.
'Bruce, I'm coming to Nepal with you tomorrow?'
'Course you are Casanova?'
'I can't stay here, I need to get away.'
'I suppose you could come, but you are pretty wasted, are you sure you want too?'
'I can't stay here. I've got the money. I'll come on the flight with you and arrange things separately if needs be. I just need to get away and you make your trips sound so exciting. Romance and adventure, that's what I want, romance and adventure.'
'Well yeah that would be brilliant,' said Bruce starting to warm to this idea.
It was settled in an instant, I was leaving London for the first time since the family holidays we took in Spain and Cornwall when I was a child. This thought motivated us both to go home and get some rest.
On the way home starving, we had a horrendous excuse for a kebab. I was sick in the street and Bruce cheered so everyone knew about it. Bruce had been complaining about how he needed the toilet all the way home. When we finally arrived he couldn't hold

it any longer and urinated down the side of the house. I told him not too. I was the good son. Then I threw up again.

Bruce and I were highly inebriated when we got home and our every movement caused unimaginable noise. My parents had never tolerated drunkenness, so just like when we were younger, we were asked to sleep in the outhouse. As we bunked down, I remembered being a child and sleeping next to my brother, but now I liked my own space. I needed to get used too it again as we were going to the Himalayas together and I knew I would have to break down my closed mind and barriers.

As I lay there, I dared to turn my phone back on and I had messages from Sophie. She was denying my accusations about her and Bryan, talking as if I was crazy, then in later messages she started sympathising with all the work I'd done and that we needed to talk. Finally she'd obviously had a drink herself because the last one simply said, 'Oh piss off to Nepal then.'

I've not seen or heard from Sophie since. I think she's with someone else now, not The Duke though – but I don't really care too much. I hope they are happy together. I feel a little bad about what I did. Actually no I don't.
I haven't spoken to work either. They were angry with me too. My parents got a lot of phone calls asking where I was, but I think this soon stopped.
The Gentleman Tramp I had tried to be as a teenager started to come back to life that night. My life was about to start again. I could now search for romance, adventure and magic.
It didn't take long to pack my bags the following morning. I would be getting the hiking equipment in Nepal, but my rucksack still felt light, it was missing something. I went upstairs to my old cupboard pulled out my gentleman's suit, dusted it off and put it in my rucksack.

With my things gathered, we headed to the airport. I felt so alive. I managed to get tickets on the same flights as Bruce and my adventure began. For too long I'd been living a life that I never wanted; a job with no meaning, a home with no comfort, a relationship with no love, a heart with no feeling and a mind without hope. Suddenly I was excited by the idea of living out my childhood fantasies; being free, searching for a passionate love, living on the road, meeting new people and experiencing the world with emotion. This was my opportunity to live the way Chaplin had described through his art, but I had no idea how close to the tramp I would actually become.

The Himalayas of Nepal

Horrendous horrible hospital! Hate, hate, hate, this hospital now! I can't wait to get out of here. The food is inedible; a grumpy nurse brings a compartmentalised cardboard cuisine to my room three times a day and I pick at the bits I like, which isn't much. One day there was some jelly for pudding and I really enjoyed that, but it wasn't sufficient.

I suppose what they give me is enough to keep me alive, but not to satisfy my hunger or cravings. A lot of people will tell you that the meaning of food is survival. Life is a desire not a meaning,' said Chaplin in an interview, and I agree with him. I desire hamburgers, pizza and chocolate milkshake, not this slop and plaster. I want to enjoy my dinner and I don't care if that means I'll die younger than healthy people.

The nurses had been giving me sponge baths, but I think that has stopped now because I was giggling too much and I think they are starting to question how sick I really am. The effects of the seizure wore off after a day or two so I shouldn't really be here. I just don't have anywhere else to go, so I'm going to pretend to feel rotten until Bruce arrives.

I haven't seen Bruce since Nepal, so I hope he's forgiven me. He's on his way to Brazil now to help me, but he better not arrive when Mariana is visiting me tomorrow, because I'm really looking forward to seeing her. It would be just like Bruce to arrive then and spoil my special moment.

I think Mariana is really concerned about me. I imagine her worrying herself sick. Despite not answering her phone when I called, she sent me a text saying she was going to come and see how I'm doing, and there was a sad face at the end of it. It must be difficult having feelings for an adventurous, dangerous guy like me. I should really think more about the effect my wild antics have on the hearts of fair maidens. After all, it's not every man who just quits his job and leaves his home to go trekking in the Himalayas.

Great Britain looked so small from up in the sky. Tiny and insignificant like a sponge floating in a bath. The wonder of ascending up higher and higher until we were shrouded in white fluffy clouds was a beautiful sensation. The troubles on my mind disintegrated into an ecstatic sense of freedom.

'Now are you sure you'll be able to handle the trek? It'll be physically demanding and you haven't done anything like this before,' Bruce said.

'I'm sure it will be fine. I expect you'll slow me down a bit though. I'll be waiting for you at the top,' I said.

'That's the spirit. I'm going to make you into a soldier. A real tough man,' Bruce said giving me a friendly punch in the arm.

'Chaplin played a World War I soldier in *Shoulder Arms*. He was the hero. I think I would be a great soldier. The hero of the war,' I said.

'So I can train you up then, can I?'

'Yes, sounds fun, but it will be me training you by the end of it.'

'Ha! I like it,' Bruce said reclining his seat and probably thumping the knees of the person behind him.

At New Delhi airport all I could see were the backs of people's heads and the luggage that rammed into my legs as I scampered after Bruce, who was slaloming in and out of a mass of bodies that were all adorned in brightly coloured clothes and flamboyant jewellery. Why do people have to walk so very slow when I'm behind them, or stop in front of me to chat to their friend or search for something in their bag? I think they do it just to annoy me, I really do.

I finally reached an even thicker mass of people staring in one direction. I suppose it must have been a queue. No one in the airport seemed to know what was going on, least of all me.

We were eventually called over to security by a smartly dressed man with a walkie-talkie and were ushered through security.

'Let's go,' said Bruce sprinting off like a frightened zebra down the long corridor of departure gates. Bruce loved all this rushing about as if it was all part of the grand adventure of his life.

Once airborne, I grew even more agitated.

'Excuse me, could I have a visa form?' I asked the stewardess.

'We don't have visa forms,' she responded failing to put my mind at rest.

'We'll sort it out when we get there,' said Bruce giving me a dirty look before turning his attentions to the stewardess. 'Sorry he doesn't get out much. So are you from India or Nepal?' he asked giving the poor girl a wink and a smile.

'India. I live in New Delhi,' said the stewardess actually engaging in the conversation and not walking off with an appalled look on her face as I'd hoped.

'Fantastic,' he said. 'I'm Bruce, we're off to climb Everest but we'll be coming back to New Delhi. I think India is a fascinating country and the women are so beautiful,' Bruce said puffing out his chest and holding out his hands to suggest he was talking specifically about her and getting the response of her delighted giggles.

Five minutes later, Bruce was leaning over me with a proud, lecherous look on his face showing me her email and phone number as she walked back to the front of the plane, hiding her blushes.

'Good start, she's lovely,' he said.

I wasn't interested. Outside the window a glorious mountain range had come into view and I overheard that this was Everest. It was so gargantuan that my mind was boggled. I didn't want to blink for fear of missing a moment of the spectacle. Looking down in greater detail, I began to distinguish between the different peaks and crevices, thin wispy clouds were scattered amongst the taller rocks and the white tops of these ancient monuments of tectonic violence led deep down until they melted into the glorious green of fields and rice plantations.

Amidst the colossal landscape I swore I could see little huts dotted around on the sides of the mountain, and this made me blink. What if they had a problem up there? How would they get help? How did they get there in the first place? I tried to imagine prehistoric settlers arguing about whether to go back the way they came or to carry on up this giant mountain. I expect it was someone like Bruce (an idiot) with the bright idea to carry on and live in the clouds. The thought of going up mountains was suddenly very real and scary, but I knew no matter what was to follow in Nepal, now that I'd seen Everest, the whole trip was a success.

Back on land, we made it through customs, despite my fears, but I couldn't find my luggage and as I walked around looking for it I could hear Bruce and that bloody raucous laugh of his.

'I need my toothbrush and my Chaplin hat,' I said.

'We can get another toothbrush and you're not dressing as Chaplin in the Himalayas,' Bruce said.

I told you he was a swine.

'Well I need my things, where are they? I knew this was a bad idea.'

'Relax, it'll turn up. We'll have another look around and then I'll ask,' Bruce said.

'Ask who?' I said. 'None of these people look like professional baggage handlers.'

'That guy is in charge of luggage,' Bruce said pointing too a man in a white shirt smoking a rolled up cigarette and spitting on the floor.

Once we finally located my bag – Bruce found it buried under other luggage and was very smug that it was him who found it – we stepped out of that frying pan of madness and into the fires of taxi chaos. Like awful celebrities walking into a paparazzi Christmas party we were surrounded by drivers and Bruce was walking off with one of them.

I got into the back of a sorry excuse for a car and clung onto my bag like a teddy bear as Bruce got in swiftly, followed by the driver and two burly men.

'Who are these people?' I whispered to Bruce.

'I don't know. Don't worry,' he replied.

'Where are you from?' asked this grinning buffoon who had climbed in the back with us.

'Well I like to think of myself as a free man, the world is my home,' said Bruce.

'We're from England,' I said as I peered out of the window at the airport like a small child being taken away from his parents.

'What a great country, we have many people come with us from England to do trekking.'

They were tour salesmen and not the Mafia-linked serial killers I had mistaken them for. This chatty chap had an extremely ghostly aura. I took an immediate dislike to him, but Bruce chewed the fat with him all right. He would have a friendly gossip with the devil, I should imagine.

Bruce had a massive trip routed out already so we simply arranged for a guide and a porter to escort me on the nine to twelve day trek of a North central section of the Himalayas called Annapurna.

'I think they have overcharged me,' I said staring at my ticket when we were finally alone in a dirty hotel room that we were going to have to share. There were two wooden beds with sorry excuses for pillows, with brown stains on them, and a little table that Bruce had already chucked loads of his stuff onto.

'It doesn't matter. It's still cheap compared with England and I don't want to mess around in Kathmandu looking for a guide.'

'Who put you in charge?' I asked.

'Do you want to stay here? Did you not look outside the window of the taxi?'

'I suppose it did look dirty.'

'Dirty! There was rubbish piled as high as the buildings, smashed up cars on the road and I saw too dogs having sex next to a restaurant.'

'Really?'

'They were doing it doggy style,' Bruce said.

That evening I picked up hiking shoes and all that sort of gear from one of the shops. It got very cold at night so I was very happy with my all-weather hiking jacket to protect me from that icy breeze. They are shiver proof you know.

On the first day, I was ready to go at 5am as I couldn't really sleep very well. I tried to wake Bruce almost straightaway, but calling his name was totally ineffective. He just grunted at me to 'get off'. So I gave him a little shake.

'Bruce, we have to get going.'

'OK, OK I'm up,' he said blinking his eyes and reaching over the side of the bed to grab a sock. I went into the bathroom for a scrub and when I returned he was lying on his bed with half his foot in a sock and his mouth wide open, snoring. I thought it prudent to give up. He's not really a morning person, Bruce. He must have had enough of that in the army. So I went outside and paced the streets awaiting the salesman and the guide.

'Right lets get cracking then,' Bruce said emerging from the doorway just as the creep salesman was walking towards me. I must have got the time wrong or something. The guide looked wise and experienced. His name was Jinsi, and he was with a quiet younger guy who we were told would be carrying my bags.

Bruce motored excitedly forward, pulling his backpack straps tighter while Jinsi took my small bag and the porter heaved up my backpack. I walked with a shameful freedom.

The driver of the coach to Pokhara, where we would start our hike, was a big, spitty man. The main thing I noticed about Nepal was the spitting. It's absolutely disgusting and it seems everyone does it. The air is thick and dirty in the cities, but I didn't feel the urge to gob all over the place even once. I think it's some sort of custom.

Everywhere you go you can hear hhhhhuuuaauuuccccckkkk poot!!! Over and over again. I even saw women doing it. I might be inclined to cancel a second date if a woman did that in England. Perhaps the women I saw were feminists and demand the right to spit too. I don't think a true gentleman would ever join in with this behaviour.

After breakfast the scenery became really impressive, rolling hills and mountains, winding roads and valleys. Absolutely beautiful! On a couple of occasions the snow capped mountains reared into view. There were a lot of shacks by the sides of the roads, kids going to school, washing lines, unbelievable amounts of trash. But what was really great was there were farm animals all over the place, just having a little wander they were and going about their business.

When we arrived in Pokhara, I was surprised to see how large and commercial it was, with backpackers from all over the world walking the streets. It was like the Disney village for Himalaya tourists. I was hoping for Nepalese culture, but everyone was speaking English and the whole place catered for the western mind. There was western food, western books and western images plastered everywhere. Fortunately the landscape was Nepalese, so that is what I tried to focus on. After our curry dinner, Bruce went off exploring the crazy fair on the other side of the lake from our hotel, and I was glad of a break from his jokes and running commentary. I just stayed in and read *The Great Gatsby*.

We did the first days trekking in three hours, forty-five minutes. It was supposed to take five hours; but good God did I suffer. Chronic shoulder pains have haunted me since I was fourteen. The doctor said it is because of a leaking valve in my heart. I had all these checks when they found out I had epilepsy. It is not what is needed when trekking the Himalayas. During a break from walking, I had slurped down cold, refreshing water with some painkillers and it relaxed me somewhat. The pain eased but the walk got steeper, hotter and more horrible. The only thing that kept me going during the full walk, in which sweat constantly dripped off my face and my vision blurred, was that bastard fitness fanatic Bruce and the ones back at the office and, seemingly, everywhere, back in England. They are spawning at an incredible rate, these people who will probably live to 150 with their Nazi-regimented vigour. They love to tell you all about their marathons and rowing machines and triathlons. I was determined to get up those mountains so that when people brag about their annoying achievements and their calorie intake, I can just mention Himalayan trekking and they will be forced to leave me alone while I eat a box of donuts.

'I was just finding my stride,' said Bruce after Jinsi led us to the first hostel on the trek and told us we would have to stop for the day to acclimatise to the altitude.

'Me too, just warming up,' I said as I sat panting into my arm. The sweat from my body was beginning to freeze as the temperature dropped rapidly.

'I like your style bro. Look at the view. Fantastic! What could be better?'

After being shown the room that I would have to share with Bruce (again), I went for a shower, or at least I scooped water on to my body as I perched near the nozzle that sprayed agonising, icy liquid into the room. I did jump under it once and the pain made me shudder and utter an array of unnatural noises.

Outside Bruce was still in the same spot, now sampling a soup with Nepalese bread. I ordered the same and the delightful warmth of it comforted me.

'Good start today bro,' said Bruce 'you did well.'

'Piece of cake,' I said.

This cockiness gave Bruce the idea of making me do a lot of press-ups and sit-ups as part of the training he'd been talking about. I don't know why I agreed too it.

'Push it, work it, one more,' he yelled as I exercised before collapsing to the floor. Then he began doing these exercises with much more energy and determination than me and suddenly there was a group of girls with us. They just appeared from nowhere, and they all started biting their thumbs and watching him. That seems to happen a lot with Old Bruce.

'Why did you make me come here? What the hell am I doing here? I'm a goofy, epileptic *Star Wars* fan. I don't belong anywhere near the Himalayas,' I said to Bruce as we clawed up a dirty path the next day.

'I told you it would be physical,' he replied. He was right about that. I hate it when Bruce is right. It was really tough. All day I kept thinking, 'Oh dear God, what have I let myself in for?'

We began at 7:30am, and seven hours later I was an angry, exhausted mess. The stench of donkey crap burnt my nostril as we headed into the final hour. Rocky step after rocky step set my legs on fire. Jinsi said the next day was even harder and we would be traversing ice. Funny how he never mentioned any of that at the beginning. I began to question his credibility. Just before we reached our next hostel we came across the donkeys who had left the shits, they were walking with sad faces and heavy loads I wanted to give their Nepalese tormentors a damn good thrashing with my stick, but realised two Nepalese men were carrying my stuff and perhaps I deserved some swift strokes too.

Reaching the hostel was a wonderful feeling and I dropped my bag in the room and, despite Bruce's attempts to get me to come out and look at the sunset, I fell asleep until supper. I was still yawning at the dinner table until spaghetti and bread was put in front of me and I attacked it like a fox at a chicken. There was only one table, but luckily it was very large, because a group of other hikers were also sitting down to eat. It didn't take long for Bruce to be the centre of attention, telling his stories at my expense.

'We were about half way up that really steep jungle section, you know the one with the waterfall, and my brother stepped in this massive donkey crap. It took him half an hour to notice,' Bruce said and was greeted with howls of laughter.

'How can you not notice for thirty minutes?' asked an annoying girl with spectacles and a screwed up face.

'He's a great thinker my brother, a genius. Little things don't bother him when he's thinking of the amazing.'

'What does he think about then?' asked a tall Swiss guy in a woolly hat.

'He thinks about shamanism, the cosmos and boy bands,' said Bruce.

'Wow,' they replied staring at me in admiration.

How exactly do you join in a conversation like this? I just didn't know what to say. 'Does Bruce even know me at all? Do I even know him? Who are these other people?' I thought. I tried so hard to think of something to say, but nothing came to mind. I felt very uncomfortable and decided to go to bed despite Bruce signalling me to come back and join him as I walked off. He looked upset when I didn't. I had been sociable the night before, but the people were too giggly and noisy and they were all loving Bruce too much. I have cursed my lonesomeness throughout life, but in Nepal I realised I just wanted to be alone, and that I have been alone so much in my life because this is what I wanted. We all choose to be the way we are. We can blame others and our circumstances, but we choose.

'I'm really hating this now,' I said to Bruce at 4:45 the next morning as we began walking up a wet slope in a chill of minus seven degrees Celsius.

'Come on it's all an adventure. You love adventure. Romance and adventure like Charlie Chaplin,' Bruce replied from ten paces ahead of me.

Unlike the other days, other walkers overtook me regularly as I sweated, shivered and desperately tried to suck air into my struggling lungs – and those that did ignited my fury. I wanted to be a peaceful, polite, kind person. I wanted to be The Gentleman Tramp, but after just a few minutes I was seething hatred like a wounded animal. I became a brute.

After forty-five minutes, I was kicking things, swearing and grunting as fit positive people filed past me. I snarled at them like a rabid dog with Jinsi getting the worst of it.

'Go slow, no problem, soon there,' said Jinsi.

'Yes, but you said that ten minutes ago,' I replied looking forwards to see nothing but the steep slope that disappeared into the darkness.

'No rush, go slow.'

'How much further?'

'Very soon, five minutes,' Jinsi said as he walked a couple of paces behind me and bumped into the back of my leg when I stopped to hold onto my knees and gasp.

'You said that earlier.'

'Before you say you can do this,' Jinsi said suddenly forgetting that I was his employer and not someone he should be disagreeing with.

'I was talked into this whole trip by your friend in the taxi. I never said anything. How far is it though?' I asked again.

'Soon, five minutes.'

'You said that before,' I said beginning to grow frustrated with the tedious conversation.

'Yes.'

'You're a liar!' I said as I felt my eyes bulging out of my head like an angry cobra. I felt the word liar in the bottom of my toes and I felt it grow in strength as it travelled up through my body and finally was released by my mouth with venom and hate.

'No, me no lie!' Jinsi said.

'You're the devil and a liar,' I said before Jinsi took a deep breath and swallowed the words of retaliation that I could sense burning in his veins. Now he was the bigger man and I felt even weaker than before. We walked the last part in uncomfortable silence.

Bruce had powered on ahead. Carrying his heavy rucksack and maintaining perfect balance, without a stick for help like I did, he climbed higher and higher –enthusiastically. His head was held proudly aloft and he smiled at locals and other climbers. He took deep, soul-enriching puffs of air that nourished his strong army trained body. At the very start he had occasionally glanced back at me, offering infuriatingly kind words of encouragement before he completely disappeared from sight.

Over the next few days we trekked, eat, slept and trekked some more. The walking was relentless and so were the demons in my head that made every footstep an utter misery. The only thing that got me moving was the people doing the same trek. I wanted to get ahead of them everyday to minimise the number of people who would see my suffering. I tried to avoid people, aware of the negativity I was giving off. Jinsi was stuck with me, caught under the responsibility of watching my every move like a devoted carer. He rarely spoke other than to point out an area of beauty or significance or make grand understatements about the length of the day's journey or the steepness of the climb. Occasionally, he would twist his body to one side to let out an array of noxious gases that had brewed in his stomach following his latest batch of Nepalese Dal Bhat, a mixture of rice and lentils. The young porter became increasingly odd, chuckling like a gibbon as we rose to a lower percentage of oxygen. Sometimes he walked with us and other times he disappeared with my bag only to turn up randomly at different points of the day, either ahead of us or catching up from behind. Occasionally the unhappiness of my ego would give way to appreciate the great beauty of where I was.

'That is spectacular,' I said as we gazed down upon the beauty of planet earth one afternoon.

'Hiking up the Himalayas to see the sun set, fantastic. What could be better?' said Bruce, just before I took a step closer to the edge of the mountain and slid on a wet rock. I rolled over on my ankle and let out a whelp. It was so painful that I collapsed to the floor taking long deep breaths. When I put my weight on it the pain intensified and I hobbled to the checkpoint making pathetic noises. The day was a blur of suffering and pain (even more than usual).

That night I took ten pills for epilepsy as Bruce gazed off into the distance with a beer in his hand. He had a serene look on his face as if his mind was blank and tranquil. Free from thought and troubles, Bruce looked more alive than any human I had ever seen before. I wanted to kill him.

The Big Fight

It was on the eighth day of walking that Bruce and I had our fight. We'd been walking up and down these stupid hills for four hours. Every time we would get to what I thought would be the top, we would be greeted by an even bigger mount that Jinsi said we would have to get up before lunch. I'd been getting angrier all day, more furious with every step. I called Bruce an egomaniacal son-of-a-bitch and Jinsi the Devil again, in the hopes that they would keep their distance. Every step increased the agonising pain in my damaged ankle as I struggled to breath. My brain felt like it wasn't mine and I was really worried about having a seizure. My focus was jittery and I could feel the electricity firing around in my head. I kept telling myself to just keep going, but that thought became less and less convincing as another voice emerged that told me to just give up and die.

An hour before the scheduled lunch-stop we reached the bottom of a hill that led to another mighty climb. It took just seven excruciating steps before I decided to admit defeat and sit on the floor. There wasn't any grass or comfy ground to rest on – oh no, grass has the good sense not to grow in such awful places. It was just rock and stone and shit. Realising I still wasn't comfy, I lay back with my head on the dirty dust ridden path and looked up at the almighty blue sky. Struggling to balance on the incline, I thought it would be a good idea to just roll sideways down to the bottom of the mount where I could relax better. I banged my head and elbows a bit, but I didn't care, I wanted to struggle on bravely no longer. It was the end for me. What was the point of continuing? The grim reaper comes for us all eventually and this seemed as good a time as any for my inevitable demise. Even Bruce had looked tired and fed up that day and Jinsi was slowing down, and he's Nepalese. I'm much less fit than those two and my ankle had swollen terribly.

The anger and frustration drifted away from my body as my life flashed before my eyes. It didn't take long. What had I been doing with my life? I hadn't lived the life I wanted, the life of The Gentleman Tramp, the life of romance and adventure.

'Jesus, are you OK,' Bruce asked as he turned around to see me lolloping down the hill like a sausage falling off a plate and land on my back with a thud.

'Fine' I said as I gazed upwardly from my position on the floor.

'Come on, no time to rest now. You've done so well,' said Bruce galloping down the hill to be by my side. 'I know your ankle hurts but it'll get better. Let's get going.' He put his hand on my shoulder as I stared of into the distance, feeling a profound relaxation. 'Come on, you just have to think positively. Everything will be fine. It's mind over matter.'

'I've been an idiot from start to finish, Bruce. I can't stop the sadness,' I said feeling my soul being embraced by infinity and my butt being scratched by stones.

'You will. It just takes time.'

'No, I'm finished. Leave me here for the animals. Get to the top. I want to stay here.'

Jinsi and Bruce began to have a serious conversation to one side as I lay there visualising eternal nothingness. I heard words like home, help and return – which my mind seemed to respond too. They came back and knelt down besides my body, and Jinsi explained the plan. We would continue to our current destination. The next day we would walk down to another village where we would hire a donkey to take me back down to Pokhara. It would take a few days, but from there I would be able to get a bus to Kathmandu and fly home.

'A donkey? I can't go on a donkey. I'll be fine here. You carry on. I like it here,' I said.

'You're being ridiculous, get up,' said Bruce.

'You have been affected by the altitude and the walking,' said Jinsi.

'I've been affected by life,' I said.

'Am I going to have to drag you the rest of the way?' asked Bruce.

'No.'

'Well then get up.'

I just lay there motionless and helpless, so Bruce grabbed my leg and began dragging me up the start of that vicious hill along the dirty rock until I got a little cross. He had no right to be dragging me, so I got up and kicked him with my bad foot, right on his big arse.

When he turned around he had madness in his eyes and he was coming for me. He shoved me violently and I backpedalled and tripped over my own feet, staggering to the floor in slow motion trying to grab at the air to stop my self from falling. I was back where I started at the bottom of the mount.

'I'm sorry, I shouldn't have done that. Just don't kick me,' Bruce said, but by the time he said the word kick, I was scrambling to my feet ready to give that bastard another good kick in the arse. I bungled my way up towards him and swung my leg wildly, it caught him in the side of the thigh and I grabbed hold of his sweaty chest in an attempt to wrestle him down.

Disappointingly, he got me first and wrapped his big, ape arm around my head as we twisted around and collapsed to the floor before rolling back down to the bottom of the hill. I swung my fists at his body as we fell, but with little impact as he tightened his grip on my face. I got one good shot in though. I know that because I heard him call out 'you little shit'. He had the good fortune of landing on top of me, so he pinned me down with my arms behind my back and yanked them so they really hurt.

'Do you give up?' he enquired.

'Yes, yes. I give up,' I said, so he let me go. Stupid Bruce! I felt the weight of him release and I had my arms back. I got to my knees as he walked away. He put his hands to his knees to catch his breath, and I saw my opportunity so ran up behind him and pushed him as hard as I could. He went over and I got in four swift kicks to the arse. I didn't care if it hurt my ankle.

'Stop kicking me in the ass,' he shouted as he grabbed my legs and tackled me to the floor giving me a solid punch to the shoulder that felt like a dagger tearing at my muscle. He was trying to make me say I give up again. He had my leg bent sideways and my arm behind my back.

'Do you give up?' he said.

'Never!' I replied, he kept twisting and yanking my arm and leg until the pain was intolerable and panic inducing.

'Do you give up?'

'No!' I said. 'Jinsi, I will give you a thousand rupees to get him off me.'

'If I let you go, will you stop fighting?' asked Bruce.

'Never!' I repeated. We lay there for what felt like another twenty minutes having different variations of this same conversation. Sometimes he pulled my arm with vicious cruelty.

'I want to let you go, but you need to promise not to try and kick me,' Bruce said.

'I will always kick you. You don't care about anyone but yourself, just as long as you're having a good time. Someone needs to kick you.'

'I'm always thinking of you. I've tried to include you in things, but you're never interested. You just want to sit around watching Charlie bloody Chaplin. Why can't you smile once in a while? And not that stupid Chaplin face, a proper smile,' said Bruce.

'Oh I'm Bruce everyone loves me, fantastic, what could be better, everything's so amazing and everyone thinks I'm brilliant. You're not brilliant, you're an idiot and I can think of hundreds of things better than climbing mountains with you. So I'll be smiling just as soon as I'm far far away from you, you rotten shit,' I said.

'You wanted to come here. I don't remember inviting you.'

'Well then, let me go.'

Bruce did let me go and I tried to kick him again but Jinsi came to stop me.

'I'm sorry. I was just trying to help you,' muttered Bruce before we began walking up that awful mountain in awkward silence as the searing pain of my bad ankle made me wretch.

'I'm sorry for earlier,' I said when we finally got to the hostel several hours of misery later. We had showered and eaten and there was nothing to do except sit outside and gaze out upon beauty, and chat.

'I was being stupid,' I continued.

'Forget it,' Bruce said, 'the mountains can drive anyone mad. I was stupid too. I'm sorry for dragging you here. I know it's not your type of thing. I should have warned you more, or gone somewhere else with you. When we get back to England we'll do something you like. Watch movies, whatever you want.'

'I want to go on more walks. Not walking up mountains though, just normal walks with trees and grass, and I want to play more sport and swim too.'

'Great, I'm in, and no more mountains, I promise.'

Bruce stood up and gave me a hug. I wasn't used to being hugged, it felt very strange and I wanted it to end quickly so I manoeuvred it into a hearty handshake.

The next morning we had both relaxed and the argument was all but forgotten as we walked down to where the donkeys were kept.

'I'd like to carry on,' said Bruce. 'But if you need me too, I can come down to Pokhara with you. From there I can see if there are any short treks I can do before I start work.'

'No, it's fine. I have plans of my own,' I said.

'What plans are they?'

'Romance and adventure! I want to search for romance and adventure.'

'Fantastic, what could be better?' Bruce had been right. I needed to make more of life.

Bruce laughed rambunctiously as I climbed onto my donkey in the giant stone courtyard overlooking the fabulous foothills and the snowy mountains above. I named my donkey Dave, and he seemed a good chap as we began to slowly plod in circles. Jinsi was looking far from happy

'What an experience, riding on a donkey in the Himalayas. I'm jealous,' said Bruce as he hitched his bag onto his shoulders ready for another long day.

'Why don't you get one?' I replied as I tried to balance on Dave's back.

'I've set my self the challenge to walk with full kit just like the Nepalese.'

'Well, you look tired. You've got weeks of this still. Get a donkey.'

There were lots of donkeys there. I had selected Dave as he looked the friendliest and his dark matted hair looked funky and spiked covering strong legs. His face was dopey, but his mouth was set upon a permanent grin. He was a cool donkey.

'No I can't, it would be cheating.'

'I think you're scared of falling off,' I said adding some chicken noises for effect.

'Fine, I'll get a donkey.'

Bruce mounted his beast, which he named Daisy.

'Go and check out some other parts of Nepal,' he said. 'What could be better?'

'See you soon, let me know about your next trip,' I said.

'I've got plans for Ethiopia and Colombia, email me from England. You can come and join me,' Bruce said as Daisy and Dave took us away from each other.

Even riding down on Dave the donkey was physically demanding. My legs ached like never before. My swollen ankle was throbbing and my big toes were black under the nail. I think I could have done the trek, maybe if I had a better pair of boots.

Every time Dave took a step down my bum bounced off the saddle. It was agony. I felt awful that Dave had to carry me about, but I was really struggling. I decided that I would try and help animals in the future, because Dave was saving my life.

As it turned out, I was glad to have some time alone with Jinsi because he began to open up about his life and we became friends. He told me that he worked whenever he could, desperately trying to support his family of six children. In the winter there is no work and by the sound of it he grows melancholy and frustrated.

'These mountains, this is my home,' said Jinsi.

On the second night of our trudge, Jinsi lit a fire outside the cosy hostel. We stood around it like cavemen and dangled our freezing feet above it. Chickens ran around and other porters and trekkers greeted us happily and wanted to be near our warm corner.

'We never make fires at home, everything is gas and electric,' I said. 'It's a shame because fires are fun. At home people spend a lot of time indoors.'

'I have had people say this often. One woman wanted her computer and telephone so much that everyday she cried until we went back. I like to be a part of nature,' Jinsi said poking the fire with a stick.

'I know I've been indoors too much. I'm going to try to get out more,' I said.

That night was fiercely dark when the fire went out, so dark I couldn't even see my hand in front of me. We gathered in a cold room with wooden tables and a small television, and Jinsi sat with the other guides and porters to chat, play cards and watch WWE wrestling.

'Come my friend, join us,' said one of the porters. I wasn't used to being referred too in this manner and it felt wonderful. We eat Dal Bat on Jinsi's recommendation and I liked it, then I tried a repulsive rice wine before watching the main event fight. All the men were upset that Randy Orton was pinned; so was I, especially after my own recent wrestling defeat. I really got into the spirit of being one of the boys and I began to realise how good it was to be part of a group of people. It felt like I was real. If only I had grown up in Nepal.

After a few more days downhill, I found the strength to give Dave a rest. I would have liked to have carried him, but I wasn't that strong. We started to go back through the villages we had passed through that first day, and they all seemed so much nicer and friendlier when going downhill. They all smiled and said *'Namaste'*, so I did the same.

At the end of the trip, I tipped Jinsi and the porter. I hope it was enough. Those guys deserve big money.

Back in Pokhara, I had some days to kill before my planned flight back to London, so I booked a trip to a national park called Chitwan. I was very excited to see some wild animals. Unfortunately, I got a bit closer to some of the animals than I'd hoped. Especially the crocodiles!

Welcome to the Jungle

I was collected from Chitwan bus station by a jeep. One of my favourite books and movies is *Jurassic Park*. Driving along dirt paths, through forests and grassland made me feel like the hero, Alan Grant. I loved it. I couldn't stop smiling. I was staying in a village compound in the middle of the jungle.

My bungalow was enchanting and peaceful; it backed out onto grassland that overlooked the enormous snaky river that separated me from the jungle. Children were out by the river feeding their cattle. The sun was firing on all cylinders and I could hear crickets chirping in the fields. My heart felt clear and free, and I was so excited to be in such a beautiful place. In the evening I was given a tour of the village; the guide spoke so proudly of the history and the customs, but said that the local people were being forced to adapt to increased tourism. I worried I was making this problem worse until my mind was put at rest by warm greetings. A small boy kicked his football toward me and I postponed the tour to pass it back and forth. Chickens ran up and began pecking at my ankles and all the villagers smiled at me, so I raised my Derbyshire hat and smiled back. Their was a wonderful sense of community, the families lived in close proximity and the population was small enough so that everyone knew each other and had clear roles. It was not like home where people shut themselves off. I have never had a conversation with any of my neighbours.

That evening, I was taken with some other tourists to see a dance show in the middle of the village. The young Nepalese men and women were incredibly talented and expressed great beauty and dignity with their movements. Not like the drunken youths I had seen in an English nightclub when I was forced to attend with Bruce one time. Those dancers were just sort of jumping up and down and shouting and thrusting their pelvic regions at people. No, these dancers were of another level.

For the crescendo of their performance some of the entertainers came into the audience to recruit more dancers, a young woman took my arm and led me up on stage to the laughter of the spectators (a gentleman never turns down the offer of a lady.) We were all dancing our way around the drummer in the middle, kicking our legs out from side to side and clapping. I tried to follow the gentleman in front of me and imitate his movements, but it was not as easy as I thought. I kept going the wrong way or mistiming my clap, so I started just doing my own dance. I like to shake my shoulders when I dance and raise my arms up and down. Sometimes I bend my knees and go low before springing up with a jump. I really like to feel the music and see where my body takes me. Yes, I really am a great dancer. You should see me go.

In the morning, I was taken for an elephant ride. I was very excited about this as you can imagine. On the outskirts of the jungle was a row of tall wooden platforms with steps leading up to the top, people were standing on the platforms and staring off towards the trees. After a few moments there came a rustling sound and the trunk of a huge beast came poking through the foliage followed by an enormous head and a majestic body. The creature lumbered out and soon two of his friends appeared on either side of him. My jaw opened aghast, and I was mesmerised as the behemoths came closer and closer. This would have been the most amazing sight I'd ever seen, had it not been for the seven or eight people the elephants were each carrying on their backs. They were ushered up to the platforms where the giggling tourists got off only to be replaced by another weight-load of people that included me.

Squashed into a corner, surrounded by an Indian family, I tried to get comfy, but it wasn't easy. I couldn't take my eyes off the skin of the elephant below me and, like a small child, I couldn't resist touching the animals leathery tough hide. It didn't feel as nice as I thought, rough and hairy it was. I think I would have preferred just to look at the elephants really, instead of clambering on top of the poor thing with all those other people. This feeling intensified as we journeyed through the jungle and the wrinkly old son-of-a-bitch that sat on the elephant's neck raised his metal stick and cracked poor Ellie over the noggin. I sat quietly the first time he did this, but I was itching with fury. The family didn't seem to care and just continued taking photos of the jungle and smiling, but when that demonic old savage thrashed his metal pipe down again, I couldn't maintain my silence.

'Stop hitting him over the head,' I said. I'm not even sure if he heard me because seconds later he was lifting the pipe again, but this time I reached over and grabbed a hold of his arm.

'Stop hitting him,' I repeated.

He turned round and opened his toothless face to utter a most disrespectful diatribe. He stared into my head with confusion and disgust – like I was the one behaving badly. I couldn't interpret his words, but just like a Chaplin movie the body language was extremely clear. He was angry that I'd grabbed his arm.

Moments later, he thumped the elephant again and I couldn't take it anymore, I backed up squashing the family behind me into the basket and lifted my legs, squeezing myself up into the basket, I carefully climbed onto my knees. The driver turned around and started shouting and trying to grab my arm.

'Get off,' I muttered climbing over the side of the basket. The elephant slowed down as the man clasped the metal chain that was attached to his feet around the throat of the pachyderm. The shouts continued and the other passengers were now also telling me to stop, but I had made up my mind. I had one foot on the side of the elephant and one foot in the basket. I was clinging on with my arms and I swung the other leg over. Holding on to the basket for dear life, I began lowering myself down. I didn't have time to think or perfect my dismount; it was all a rushed panic. I landed on the ground from about six feet up and let out a wail of agony as I landed on my bad ankle. Then I began walking angrily back in the direction from which we had come. The shouts from the driver continued and I sensed he was turning the elephant around. I didn't look back. I wanted to get away from that thug and his cruelty so I walked as fast as my ankle would allow and headed into the jungle alone.

I believe it must have taken about twenty-five minutes until I lost my confidence in where I was going. It all looked so similar, but I didn't believe that I had changed direction at any time. I should really have been back to the car park in that time, but no, I was still in thick jungle. Was I going in the right direction? My ankle really hurt. I was of course very lucky not to have been more seriously injured from this daredevil stunt, but that was of little comfort as I hobbled along desperate for water. I didn't panic, not straightaway at least. It took a while for me to start thinking about the wild animals.

I knew there weren't any lions and I was really hoping that tigers were nocturnal. I think I'd heard that somewhere before. The night before, the guide had been talking about sloth bears. They had attacked quite a few tourists and seriously mauled them before help arrived. There was also the rhino risk. Strong, powerful, quick and with those pointy horns that poacher's steal, I didn't want to come across a rhino. I began to place my feet with added care in hopes of not alerting any beasts to my presence. I considered calling for help, but I thought that might disturb a sleepy tiger that could be just metres away. I was sweating a lot and I must have been a real stink to any animal in the area. Maybe a horrible, violating stench or maybe the smell of dinner, I don't know which would be worse. My heart began to thump louder as my breaths were getting deeper. I wanted to be a chameleon, undetectable in the jungle. I think in total I spent about two to three hours wandering around. 'Surely people were out looking for me after I jumped off the elephant,' I thought.

The first animals I came across were a family of deer. That may sound pretty tame, but they really startled me and they had a menacing look in their eyes. It was the unpredictability of them that frightened me. One minute they were totally still and then they were leaping off into the trees making a hell of a racket. Beautiful creatures really, only I should have liked to have observed them under better circumstances.

You wouldn't believe the relief I felt when I came to the river, for I knew that my bungalow was on the other side. I traced the watery expanse with my eyes, and I could see where the hotel compound was. It would be a bit of a walk once I'd crossed the bridge, which was in the other direction, but I was just so happy that I knew where I was. I quickened my pace as I headed for the bridge. I was feeling so grateful to have a sense of direction. However, I was stopped dead in my tracks by what I could see lurking under the bridge, next to the bridge and past the bridge. Crocodiles!

My heart stopped and I froze in panic. There were five of them in total; at least that's how many I could see, maybe there were more in the water. None of them were moving and they were all basking in the sun. A couple of them had their mouths wide open as if they were waiting to be fed, but they didn't move at all. It crossed my mind that perhaps they weren't real and just models for tourists to look at. I didn't particularly want to take that chance and so turned around to go the other way. Surely there was another bridge in the other direction. As I began walking along the river I saw more and more crocodiles just lying there in the bank. 'Oh no! Oh no! Oh no! I thought while trying to weigh up my options.

Option 1: Go back into the jungles and look for help; this could lead to getting even more lost or being mauled by a rhino or a sloth bear.

Option 2: Try to sneak past the crocodiles and over the bridge to safety.

Option 3: Stay exactly where I was and shit myself.

After I had taken the third option, I decided to cross the bridge. I didn't feel that standing still could lead to anything good, I was just waiting for trouble. So I headed back for the bridge and decided to just go for it. No sneaking around, no tiptoes, just walk up to the bridge and get across it.

I could see the first one out of the corner of my eye as I approached the bridge, not as big as some of the others but still terrifying. He was on the bank down the slope below me, facing the other way, he was not moving. The next one was higher up and sideways so he could see me, I think. He was absolutely massive and his mouth was wide apart with gigantic, sharp fangs. His eyes just sat motionless in his face, dead to the world, I hoped. I just kept walking and he was soon behind me. The next croc was directly under the bridge and I didn't think he was a threat because of the effort it would take to get up the slope and round the bridge. It was the two that sat on the same level as me a few metres past the bridge that were the problem. I was actually walking closer towards them and there was a ghastly set of birds in the sky making a terrible noise. I waved at them to shut up. I really tried to just focus on the bridge and, just get to the bridge and across.

As I lay my first foot on that wooden plank, I was so relieved and I walked even faster as I headed for the other side. About a third of the way across, I felt like I had made it. I could sense none of them were moving, so I stopped and turned around. Just as I suspected the crocodiles were still, so after staring at them for a minute or two I began retracing my steps for a closer look. They really weren't moving; maybe they were dead. Maybe they weren't real crocodiles. I kept taking a few more steps and then stopping to look at them, then a few more steps. It was really exciting, I wanted to be part of the crocodile gang; they looked like chilled out guys, they looked like they knew stuff. I was really quite close by now and enjoyed just being with them. 'Surely just another couple of steps would be OK,' I thought.

But as soon as I moved, so did one of the crocs. His eyes instantly became alive and settled on me. He lifted his head and he was moving towards me. I could read his mind – he was hungry and I was his dinner. His tail swung and he was moving like a dart as I turned and ran as fast as my ankle would allow. I didn't look back, not even when I was to the end of the bridge. I just kept heading for the village and my bungalow.

It wasn't until I was safely at the entrance to the village and I was greeted by some wonderful children, that I relaxed. The children were pointing towards the river. I didn't want to look, what if that awful croc was there and coming after me. But they kept saying 'look, look'. So I turned my head to see. Across the water was the most curious chap sipping from the river. Gigantic but beautiful, like a living tank, he slurped and slurped. The rhino wasn't far from where I had been earlier – he was a magnificent sight. I was so glad to be watching him from safety and that I hadn't gone back into the jungle. I stood with the children, staring at this wonderful creature in awe. It was a special moment; I had a newfound appreciation for existence.

That night I drunk and eat so much, savouring every morsel of taste and fulfilment.

After this excitement, I just wanted to sit in the grass and read or walk around the village until it was time to leave Chitwan. I needed to rest my ankle, which I had bandaged by a local doctor. I was lectured about my dangerous actions as many people had been out looking for me. I just nodded and said sorry. I'm good at doing that.

Finally, I took a bus to Pokhara and then flew to Kathmandu. It was time for me to go home.

Standing in the monotonous cue, waiting to check in to my flight to New Delhi, I looked at the other passengers and wondered about their final destination. There were definitely Indians and Germans going to their respective countries. I felt jealous of them, I wanted to be going somewhere other than England. I'd spent enough time in England. I was fed up of the soul-destroying routine and the meaningless human contact. I still had quite a lot of money; maybe £7,000 give or take. Surely it wouldn't hurt to see what other destinations were available and how much flights would cost.

The lady gave me a list of possible destinations from New Delhi and I was immediately fascinated by Bangkok. What an adventure that would be. I remembered Mariana saying she would love to go to Thailand, so it must be good, I thought.

Before I booked the tickets I asked my self a question. The same question Dr. Jove had asked me. What would Charlie Chaplin do? Get on the plane with a smile and a skip was the answer. So I said goodbye to Nepal and my negativity. I was no longer willing to be miserable. It was time to start enjoying myself, so I checked in and boarded the plane to Thailand via New Delhi.

In the air I waved goodbye to the Himalayas and I thought of Bruce powering up those hills encouraging everyone with cries of 'Fantastic. What could be better?'

As I sat squashed in the horrible aeroplane, experiencing sickening turbulence while trying to eat a disgusting tasteless meal, I really couldn't have agreed with Bruce more.

Party Party Party

Thailand is another dimension, one in which the gluttony and indulgence of tourists is exploited with friendly smiles. It was here that I embarked upon a new life of enjoyment and fun.

I didn't really like it very much.

As I stepped off the plane at Bangkok airport, I was hit by a wave of heat and humidity, as though I was being attacked by a thirty-foot hairdryer. The airport was clean and sterile, a very ordinary public building, but the smiles of the Thai people gave it a feeling of excitement. That's what I loved about Thailand, the infectious smiles.

I didn't stay in Bangkok for more than a few days. It was a big, dirty city and I wanted to go to the beach so, after a long bus journey, I got on an overnight boat to the infamous Koh Samui. I had read and heard a lot about this large and populous island in the gulf of Thailand. Apparently, it boasted delicious local cuisine, clean sandy beaches, calm seas and had a host of relaxing and pleasurable activities such as yawning yoga, calamitous canoes, jumping jet-ski's, marvellous marine-life and meditative massage. What's more, the locals were supposed to be even friendlier and smilier than in Bangkok, with the most beautiful women on earth and total relaxation guaranteed. 'It's like Disneyland for grown-ups,' said a toothless, drunken old man in one of my Bangkok hostels. 'You can live like a king there.'

I boarded the tiny boat nervously, as I was unsure of my sea legs, and I was ushered down to the sleeping quarters with the rest of the passengers. The room was long and rectangular with about sixty mattresses on the floor. It was a window-less room, dusty and wooden, with dim orange lights dangling above casting a Halloween glow to the evening. People were sitting around chatting and, after finding my own little space next to the doorway so that I would only have one neighbour and not two, I settled down to read the autobiography of Charles Spencer Chaplin for the thirty-third time. When the bed next to me was finally taken, it was by a bearded Thai man wearing spectacles, he was trying to juggle looking after all of his five children – that were sandwiched between him and his beautiful but tired-looking wife. The children's ages ranged from a tiny baby, no more than a few months old, to a moody looking chap with a baseball cap and a handheld computer game. They were going through their civilised night-time routines such as singing songs, playing with cards that had pictures of animals on them, and one-by-one going to the bathroom to return in proper pyjamas. The father sat one of his daughters next to him to read her a story, and she couldn't help but slap me on the leg every time there was something exciting in the adventures of the cartoon dog. I felt really bad that I was somehow in the way of this family who were making the most of this uncomfortable trip with their wonderful attitude and rattling good spirit.

I was fully dressed in my Chaplin suit and hadn't even brushed my teeth. I used my bag as a pillow, but barely slept. I was definitely inferior to this lovely family. I was an awkward invader.

Opposite my mattress was about a metre of wooden corridor that separated the two long lines of beds. People would traipse up and down it to go to the big kettle on the other side of the door or go outside to get some fresh air or use the toilet – they would usually wake up anyone with the audacity to try and sleep. The mattresses were slim so I couldn't curl up, and short enough so my toes came off the end of my bed. Directly across from me was a young Thai couple, the eager doe-eyed female had rubbed lotion on the man's limp, runner-bean arm. She got up to make him some tea, returning with the mug of hot water and the milk and sugar to mix until receiving his approval. She had to get up to put it all back and bumped into my feet again, and then several more time as she stood fluffing his pillows. He did absolutely nothing. At first I thought it was rather sweet, it was nice that she was enjoying looking after her man, old fashioned and romantic. However, when I saw her washing his face with a flannel I thought it a bit ridiculous. I wasn't sure if he was this terrible man making his wife do everything for him or if it was her bossing him around and treating him like a child. They both seemed happy anyway. Next to them was a western pair – a striking blonde Scandinavian girl who was chuckling over a comic book and bobbing her head to earphones, and a dark-haired, muscular chap with a baseball hat pulled over his face as he lay down to sleep for the entire journey. Occasionally, she would wake him and ask him if he wanted something to drink and he would hold onto his head and moan as if he had the most terrible headache, before rolling over to sleep some more.

It was a long and uncomfortable night and I was very glad that good old Charlie Chaplin was there to keep me company. I imagine that the workhouses he'd been in as a child were a bit like that boat – cramped, dirty and with no privacy.

We arrived early in the morning and I got a taxi to the beach and booked a bungalow for a few nights. The bungalow was infested with cockroaches and lizards, and it had a really uncomfortable looking wooden bed and only a couple of blankets. The toilet was a hole dug into the floor and the tap spluttered out dirty water. It was right on the beach though, so I was very happy with it indeed. I could hear the waves breaking on the shore as I lay in bed and got some much needed sleep.

I didn't wake up and make it to the beach until late afternoon. It didn't cross my mind when I stepped onto the soft golden sand that crinkled beneath my toes that I was about to embark upon an eighteen-hour long party. I was wearing just baggy shorts from the waist down, but from the waist up I was in full Chaplin attire.

'Jeeezus, aren't you hot in those clothes?' came a voice from behind. I looked over to see the Scandinavian girl sunbathing with a coconut in her hand and sunglasses on her head. I nervously looked away and continued walking. 'Do you speak English?' she continued. This was when I realised I was being terribly rude and turned to talk to her.

'Sorry, yes I am English. It's hot in any clothes. I like to dress smart,' I said.

'But you're on the beach. You can't wear a suit on the beach,' she replied laughing. We continued to chit chat. Her name was

Nico, she was charming and invited me to sit with her. I thought perhaps my dreams of romance had come true. She told me about herself – how she had been travelling around Asia for some time – as she began to sprinkle this green stuff onto a cigarette paper.

She rolled it up and lit it.

'Would you like some of this?' she asked.

I never turn down an offer from a lady, so I took it with a smile and put it to my lips. It was hot as I inhaled and I could feel my lips burning with the crackle of the paper as the end of the cigarette glowed a fierce red. The stench of it was overpowering and made my eyes water as the thick smoke made it's way into my lungs. I had to swallow to stop the coughing. The blood rushed to my head and all I could taste was ash and burning paper. After a couple more puffs the party had started.

'Is it illegal to smoke this stuff here?' I asked.

'Yes, but don't worry. Nobody cares here. Well the police care, but they are not here. Don't worry.'

'I think I'm sinking into the sand,' I said.

'You won't sink into the sand.'

'Do you think there are dragons in the sea?'

'No, I don't think there are dragons,' she said.

'Are you sure?'

'I hope not or Jordon is in trouble. He is out there on a jet ski.'

I looked out to where Nico was pointing and saw water bubbling up like soap under a speed machine that cut through the water and bounced up and down on the waves.

'Woohoooo,' were the shouts of the driver, who held one arm up in the air as he stood up on his wave runner. He was heading towards the beach at full throttle and showed no signs of slowing down. Grinning from ear to ear with sparkling teeth he raced into the shallows and manoeuvred the boat onto the beach.

'Man that was fun! You have to have a go on one of those things Nico. They are awesome,' he said as he approached, dripping water on to us as he reached for a bottle of drink before slumping down. 'Hey, you were on the boat last night. I'm Jordon, nice to meet you.'

'The pleasure is all mine,' I said.

'Aren't you hot in those clothes?'

'Not as hot as I was,' I replied.

The pair of them were terribly friendly and they invited me to go to dinner with them.

As I fiddled with my chopsticks trying to scoop sticky rice into my face, Jordon explained how he had lived in Thailand for over a year as a teacher and was now travelling before he had to go home.

'Ah man it's been freakin' awesome! I was making enough money to live in a nice house, go out three times a week and save up to go on trips to amazing places like this. Did you have to save up for your trip?'

'I was saving for a wedding, but came here instead.'

Good move. This is much better. The people are so nice; the food is great; the weather is fantastic,' Jordon said.

'How do you know it's better? Have you ever had a wedding? Maybe he loved this girl,' Nico said.

'She could have come with him if she loved him. Better than an expensive wedding. He was offering her an amazing experience so she should've taken it,' Jordon said.

'People have responsibilities in the real world. It's not always so simple. Life is hard. People have jobs and bills and families,' Nico said.

'I know that! On the farm in Saskatchewan it gets to minus forty in the winter. That's life being hard, there is no fun or fashion or socialising. You just try to keep warm for six months. Then you have to spend the entire summer working your ass off to get a decent harvest to keep you going through the winter. Twelve-hour days I work and then I have to fit in my studies. I'm just saying that coming somewhere like Thailand is a better option than enduring a hard life. This girlfriend of yours should have known that. Sounds like you're better off without her.'

'I didn't invite her, she was cheating and she was also mean,' I said.

'She cheated on you. Then you definitely did the right thing coming here. It's awful, but now you can party with us,' said Nico.

'That's right, we're going to tear this island up tonight,' said Jordon.

'Can't wait,' I said.

I hadn't known what to order, so Nico ordered for me. There were bowls of different things all over the table; vegetable dishes, chicken dishes, pork, fish, rice, omelettes and soups. The table was full and there were bottles of beer sitting in ice. Women in tight red dresses stood by the table and every time I finished my glass of beer one of them would fill it right up again. There was something called jungle curry, a chicken dish with a light red sauce, which had tasted great to start, but after a few seconds my mouth began to tingle and then sting. I licked my lips as the burning began. I listened to Nico talk about Danish pop music as I reached for more beer and emptied the glass.

'More beer please, it's hot.'

My mouth would not stop burning, and the others told me that my face was going red as tears streamed down my face. I wiped my eyes, but I must have had some curry on my hands because then my eyes started burning too. I grabbed a napkin to rub my eyes and tried to scoop my mouth out. I breathed hard to get some soothing cold air onto my tongue and drunk more and more beer.

'You don't like spicy?' asked the waitress.

'Yes it's delicious,' I said as I opened my mouth as wide as it would go, crying into my napkin and drinking more and more beer.

'There are things that piss me off in Thailand. Like they don't warn you when something's going to burn your mouth to pieces,' said Jordon.

'It's not that spicy. You two need to man up. I'm more pissed off about the racism and the sexism than spicy food. I'm pissed off about poor people being used by these rich, fat western assholes,' said Nico looking across at a table of American or German businessmen dressed in golf clothes who were stuffing their faces and putting their hands all over the multitude of young prostitutes that they had on their table.

'How un-gentlemanly,' I said.

'I would kill myself if I was one of those guys,' Jordon said.

After dinner we went to a beach bar and got some cocktails. All different colours they were, with umbrellas and fruits sticking out of them. They tasted quite sweet so I didn't suspect I would get so drunk.

'You are both very, very lovely people,' I said. 'I didn't know people were so nice. I thought they were all a bunch of bloody bastards. The Thai people too. So nice and lovely, I love it all,' I said.

In another bar, there were far more people and live music, and we moved from cocktails to what Jordon called 'a bucket of joy'. It was a foul concoction of vodka, caffeine, ice and God knows what else. We had one each. Every sip was repulsive and I was beginning to feel sick. Once I had made it to halfway through the buckets, I was declaring my love for everyone with such enthusiasm that I got up and climbed on the table to dance around like a crazed Ape. Nico stood up to dance too and Jordon was clapping. Pretty soon nobody was watching the band, they were all watching me and clapping and cheering to my wonderful dance moves. After the dancing in the Nepalese village and now this, I was really beginning to get a taste for performance. It made me feel alive. The owner of the bar came over with free tequila shots to express his enjoyment at my performance. I drank it down and suddenly didn't feel too good. I excused myself and ran to the toilet where I regurgitated beer, the bucket of joy, cocktails and the tequila. But I went straight back and started drinking again, my head hurt but it was time to enjoy myself and party. Bruce would be so proud of me.

Next we went to a club and drank some more beer. There were Thai girls in the shortest of dresses and some of them were rubbing their bottoms against me. I thought this most odd. I think you really need to romance a lady before any of that sort of funny business. Jordon was trying to get me to dance with these girls, but I was just enjoying the music. Nico was dancing a lot too, she waved her arms around and her blonde hair swayed around amid a sea of dark hair.

This dancing went on for some time before Nico said she was going back now and that she would hopefully see me tomorrow. She kissed Jordon goodbye and when she was gone Jordon said we should go to this other bar he knew about.

'Why the hell not?' I said.

We walked for some time before we reached an unadvertised building with four very large men standing outside.

'I think this is the place,' said Jordon. 'My buddy told me about it, it's a ping pong bar.'

The men at the door took a great deal of money from us before leading us down a long, dark corridor. With every step further into this building the dance music grew louder and the smell of tobacco grew stronger. Finally there was some light and we reached a big smoke-filled room. A few men sat in dark corners sipping whiskey and ogling the centrepiece of the stage. I looked to see the object of their lecherous fascination and saw a sexual gymnastics session going on between a hairy-buttocked fat man and a skinny woman with her legs over her head. I quickly looked away again as we were led to a table. Jordon ordered a couple of beers, and before long we were joined on either side by some women in their underwear.

'You very handsome man,' said the lady by my side as she put an arm around me.

'Thanks. You're nice too,' I said.

'You buy me drink?'

'Maybe later,' I said.

When the repulsive sex act finished there was a small gap in the entertainment before the main event. A woman got onto the stage and started to perform a variety of tricks that all focused around the theme of her lady parts. She used her vagina to open a bottle of beer, fire Ping-Pong balls across the room and seemingly eat a banana. My favourite part of this bizarre show came moments later when some of the women dragged Jordon up on to the stage despite his protests.

'No, I really prefer not too,' he said.

I was of course full of encouragement. On stage they pulled Jordon's shirt over his head and lay him on the stage. The Ping-Pong lady managed to grasp a big felt pen inside herself before squatting over him and gyrating. When Jordon stood up he had Bad Boy written on his chest. I found this highly amusing and it became even funnier when he came to sit down looking very embarrassed.

The lady next to me had left the table for a while, but when she returned she began kissing my neck.

'Be careful, I think she's a dude,' said Jordon.

I had not even considered this, but suddenly she seemed a lot less attractive as I started to inch away from her. In that dark room there was not enough evidence to confirm either way. This made me start to feel a little unwell again, a problem that got worse when I took a big mouthful from my glass only to notice a Ping-Pong ball floating on top of the frothy beverage. This prompted my second vomit of the evening, and when I returned from the bathroom I was adamant that I wanted to leave.

We paid our bill and headed for our beach bungalows. However, before we made it home we passed a maze of other bars that were nice and quiet and that had pool tables. Jordon suggested a game, and under the neon lights listening to music from the 1980s and 90s, I was given a thrashing. He needed a greater challenge so played against one of the bar girls, who I thought definitely looked like a man. She was giving him a run for his money as I began swaying back and forth to the *Titanic* song by Celine Dion. There was a table of Thai girls in very low-cut tops and short skirts giggling at me so I invited them to join me and one of them became my Kate Winslett as I shouted, 'I'm the King of the world,' like Leonardo DiCaprio. I brought her a drink because she was endearing and beautiful, with a flower in her hair and a sparkle in her eye. Her name was Eve and for the first time in Thailand I began to feel twitches in my trousers. She asked if I could buy a drink for her friend Som, who was equally delightful. Som was dressed in blue with a full smile and a sensual laugh. We began to talk as they pressed their thighs against me. I was overcome with a breathless fancy and my heart was thumping about in my heart like an overexcited rabbit. After a couple more drinks, Eve started to passionately kiss me as Som rubbed my leg.
  'You want we come home with you?' said Eve.
  'That would be very nice,' I said totally confused and bewitched. 'I don't have a very big room though.'
  'It's OK, we take you to good hotel for tonight,' said Som. I said goodbye to Jordon as he doubled over with laughter and I departed with the two ladies on my arm.
  The hotel was fabulous, very expensive. Too expensive, but as I stood under a hot shower with two women sponging me down and lathering me up with soap, I really didn't care.
'This is amazing,' I said as Eve lay on top of me kissing me, and Som sat beside me stroking my arm. Eve sat up and Som took her

turn to kiss me with her wet soft, tasty lips. The smell of their hair was intoxicating as my hands wandered all over their bodies. The drunkenness in my mind was falling away and I felt very serious and confused. This is not the sort of thing that happens to me. I'd only ever made love to Sophie, and now I had two women pleasuring me at the same time. I felt like I was watching a movie of somebody else, or that I was going to wake up any moment from a deep sleep. It didn't feel natural as we kissed on the bed until I put my lips to Som's neck and she moaned in a delicious sensual tone, I then began to feel like it was real and my repressed libido emerged from my uptight body and I totally lost myself in the moment.

I was not worthy of this magical moment but 'who cares', I thought as Som mounted me and started bouncing up and down while Eve kissed my neck and chest. After a few minutes, she was going faster and faster as I lay there doing nothing. I got the most pleasure from watching her enjoyment and her soft skin felt wonderful in my hands. I really can't imagine anything nicer to touch than the soft skin of those women. I fell in love with Eve's buttocks after she asked me to make love to her. I fell in love with Som's breast as they pressed against me. I fell in love with Eve's body when we embraced, but I fell in love with both of their hearts for doing such kind things too an unattractive, shy and quiet Gentleman Tramp. The episode finished as I moved up and down on top of Eve as Som gently rubbed my back. When we finished, I went to the bathroom and nearly collapsed to the floor. My legs felt like jelly. I went to bed and we slept in one big cuddle. Actually, I didn't sleep. I just lay there with a content grin on my face. In the morning, Som made love to me again while Eve was in the shower. During this passionate moment I could not stop from calling out, 'I love you.' She purred like a happy cat after her crescendo of energy.

I went to the bank while they dressed and I gave them both a lot of money. They said it was five times more than they were expecting. I was glad that I hadn't given them too little. I took them for breakfast and afterwards they both kissed me on the cheek and left. I never saw either of them again.

That was my wild night of partying, my time of fun and enjoyment. I felt very strange after that night, like I had become somebody else. I don't think that I wanted to be that party person. It didn't feel like me. It didn't feel like The Gentleman Tramp. So I stopped with the crazy fun; sort of.

OK, so I did one other stupid thing. I took hallucinogenic drugs a few days later. They messed me up quite badly. Oh and then I got into a relationship with a girl from a massage parlour and lost most of my money, but nothing else stupid, I promise.

Magic Mushroom Milkshake

Over the next few days, I grew more and more appalled by my fellow man. The gluttony in me was awakened everywhere – women, food, sun, motorbikes, drugs, alcohol, speedboats. It was all right there, and easy to attain. The greed of others reminded me of myself too much to find other tourists tolerable. I read books by Hawking and the Dalai Lama that I desperately wanted to understand. Unburdened by genius, I feared my ability to make virtuous decision. I spent time with Nico and Jordon and they became great friends, but in the evenings I drank Coca-Cola and went to bed early.

About a week after the massive party, Jordon and Nico were headed for Haad Rin beach on Koh Phangan. When they invited me to go with them, I jumped at the chance to see a new island. I didn't realise it was for the wild, full-moon party.

My room on Koh Phangan was much better. It had air conditioning, a television, a hot shower, a fridge and a proper toilet. All these things came in handy during that crazy night of noise and shouting. I refused to go to the full moon madness, but it felt like a long night in my room. Next morning I decided to go out for a stroll on the beach just as the party was drawing to a close.

Dawn saw the end of the drunks and brought out the nature loving, healthy people. The turn around was instantaneous as inebriated embraces became muscle stretches, motorbikes became dogs and sickness became smiles. I walked the beach from end to end. I really wanted to feel healthy again after that awful night of debauchery in Samui, and I was trying to eat well and exercise as much as my bad ankle would allow. I was definitely off alcohol. I must have seemed a little boring.

'Why don't you want to party?' asked Nico one afternoon.

'I don't like myself at parties. It's so noisy and so many people acting strange,' I replied.

'They are having fun.'

'I know, but I don't want too anymore.'

'You don't want to have fun?'

'I don't know.'

'YOLO!' replied Nico. I still don't know what this means.

At night, I sometimes eat with my new friends and other times alone. I didn't like eating alone too much. I went for an all-you-can-eat barbecue one time. I could feel the indulgence crossing a line, like the most disgusting of gluttons I pigged out from dusk until it was pitch black, eventually emerging from my trough with BBQ sauce smeared across my face and my belly stretching my shorts to breaking point. It was a large restaurant, and early as it was I was the only customer until a jolly fat man arrived and sat at the table next to me. He ordered beer and a surf and turf. I thought perhaps he wanted to make small talk, but I couldn't bring myself to look at him. His greed was a reflection of my own and it was making me feel ashamed.

Every night on Haad Rin, I would notice bright neon flashing lights half way up the mountain at the end of the beach. The lights aimed to attract customers, to look fun and exciting in the same way that a clown dresses to amuse people. It also achieved the same terrifying aura of bad things lurking under the surface. The glow of the neon lights was beckoning me, I can't deny. I felt like I had to go up there in the same way I just had to look when one of the fat European men in speedos strutted along the beach.

It was on a boiling hot morning that I finally decided to go up there. I'd been playing Frisbee with Nico and Jordon, but they had gone shopping and I was full of energy. I set forth like an intrepid explorer and gingerly made my way up the cragged, uneven rocks. I was still feeling a great deal of discomfort in my ankle, and I wondered if Bruce was still traipsing up those mountains, as I went higher and higher towards this mysterious place of night-time luminosity I was definitely glad I was not Bruce. He was as hard as nails to still be doing that. The walk up was eerily quiet, but there were some wooden signs just to the side of the rocky path that were dug into the dry earth. Thai lettering was painted on the signs in blood red and the professionalisms of the workmanship assured me I was headed for a genuine and exciting destination.

When I finally arrived, I was welcome by a dark-eyed Thai man with slicked back hair who was smoking a pipe and eyeing me suspiciously.
'Where you from?' he asked.
'England.'
'Why are you here?'
'I saw the lights at night and I wondered what was up here,' I replied.
'OK, take a seat.'
He went over to his table to fetch a laminated handwritten menu that he passed to me. Unfortunately it was all in Thai, so I asked what was on offer.
'Coffee,' he said.
'Do you have any food?' I asked.
'No. No food. Coffee,' he replied.
'OK, I'll have a coffee with milk and sugar,' I said as he walked off behind his desk and started looking through cupboards. It was a magnificent view from up there. I could peruse the whole beach and jungle that stretched as far as the eye could see. I watched as people sunbathed and swam and played games below. When I got my coffee it was black and unsweetened.
'So what you want? Some weed, marijuana, coke, mushroom, ecstasy?'
'No thanks, the coffee is great.'
'You come all the way up here for coffee? You don't want to try my special milkshake?' he asked.
'No thanks, coffee is great.'
'My milkshake is very good. The best you will ever try.'
'OK, I'll have a milkshake. It sounds good.'

I'm not a total idiot, I did notice that the milkshake didn't taste very nice and probably wasn't a normal milkshake. I thought perhaps the milk had gone bad, but I really didn't think it was made of hallucinogenic, magic mushrooms. I didn't realise anything was too odd until I'd finished the milkshake and noticed I was no longer talking to a hung-over Thai man in a mountain café, I was now talking to a fang-toothed, pale-faced vampire with two gaping holes where his eyes should be and blood dripping from the corners of his mouth. Fortunately, I had already paid so quickly headed for the steps in the midst of the vampire explaining that the milkshake was full of mushrooms.

On the way down the steps, I felt the hot sun burning through my pale skin, I looked at my hands and they had turned fluorescent pink and were pulsating and stretching all over the place, they felt heavy as if they were rubber gloves that had been filled with water. The fear kicked in and I took each step more and more carefully. I was Indiana Jones traversing a booby-trapped floor. Up in the sky the sun was blazing. It was calm, but I knew the dragons were on their way. It was just a matter of time.

As I got onto the sand a whole new universe opened up to me, I opened my arms wide to embrace it all and I skipped along the sand until my ankle hurt again and I had to sit down. I picked up a handful of sand and poured it slowly into my other hand. The way it moved, the trickle of the grain, it was all so fascinating. I lay down propped up on my elbows to study it in greater detail. That is when the scorpions came. They were everywhere, in the sand, crawling over my body, inside my clothes. When I went to brush them away they disappeared for a few seconds only to reappear again and head towards my face. I rolled over to escape them but now I was getting covered in sand. I had more and more sand on me. It was multiplying. I was going to turn into sand, morphing from man to sand like the T1000 from *Terminator 2*. 'Get off me,' I said stripping off and running to the sea.

In the water everything was much more pleasant. It was beautiful. The water was so clean and pure. I jumped up and down splashing the water from side to side and chuckling manically. I dived down to the bottom and held my breath and shut my eyes. For a moment I was the ocean – powerful and eternal. When I looked to the shore, I saw that the movements of the beach people were gymnastic and flamboyant. They looked like clowns performing and it was beautiful. Then those goddam dragons came; they twisted and turned in the sky. Diving and darting around leaving a stream of colours like an aeroplane show. They were coming for me and I had to get to safety.

I found refuge in a nearby café and a young Thai lady came to serve me. Her big smile lifted my spirits. I ordered a lemon slushy and I gulped it down before ordering several more. The hydration and the goodness seemed to percolate my entire being. 'When would I snap out of the trip?' I thought as I left the café and walked and walked seeing snakes slithering along the floor with their muscular green and black-striped bodies and their little heads that would turn around to laugh and hiss at me. I prayed for sanity.

I bumped into Jordon and Nico and the familiar faces pulled me somewhat to my senses. I could see the wisdom of an owl and the strength of a puma in Jordon's face. Nico was wearing a bikini and her tanned golden skin gave her the appearance of a Greek goddess as the white wings of an angel began to emerge from her back and flap in the sunlight. My god, she was lovely.
'What have you been doing?' asked Nico.
'I went for a milkshake in the place with the lights,' I replied.
'Seriously. What the fuck, that place is for drugs. Why did you go there?'
'It was colourful, like a circus,' I said.
'So you had a milkshake, a mushroom milkshake?' Jordon asked.
'I had a milkshake and now I keep seeing strange things and funny colour,' I said. 'You're face, it's like a panther.'
'Are you enjoying it?' asked Nico.
'I was, but then it was horrible.'
'Dude, you should go to bed, sleep it off,' said Jordon.
'Which way is bed?'
'We'll take you back. Holy shit I don't believe you did that,' said Nico, flapping her wings.

When I was in bed the weather took an awful turn for the worse. Black clouds descended and cast darkness over my hotel room. The splatter of rain began quite gently but it quickly escalated to a full-blown artillery attack on the windows. There was no surcease from the barrage of watery sheets that slapped against the hotel room. I gazed out and it looked like the world had been turned upside down and the ocean was falling. Thunder and lightning flashed in the sky until I couldn't take it anymore and hid under my duvet in the foetal position with cold sweat clinging to my body. My brain continued to play unpleasant tricks on me, and the space/time continuum was no longer obeying the laws of physics. I'm so glad that I eventually fell asleep as the panic was becoming deeply unpleasant.

I awoke showered and felt strung out, but more focused. The hallucinations had subsided and I just felt like I was on a cloud. I needed to get out and away from my mind, so I went to an internet café to email Mariana.
Mariana would save me.

Hi Mariana,
  Wow, long time no speak. Sorry I haven't been in touch more but I've really missed you a lot. You are not somebody that I will ever forget. How are you? What are you doing now? I am currently in Thailand. It's very beautiful, but I think I was partying too much. I feel crazy. I left England because it was boring. I didn't like my job and I split up with my girlfriend, so I want to see some of the world. I also went to Nepal with Bruce. It was amazing in the Himalayas and I even saw some wild animals in the jungle. I am going to the beach now. I hope you are having a nice day in Brazil. You are so amazing xx

Next to the café was a clean looking and well-lit massage parlour with a pile of well-arranged shoes outside. As I walked past, I was greeted by a sad looking, but beautiful, woman with hair that stretched all the way down to her waist. She asked if I would like to come in.
'I would like an oil massage please,' I said as I went in and began clumsily untying the laces on my Chaplin shoes and faking the confidence I'd been observing in Jordon and Nico. I was still feeling very strange and was desperate to have some human contact.

'Lay down here. My name Mon,' she said as she oiled me up with great tenderness, it felt lovely and relaxing. 'Oh, you feel stressed, you must meditate.'

'Really, does that work?'

'Oh yes, I love to go to temple and give to the monk. I feel good and no worry after this. You have a massage before?'

'No, I'm shy.'

'Buddha says you cannot be shy to be good man. You believe in Buddha?'

'I believe in shy.'

'You believe in shy, if you like girl then how does she know it if you shy and don't say?'

How delightful it was to have a lovely chat after hours of manic solitude while being cured of my aches and pains.

'Do you have a big family Mon?'

'Oh you remember my name, very good! Yes, four brother and three sister. I youngest, but I toughest too,' she said. 'Why you laugh?'

'No reason. I believe you.'

'You must believe me. You have brother and sister?'

'A brother. He's in Nepal.'

'Very beautiful. Why he in Nepal and you Thailand? What wrong with England?'

'Nothing really. I don't know.'

During our chat, Mon explained that she only got paid forty percent of customer intake and had no real salary. I tipped the same value as the massage saying it was for her and her family to keep well. She was very pleased. I said I would take Mon for dinner in Koh Samui as she was only working in Koh Phangan for a couple of days, and normally works very near to where I'd been staying before. She said she'd seen me walking past. How wonderful when life can throw up new opportunities.

After the massage, I returned to the internet café in the hope that I had an immediate response from Mariana. When I saw that I didn't, I went onto YouTube and typed in Chaplin.

'He's my hero; he's my absolute hero. He's amazing,' I thought as I watched a montage of his greatest comedy business followed by some clips of his hypnotic smile accompanied by some of his finest musical compositions.

After that surreal and bizarre day and the general fatigue and madness of my travels, I was home. I clicked on some of his short films such as *A Dog's Life* and *The Vagabond*, before going through *The Circus* and *City Lights* – cutting quickly to all my favourite scenes. Watching Chaplin again was like getting into a warm bath and I turned the sound up on my headphones as loud as it would go, I leaned forward in my chair in a state of bliss. Still occasionally getting confused, I watched Chaplin in awe. The part of my subconscious that he so profoundly influenced seemed to ignite and a new idea started to take hold of me, the idea to live homeless on the streets like my hero, in a search for romance and adventure. I wanted to understand this tramp character. I wanted to feel his feelings and think his thoughts. I wanted to battle with hardship and be dignified in the most undignified circumstances. The idea was formulated there and then, it would take a little longer to grow and solidify but the seed was planted and the inevitability of my future was clear. I was to be The Tramp in the modern world. I just didn't know where and when it would begin.

Awakening

Laying on the beach day after day, going on walks through jungle and still suffering the effects of the hallucinogenic milkshake – the words of the Dalai Lama and Stephen Hawking, that I had persisted in reading, were beginning to make sense. I began to see the world as a vast living organism floating in an infinite universe of which I am only a tiny atomic part. With this knowledge I was beginning to feel totally relaxed, my mind was emptied of my fear and prejudice and I felt open to everything and generous with my love. I was living in the moment. I was meditative. I was calm.

Nico and Jordon had already left the islands and were headed to Chiang Mai to continue their adventure. I considered going with them, as it would have saved me money and provided me with companionship, but two is company, three's a crowd and I had my own adventures to be getting on with.

It took a week of beach living back on Samui, until I finally got my date with Mon. I had telephoned her and we'd agreed to meet at the cinema at midday on a Tuesday. We were going to see a James Bond film.

'I like James Bond, he's my boyfriend,' Mon said as we walked around the big entertainment centre, past teenagers glued to the screens of arcade machines and a bowling alley that was deserted, but for a long-suffering mother trying to put her daughter's fingers in a big ball.
'Really, I'm jealous,' I said.
'Why? You want to be James Bond boyfriend?'
'No.' I stifled a giggle, my brain could not come up with any kind of humorous response, I wish I was smarter, I wish I was better at this kind of fooling, I really do.
We sat in an American franchised café and had ice coffee. Outside the sun was scorching, a real blistering day. I had no intention of leaving the comforts of air conditioning as every time I

raised my eyebrows or stretched my face to laugh or yawn, I could feel my skin pulling tight. It was like someone had stretched a tiny balloon over my head and cut out a couple of eyeholes, definitely time for a break from the sun.

'Why don't you have a girlfriend in England?' Mon asked looking down at her drink and crushing the ice with her straw.

'I did, but it's finished now,' I replied. The life I had with Sophie seemed so far away, but it was only a couple of months ago that I planned to marry her.

'Why finished'?

'She was with another man.'

'I know how this feels. My boyfriend was from Italy and we were together for a long time. I went home one day and there was a woman's sexy underwear under the chair. He say, "Oh I buy you a gift." I laugh at this. Does he think I'm so stupid? "Why you think I so stupid?" I say. "You fucked a girl here." He keep lie and lie. It made me laugh he can lie like this, but I didn't get mad. Buddhism is not about being angry or getting revenge, but to be calm. I go home, I go to temple, give to monk and I see family, but it really hurt me. I'm scared of this hurt.'

'It's a horrible feeling, but I'm better now, are you?'

'I'm OK. It's good you feel better, very good. Have you slept with a bar girl in Thailand?'

'Yes, but I don't want to do that anymore,' I replied in shock at the directness of the question.

'Why don't you want to do that anymore?'

I hid my face and drunk my ice coffee. I knew what I was thinking, but I was not sure I should say it. I was feeling strong loving emotion in my heart, but I didn't know if this was caused by Mon or by my relaxation.

'I don't know. It's not a nice thing to do. I want to be a gentleman.'

'Why is it not nice? The girl, she needs money to help her family. The man, he is lonely and he needs to be with a woman. Why is this bad?'

'People think it's bad in England. Sex is supposed to be about love not money. Women work normal jobs and if they sell their bodies people call them names.'

'Call them names? Buddha says we should not judge others. How else do they make money? I have friends, they do this and they like to do. They like to help family and they like the falang man and sometimes the falang man will marry them. How can we say is bad? Everyone is just trying to survive and be happy. No, we can not judge.'

'I don't know, people at home think its bad for women.'

'Because they have a choice, they have money. Here we need money too. I can give massage, but some, they can't do this.'

'It's just that I want romance. After I was with a bar girl I didn't feel happy. I didn't feel like myself.'

'For Thai people we must be happy, must be kind. Buddha says this is important and we must feel good. So it is good you don't do, if this is how you feel.'

I was becoming more and more interested in Buddhism as it seemed to offer so many solutions. Maybe I was just becoming more and more interested in Mon, but I really wanted to learn how to meditate properly and I wanted to visit temples. I had heard about the temples of Angkor in Cambodia, they sounded really spectacular.

We chatted for about two hours before getting a taxi back to the beach where we had some sort of fish dinner with noodles and vegetables and Mojitos.

'We must give good things to our body. I don't eat meat much, but I like fish and vegetables,' Mon said as she played with the last of her dinner. 'What food you like to eat'?

'Spaghetti, burgers and pizza,' I replied.

'You naughty man, not good for you, make you sad, feel unhealthy. Not good for you.'

I ordered ice cream, what a selection. The cold strawberry flavour was the perfect end to the meal. I find healthy things never fill me up and I'm never content until I've bloated myself. After dinner Mon took me to this massive nightclub called Green Mango.

'I don't like this place. It's too noisy,' I said.

There was loud dance music that operated on an ugly frequency that upset my biorhythms, it was shaking the floor and rattling the tables. It was early, but I could already see drunken European buffoons, you know the type, people like what I had been just a week or two before dancing on tables.

'You like this place?' I asked.

'Not all the time; but sometime I like to come with my friend to dance and have fun. I can see you don't like.'

We went for more drinks on the beach, where there was another party, and we sat on pillows with a table between us.

'No thank you,' I said as a child approached me with a flower necklace.

She didn't move from her position and there was no mistaking the dirty looks she gave me when they were joined by uncomfortable winey sounds. From a distance this little girl had looked so sweet, but after refusing her necklace her vibrations altered, suddenly the soul of an evil old woman was staring into my brain like a dementor. I caved and bought the necklaces, which she put on me, and Mon, kissing us both on the cheek. The money was probably going to an alcoholic dad or mum – it was very distasteful.

Mon and I walked back to the hotel room talking of the future. She was going to have to stay and work in Samui for the foreseeable future, but she wanted to go home desperately.

'Why do you want to go home?' I asked.

'To relax with my family and care for them. This is important, at home I get up early, go to temple. It sounds boring, but this is real. Here there is too much and I hurt here, but I must make money for mother and father because my brother, he died last year and my sister, she sick. I must work. All of children, we work.'

The idea of home was still repellent to me. I sort of envied Mon's desire to go home. It was a virtuous goal.

'What will you do now?' Mon asked back in the hotel room, she was lying down on the bed next to me and we were holding hands?

'I think maybe I would like to stay in Thailand. I like it here. My friend Jordon teaches English here, maybe I'll do that.'

Mon sat up and moved closer. 'If you live here you must have a girlfriend.'

'I want you to be my girlfriend.'

I probably shouldn't have said this, but the smell of Mon and the feeling of her hand electrified me. It had been a special day and my heart was aching with powerful love that I wanted to explode onto the world.

'You want I be your girlfriend? I'm not sure you really think. Have to be good boyfriend. Not to fuck other women.'

'You don't want to be my girlfriend?'

'Yes, I want, but I not sure you want. I am scared you are lying. Call me tomorrow and we see if you still think,' said Mon kissing me on the cheek and putting on her sandals before leaving.

The next day all I could think about was seeing her again. I was still enjoying a break from the sun so I went for one of my burgers, then checked my email. Mariana had replied.
Hello,

It's so good to hear from you. I have missed you a lot too and I don't forget you either. I totally understand about hating your job I don't blame you for leaving I have wanted to do this before. So bad about your girlfriend, but these things happen and you are still you. I am good, in Brazil again. I was travelling before for my study of fashion and media, and to see a friend, but Brazil is the best. It's OK, you party hard, haha, it is fun. Your travels with your brother sound amazing. I don't think I can climb mountains like this. Thailand must be so beautiful I wish I was there away from everything. How is your family? Do you still dress like Charlie Chaplin? Haha. Take good care.
Mariana

On Mariana's social network page the most beautiful smiley face in the universe appeared on my screen, but I didn't write back just then, I thought I'd wait until I knew what I was doing.

Later, I called Mon and she came to meet me. We went for drinks, but she said she couldn't have dinner as she was meeting friends. She came back to my hotel for a bit and we watched a terrible film starring Steve Martin as the father of twelve kids and numerous grandchildren. I did the fake yawning move and put my arm around her. In this position the poor acting and bad script of the film transformed into a delightful feel good romp that I could write a glowing review about. I blissfully cuddled up with her until the movie finished and she left. The cuddling had got me somewhat excitable and Thailand is not the best place to be in this kind of a mood.

I wandered around and had a couple of drinks. I was talked into a game of pool, but left when one of the girls started rubbing her bum up against me. I was practically dragged back into Green Mango by another gorgeous, soft-skinned juicy lipped woman who lifted her short skirt to flash her knickers at me as I followed her, but as soon as she went to get the drink that she had talked me into paying for, I ran out.

Women seemed to be after me everywhere. It's not that I was suddenly charming or anything – a lonely, single guy is a volcano ready to erupt with love and money and the Thai people know it is all. I really wanted to see what was happening with Mon, so I went home and released my tension. I really wish I hadn't for I was woken by a knock at my door. It was Mon and she seemed a little worse for wear.

Dragging me into the showers she took off my clothes before leaving the room, returning dressed in nothing but a shower cap, and then she started spraying me down, and washing me all over with a flannel.

'Now you go, I must wash my body,' she said. I went back to the bed and wrapped myself in a towel before lying down.

'I go on top,' she said as she approached me still wearing the shower cap. 'I no have sex for one year, so I want go on top.'

I was lacking in energy and reserves and it was an awkward bumpy experience. She seemed to enjoy it eventually, at first it seemed like she was doing a chore.

'OK, now you can go on top.'

A gentleman should never deny the request of a lady, so I gave my all and some vigour was conjured by her beauty. I think a bit of romance and build up would have improved the situation though, I really do. I did not achieve the goal and gave up. I just wanted her to be satisfied. I was already as happy as can be.

'Now you can't be fuck other woman,' she said.

'No, I won't,' I said.

The purple patch of sex continued for some days. I really got into my stride. Like when John McEnroe came out of retirement for another shot at the Wimbledon title, I really started showing some class and style. Mon became magnificent. Very good days they were, for a while anyway. Then it became dark.

My money was drying up and Mon began requesting clothes and gifts in addition to the food and bed I was providing her with. Concerned that without the money she wouldn't want to be with me anymore, I turned down some of her requests to test the outcome.

'You must go back England, make money for us, then come Thailand, buy house for us.'

'How can we be together if we are in different countries?'

'If you love, you do. My friends have boyfriends in different countries.'

'It sounds difficult.'

'I can't stay Samui. My sister she sick, I want go home. I need 2000 baht. You come?' All these requests came quick and fast and it was overwhelming. I started looking for a way out, just like I had when I was with Sophie. That claustrophobic feeling, the sweaty panic, the run away voice in my head was in overdrive. I'd gotten what I wanted from Mon – sex and promise of love, and now I was no longer interested and she was a headache.

'I will give you the money to see your family, but I'm not going with you. I want to go home.'

'When will you come back' she asked?

'I don't know. We can email each other.'

'No email bad, email cause bad heart. Why you go home?'

'I need to make more money.'

'So you come back?'

'Probably not, no.'

'You say you love me and you want to be my boyfriend. You are just lies.'

'I did, but I didn't think it through.'

'It's OK, I not angry, Buddha never angry. I just want truth not lies.'

'I did love you, but I want to go home.'

'You must do what you want, but I not wait for you. If you change your mind, I'm not here. Understand?'

'Yes, sorry.'

Before you go, you must see temples. It good for you, because I love, I want you see this. I want you to understand Buddhism.'

Mon had seen falang men coming back to Samui year after year, playing games with the same women. She didn't want to be like this, she said she wanted long love. I didn't really want to go home, I just wanted to get away from Mon. Despite feeling I'd had a spiritual awakening, I was still basically a horrible person, so I thought going to temples and learning more about Buddhism was probably a good idea. I couldn't come all this way just for beaches and booze. I should see something amazing and learn.

When I left, Mon gave me a present and I gave her quite a lot of money. I just felt I should. I didn't open the gift, as I wanted to save it for a special occasion. I hugged Mon and I didn't want to let her go, the warmth of her and the feeling inside me was painfully delightful. It was her who ended up pushing me away, I got in a taxi for the airport and she slammed the door before waving through the window. I deserved to be alone. I had brought it on my self, again.

I headed for Cambodia to escape from luxury and pleasure. I didn't feel I deserved either of those things, and the romance with Mon had ended up terrifying me. I was too immature, too selfish. I thought that if I did some good for others then I might grow up a bit – might feel less selfish, might see some truths. I might become a better, happier person. I also thought lots of women would love me if I told them I helped poor people. I thought they would probably want to have sex with me if they thought I was a great guy that helped others. I'd had a taste of being sexually popular in Thailand and I liked it. Unfortunately, it came at the same time as my spiritual awakening began to accelerate and I knew my temporary popularity was as illusory as the life I'd had at home. I wanted to continue my journey and my search for romance and adventure, but I wanted it to feel genuine. I wanted to find reality.

The Witch Doctor

I clung on to the metal bars of the shaky old tuk-tuk as it reached maximum acceleration over the gloriously bumpy roads. Ploughing through the vast green of the open grassland, Pierrie's shirt was flapping in the wind as he steered round the corner into a fresh deserted expanse. The image of a bird of prey and the word Daredevil were stencilled on the back of his fire red helmet. Pierrie was a chunky young Cambodian man with a placid face and a calm quiet demeanour. For the three days that I spent touring the Angkor temples of Cambodia, Pierrie was my driver. He would pick me up from my hostel in the morning and drive me from place to place before dropping me off when it got dark.

I'd chosen the worst possible time to have my Chaplin suit washed. Despite appreciating the coolness of summer clothes, they didn't provide me with the dignity I require. As Pierrie pulled up to the giant car park of the first archaeological attraction I stretched my leg over the tuk-tuk door and heard a terrible tear, looking down I could see my bright red underwear proudly exposed between the gaping rip in my crotch.

Pierrie pointed me in the direction of a two-kilometre hike to the ancient symbols of the Suryavarman people. The hole in my shorts grew larger and larger as I traversed the slippery rocks, barricades of chopped timber, thorny branches and puddles of sludgy filth that blocked the path.

By the time I reached the attraction, I was as dirty as a Celtic warrior and drenched in sweat. My shorts were shredded so badly that my thighs and underwear were visible to all, so I had to cover myself with my hands like a footballer defending a free kick. I looked at the stone markings and headed straight back for the sanctuary of the tuk-tuk. I passed couples, families, school excursions and the elderly on my way out of that awful jungle, feeling like a disgraceful man. When I finally got to civilisation, I went straight past Pierrie to some women who were calling out for me to buy a shirt.

'Shorts, I need shorts,' I said pointing out my predicament.

'Yes we have many, come with me, I take care of you,' replied the woman I had focused my attention upon. Inside her establishment there was an array of fashion choices, but no shorts. She showed me a rack of colourful baggy trousers.

'Do you have any men's ones?' I asked.

'Yes, these all for men. You look handsome in these,' she said picking up a pair and holding them to my leg.

'Are you sure? They look a bit feminine.'

'No, for men, very handsome. You try on.'

I selected a dark blue pair, with elephants all over them, as they looked the most gentlemanly. In the changing room, sweat poured off me so that my clothes stuck to my body. It was a ghastly affair.

'You want shirt too?' she asked, walking in on me with my shorts down and my T-shirt over my head. Without thinking I put on the new shirt.

'You very hot. You want cold water?' she asked.

'Yes please,' I replied.

'No problem, I take care you.'

She returned with the most delicious water I had ever tasted. I had no idea water could taste so good. She then showed me on a calculator what I owed. I pulled a handful of notes out of my wallet and gave them to her without counting. Her eyes came alive and a smile spread across her face as she wrapped me in a warm hug.

'You a very kind man,' she said as I left to return to Pierrie. I was a bit silly with the money I threw around in Asia, but what price can you put on a bit of mothering when you find yourself in such a predicament. I should have given her more.

During the following days of looking at temples, my imagination was ignited with visions of lost ancient civilisations and rituals. My favourite temple was this one in an over-grown jungle that reminded me of adventure movies. The only place I didn't like was the floating village. I think it was the second day of temple seeing that I found myself the only passenger on a wooden boat painted bright yellow and covered in small bullet-sized holes. It seemed Pierrie was a ships captain as well as a daredevil tuk-tuk driver, he twisted the wheel this way and that, kicked boats out of our way, jumped on and off different vessels to clear the path and manoeuvred the ship through the still convoy. We sailed through a village on stilts. Schools, hospital, houses and shops all erected above rising deep water that never dried out. The residents would transport themselves around using rowboats, swings and just by swimming. Dogs, pigs, chickens and humans all existed in this watery world. I can't imagine living anywhere more horrible than above a river. The heat and the stench of caught fish and dirty water, the unsanitary conditions, the scolding heat, the rats, mosquitoes and other vermin, the difficulty in finding privacy and escaping your neighbour, the sheer madness of it. I didn't know places like that existed, and I don't know how people survive in those communities. I would rather live anywhere but there- anywhere! The boat went past the whole village, but these people weren't waving, they clearly see enough tourists who treat them like zoo animals to be gawped at. I tried not to do that, it's un-gentlemanly to stare but my goodness it was a challenge, I was curious.

'For more money this man can take you on the rowing boat,' said Pierrie pointing to a man in a blue shirt and a cowboy hat, paddling his way around us.
'OK, no problem,' I said handing over more cash. It wasn't like I was going to be returning. I upset the balance of the boatman with my clumsy boarding and he instructed me on where to sit, but I was most uncomfortable. Every time I moved the vessel threatened to capsize and I didn't fancy going in that grim water. We went closer to some homes and then into the floating forest, a surreal ecosystem of trees and plants submerged by four metres of water. The boatman kept showing me things he'd grabbed out of the water, like snails and weeds, and asking me to eat them. I said no as politely as possible. I wanted to be open minded, but snails and weeds growing out of filthy water? How undignified; the idea was too much for me. The peacefulness was magical, like something from a Grimm fairytale, I imagined goblins and witches and enchantment as the boatman whistled and the crickets chirped.

I was relieved when I was back on the big boat with Pierrie, and even more so when we eventually reached dry land, but after being encouraged to jump from the boat I landed hard on the wet floor below and sunk about a foot. I dug my feet out of their trenches and slipped on the floor and landed face first in the wet mud. Wiping soggy crud out of my eyes I looked up to see Pierrie with his normal facial expression as the rain started to come down. The heavens collapsed as we walked through the car park and I flung huge globs of muck away from my body. By the time we reached the next temple, the rain had stopped and the sun was as hot as ever. So much so that the mud soon dried and I looked like something excavated from an archaeological dig.

At the final temple of mud day I was talked into buying some paintings. I initially dismissed this art before realising what a wonderful gift they would make for Mariana. I could mail them to her. I could imagine her smiling to see such wonderful images. The salesman was a Cambodian street urchin, a child, I was growing very fond of these entrepreneurial ragamuffins that ran up to me at every temple with a tray of goodies and a sob story about how they wanted money to go to school. I was a soft touch compared to the Chinese tourists because I enjoyed talking with the Asian Artful Dodgers who talked me into coughing up a little dough. Chaplin was like these kids in the poor houses of his youth, taking any work he could get. I find it highly inspiring and I'd been giving away plenty of dollar bills while chatting to these hardworking boys and girls. I imagined my bank account was dwindling fast.

After seeing all the temples, I began my enquiries into helping people like these poor kids. I asked in hotels and hostels and scoured the internet for volunteer work but with little success. Wandering around Siam Reap, I bumped into Pierrie and told him I was a little bored.

'I can show you my village. My father is the medicine man. Would you like to meet him?' asked Pierrie. I jumped at the opportunity.

I had to duck my head as I went into the treatment room, which was a small annexe on Pierrie's family home. The room was totally bare with the exception of candles burning next to a Buddha statue, a small table and a trunk that seemed to glow with mystery. I imagined it held ointments and medicines manifested from the land. There were a couple of paintings on the wall, one of Buddha and a magic eye painting.

The witch doctor sat in the middle of the room with his legs crossed and tucked underneath each other. He was barefoot and topless wearing nothing but an orange shawl wrapped from his waist to his knees. His head was totally bald and his skin was wrinkled; yet he looked powerful and energetic. His back and shoulders were perfectly straight and his head was poised parallel to the floor. His eyes were closed, but he sensed our presence and welcomed us.

'I say to him you are an Englishman of great learning,' said Pierrie. I had never been described as this before.

'How kind,' I thought.

With Pierrie being such a quiet chap we spoke with brevity and it was all very awkward, the three of us sitting down on the floor as we were.

'You can stay and see him treat the patients,' said Pierrie.

'Thanks, that's a great honour.' I said. With each patient he began with a period of silence as soon as they had told him their troubles, then he would rub an ointment on the problem area, say a few words and then spit on them several times before bandaging if necessary and then continuing with further quiet meditation. It wasn't like the spitting in Nepal, it was controlled and the patients welcomed it. He asked if I had any problems.

'I have epilepsy,' I said and Pierrie translated. Neither of them understood, so I began pointing at my head and acting out an epileptic seizure. I thought it was a pretty good performance.

'He can help, yes,' said Pierrie. I was very excited by this as I was not a fan of pills and if I got better I could relax so much more.

We sat in quiet meditation, and then the witch doctor said some words, he leaned closer and then spat on my head and patted my hair.

'You will have to come back many times to be cured,' translated Pierrie.'

I wish he'd told me this before the spitting. We sat on the floor and drank tea and I asked them to show me how to meditate. I tried hard, but it was so uncomfortable that my aching legs and back were all I could think about. I imagined Chaplin meditating. He'd be thinking of jokes and funny expressions to start with, but then the silence of mind would come. This is what I really wanted, silence of mind. It didn't seem to be coming though as my legs were too uncomfortable so, after a while I stood up because I didn't know the etiquette. I might have been there all night if I hadn't made this brave move. Pierrie and his nephew took me for a walk through the village. I kept walking in puddles and the dogs barked at me.

Drinking beer at his brother's house got me to feeling quite inebriated. I was glad to get back to my hostel.

In the morning, the big hairy hostel owner approached me and said that he had recommended me to some volunteer groups and they said they were eager for help.

I went off the next day with a young American woman to help a family who had recently been re-homed after living on a rubbish dump. Pierrie was our driver and translator and I was taken to a hot smelly market where I brought tools and equipment for the job. We went to the scant and dilapidated house and the mother, who was sitting in the corner nursing her newborn, invited me in. She smiled, but I sensed she was suspicious of me until I got to work nailing mesh to the windows. Pierrie said that by stopping mosquitoes coming in and spreading Dengue fever I was performing a great kindness.

It was lovely to be accepted into this modest home and to do something productive after so long sat on a beach. The children became curious to my work and soon began handing me nails and holding the mesh still for measuring. Before long they were doing the hammering themselves and even the three-year-old daughter had a go. They were very smart and I had brought plentiful supplies, so was confident they would be experts in doing this job themselves when the mesh needed replacing. When all the windows were covered I went around their garden picking up garbage. I filled three black sacs that we took for disposal when it was time to leave. Unfortunately, that was all the help I was needed for.

A couple of days later, I was asked by another volunteer group to go to a local orphanage to help out, I was given directions and sent alone. I felt very uncomfortable as I entered the huge silent compound early in the morning as I was an intruder to a private place and I desperately hoped to find an adult as I walked around the internal perimeter looking into doors to see children sleeping or getting ready for lessons. A loud ringing bell slammed my eardrums and children began to file out into the compound like ants heading for a fresh carcass. They instantly mobbed me, pulled at my clothes, screamed and fought for my attention. When the teacher eventually rescued me, I explained I had been sent to help, but they didn't know what I was talking about. They asked if I could speak the language and when I confessed that I couldn't I really questioned what I was doing there. I apologised for the misunderstanding and left feeling very cross with the people who sent me there.

That day I continued searching on the internet for properly organised project that I could get my teeth into. I found several interesting companies with good volunteer programmes, but they weren't offering anything in Cambodia. I looked at the possible locations and was intrigued by Sri Lanka and Uganda, but then I noticed Brazil. I could do a month's volunteer work teaching and working with children in the favelas of Rio de Janeiro for £1,200 with accommodation provided. I still had three to four thousand pounds left. I filled in my details and sent off an email, and within half an hour I was booked to start in just a few days time. I searched for flights to get me from Cambodia to Brazil and booked them too. I couldn't wait to get to work helping the kids, but even more excitingly, I was going to see Mariana again.

Rio de Janeiro

Everyday I would get the same bus from the business district of Rio de Janeiro and I would look around to see tall, glass buildings emerging from the cracked pavements and stretching to the heavens. I usually had to wait at the station as insane temperatures made me gasp for water and scour the floor for shade while workers filed towards their places of business like cattle being shepherded towards slaughter. They wore smart, uncomfortably hot looking clothes and sunglasses as they sped towards the comfort of air conditioning. Dodging and overtaking fellow workers, the cattle also had to rush past homeless vagabonds whilst being careful to ensure their clean attire never brushed against the dirt encrusted poverty of tramp clothes. They avoided looking at the desperate eyes, sun-battered skin or matted hair of these men and women, yet there seemed to be a tolerance between rich and poor that I don't think exists in Europe – a recognition that they were in parallel universes that lay right on top of each other. The disparity appeared enormous, but the tramps didn't look out of place in this world of commerce. On the contrary they looked more at home than the workers and they were not pleading for recognition, the quantity of them made their existence undeniable.

My destination was the same everyday – an impoverished favela that had not been pacified by the Brazilian police. I was there in an attempt to teach the local children and teenagers of this community.

As I stepped off the bus one day, I saw a child crying as his mother washed him in a fountain across the street, I felt bad passing the poor boy as I like to have privacy for my bath time. The local buildings appeared dusty, rotten and slanted, glancing through the doorways I saw families crammed into small rooms, gathered around tiny televisions to watch news or cartoon shows. Doberman dogs walked freely about the favela in packs, making me feel nervous. As I continued to the school building, a man with a missing eye bumped into me violently, hatred burning out of his soul, making me think the collision was not accidental. If I had a missing eye I would get an eye patch, but his wound was fully on display, rotten and sore it protruded from his face.

On the other side of the dirt street was a group of young men playing barefoot football. They had an audience of adolescent girls who watched with a sultry attitude as they played music out of a portable radio and shouted encouragement and abuse to the players. It didn't look like the competitive football games I had to play at school though; it looked more like co-operative posing as they helped each other keep the ball off the floor and over-exaggerated every movement for the spectators. As I neared the entrance of the school an old woman came out of a shop to my side and stopped in front of me to cough germs all over the place. I covered my mouth and nose before looking down to see dark red welts covering her legs, and calloused feet squeezing out of battered sandals.

I was very glad to get into the school where I was greeted by the owners who gave me a glass of water, lead me into the classroom and turned on the fan. I should point out that I never made this journey alone. A very friendly girl from New York called Ayla was with me, she had long, dark hair and sparkly blue eyes. I liked Ayla.

We had about an hour before the students arrived that day and it was too hot to do anything but sit and sip water.

'How did you get all those scars on your legs?' I asked. There were about twenty long white marks on Ayla's soft pale skin, leading right up to her denim jean-shorts. I had been noticing these wounds for some time and had become so curious that I could not stop staring, so my fear of asking was eventually overcome by my fear of appearing un-gentlemanly. 'I hope you don't mind me asking.'

'No not at all, my sister and me had this big fight one night. Her dog was there and he got really protective over her and just went for me,' Ayla said as she concentrated on a picture of flowers she was drawing. It was beautifully coloured.

'With his teeth?'

'No, his claws. It was awful, there was blood everywhere and my sister was crying like crazy. He's usually a good dog, but he just flipped out.'

'I didn't know dogs had claws like that.'

'Not anymore, we got them clipped after he did that.'

'She still has the dog?' I asked.

'Yeah. She loves that dog. So, what are you going to be teaching today? I haven't really thought about it.'

'I'm going to teach Charlie Chaplin. We will use that old computer in the other room to watch some clips from the internet and then perform plays.'

'That sounds amazing. I want to do that.'

I stood at the front of the classroom pointing to crudely drawn pictures on a dirty whiteboard, asking a group of sullen teenagers to repeat the words for different items of clothing. Twelve faces stared back at me with their mouths gawping and their eyes devoid of thought or emotion. Only Lorena and Yasmin repeated the words. This wasn't working, so I tried to just start a conversation.

'Diego, how are you?' Diego jumped at the sound of his name. I didn't want to pick on the poor lad, but he was half asleep and I thought he would enjoy things more if he took part. He smiled widely, thinking this to be an acceptable response. He reminded me of my self as a boy.

'How are you?' I repeated.

'How are you?' said Diego.

Yasmin started shouting at him. I think she was saying that everyday I asked 'how are you?' He should know what to say by now.

Como você está? Não basta repetir ele. Isso é fácil fazemos isso todos os dias. Você diz que eu estou bem. I AM FINE!' said Yasmin with an infuriated tone as Diego turned back to me with his eyes wide open and stiffness to his body.

'I am fine,' said Diego.

I had been struggling with these lessons and although we had fun, played games and there was often smiling and laughing, the teaching of English was frustrating. Lorena and Yasmin spoke the language very well and picked up new vocabulary fast. I became dependent on them translating everything back to the other students and spent too much time talking to them and not focusing on the other pupils. Lorena was very helpful and always volunteered to help. Yasmin was more moody and helped me by shouting at the other students, but she was very nice too. I really liked all those kids.

It was time to execute my Charlie Chaplin plan. I led the group of teenagers into the computer room and they sat on the floor chatting among themselves and doodling on notepads. Ayla's class of younger children came to join us and I introduced Charlie Chaplin as I pressed play on a YouTube montage of his wonderful comedy.
They stared blankly for a minute and I was in a cold sweat, anxious to see how my hero would be perceived. Then the laughter began, first it was just a few chuckles, but then it increased and spread to loud riotous roars. I didn't know what they were laughing at, for I was watching their faces and not the screen. They were elbowing each other and pointing with wide smiles and big laughs, it was wonderful to see. When everyone began to applaud, I turned to see what had impressed them so much. I looked at the computer and Charlie the tramp was kicking a policeman repeatedly in the butt.

After the film ended, I explained that I wanted them to plan short silent plays that they could perform for each other. We were going to communicate without talking. They stared at me blankly until Lorena repeated my instructions in Portuguese and Yasmin shouted at everyone, they laughed at whatever she was saying.

The big performances came and they were magnificent. The children were communicating their fears and concerns in the style of Chaplin. Yasmin was dragged off by two nasty police officers after stealing a loaf of bread. They had chased her around the room and tripped over chairs before getting hold of her. She was left miserable in jail before performing a daring escape where she kicked the police officers' butts.
Some younger children acted out scenes in which one of them was a dog and they were desperately trying to get food. Rubbing

their bellies they stole from a shopkeeper every time he turned his back. The shopkeeper looked bemused by the ever-decreasing amount of goodies on his table. Diego played a factory worker going mad and tripping over equipment before chasing everyone trying to tighten their ears and noses with imaginary spanners. Lorena and Gabriella played automatons hitting each other with pillows and laughing in robotic style while hiding from the police.

As some of these dramatics developed new themes and ideas came into play such as drugs, guns and prostitutes, but I don't know where they got these ideas.

'Charlie Chaplin, is he dead?' Lorena asked at the end of the day.

'Yes he is dead,' I replied.

'I think he's cool,' Lorena said. She smiled, with braces on her teeth and innocence in her eyes. I couldn't help but think that the future will be a fantastic place. We began having art sessions, played sports outside and did more drama after that day. I wanted the kids to express themselves, not to worry about learning English, as I didn't think they really needed to know English that much. I tried to learn some Portuguese, but it was tough for me, I'm not very intelligent.

'That was awesome,' said Ayla on the bus home. My chest puffed out and my shoulders went back.

In the evenings, I would sit outside in the guesthouse high up in the hills where many of the volunteers were staying. I would gaze down upon the city of twinkling light and beauty and think about what was going on below, often wondering if Mariana was down there. I would sit and talk to Ayla before she went for her big nights out. I never saw her return home, but she was always ready to go in the morning, no matter how much she had been partying.

'I'm not going out tonight,' said Ayla one evening. 'I keep making too many bad decisions.'

'What kind of decisions?' I asked.

'Decisions about guys,' she said. I think maybe she wanted to tell me more, but I didn't really ask. She went out about an hour later.

I was sharing a room with another New Yorker called Josh. He had worked in stocks and shares after college and as a cocktail waiter. He was also an underwear model and a lot of people were impressed by that – especially girls. I wasn't. I could stand around in my underwear just as good as him, so I really don't see what's so special about him for doing that. He was nice though and one evening he said he liked sharing a room with me, because before he was sharing a room with a lot of girls who kept trying to get into bed with him. He said Ayla was the worst for doing that, especially when she came back drunk.

'Sounds terrible,' I said.

'Yeah, I didn't come here for that shit. I came to help kids and to chill out and read some books. I need to clear my head from home. If I hook up with someone it will be with a Brazilian girl. I love the Brazil ass. Thick and juicy, they are awesome.'

'They are rather wonderful,' I said.

'I'm trying to get over my ex as well, so I don't want to get into anything really. Have you ever been in love?' he asked

'Sort of. Maybe it was infatuation.'

'That's not the same thing,' said Josh.

'It is the same thing. I love Mariana.'

'The Brazilian chick? I thought you said you were just friends. You will get the real thing soon. I know you will.'

'It is the real thing. I love Mariana.'

'So when will I meet this famous girl?'

'She's coming here for my birthday party next week. You're coming aren't you?'

'For sure I wouldn't miss it.'

I had met with Mariana in my first week in Rio, but I'd felt very jetlagged and a bit sick. We went for a coffee and talked about times in London and what we had been up to. When we went our separate ways she said she had a lot of work, but would come to see me for my birthday. She kissed me on both cheeks. It was heavenly, better than the threesome in Thailand by miles. In fact it was so wonderful that I nearly got run over on the way home, I was lost in a dreamy world of magical delight and had no comprehension of the world around me. Speeding traffic was but a peripheral reality until it nearly killed me.

On my birthday, the kids at the favela brought me food and cakes and they all came to shake my hand or kiss me on the cheek. I had also brought food and we had a lovely little party. When it was time for them to go, they sang happy birthday for me and I felt like a very rich man. Ayla looked a little worse for wear that day, her eyes looked droopier than normal and she was not her usual talkative self, so she was even happier about the party than me as she got to sit in the corner and rest.

On the way home I stopped to get beers, wines and foods and took it back to start cooking on the barbecue. With the smell of steak and sausage people began arriving out of their rooms to join me. I was a wonderful host handing out beers as they sat and talked and began playing card games while Josh and Ayla helped me cook. By the time Mariana arrived the party was in full swing and I must have looked very popular.

She came in and everyone's eyes went to her as if a movie star had just entered. She was even more beautiful than ever, even more spectacular, adorable intelligent and wise. Her sweet smile was like a golden drop of sun on a cold day, her hair black, smooth and straight was as soft as unicorn fur and it swung deliciously across her shoulders. Her elegant body screamed to be embraced – she was a miracle to me.

I began passing out the food and everyone eat. I don't think it was enough to satisfy their appetites, but they began drinking a lot and forgot of their hunger. I stayed to one side ignoring the games and chatted with my great love.
'This is a great party. You have made a lot of friends. It is great for you. I would love to travel more like this and to help people. I must follow your example,' said Mariana not realising that, besides a few friendly people, most of the guests were there for the free food and drink or to stare at Josh's muscles.
'It's great and the kids in the favela are so nice. Today they brought me food and cake and sang me happy birthday. They are so cool,' I said.
'That's great, they like you, because you are kind to them. We must all be kind. Today I was driving in Niteroi and there was a poor man sitting on the street and this rich man walked past him and spat on him. It was disgusting and I got so angry that I was banging my fists on the steering wheel and shouting out the

window. The rich man thought I was shouting at the poor man, so I stopped and told him I was shouting at him. He said he was upset that the poor man was near his house, but this is no reason for cruelty I told him. We must all love each other I said, but he wasn't listening. They are both just men, so why is one so lucky and the other so unfortunate? I hate it. I am proud that you are doing this teaching. You are very brave, the communities can be dangerous.'

'It doesn't scare me,' I said sticking out my chest and waving away the idea of fear. 'I was in the Himalayas. That didn't scare me either.'

'Well you must be careful,' Mariana said, laughing.

Mariana spoke Portuguese, English, Spanish, German and French I could barely speak at all. She loved to meet new people and was friendly to everyone at the party. Having a natural curiosity to the beauty of humanity, she asked everyone questions and they would talk about themselves. Yet it was to me that she gave two more enchanting kisses on the cheek when she left – happiness is a kiss from Mariana.

Josh had come over to invite us to play a drinking game, but Mariana said she had to be leaving as she had work early in the morning.

'No problem, it was great meeting you. This guy is always telling me about you,' said Josh.

'I hope he is saying good things,' said Mariana.

'Really good things. He said he couldn't even talk before he met you. Is that true?'

'I don't know about before, but he start talking to me yes.'

Mariana had invited me to meet all her friends in a week's time. They were all going to the beach and then to a film festival and she wanted me to come. I was very enthusiastic about this. I had heard so much about Mariana's friends.

'Oh my God you are so lucky! She's gorgeous,' said Ayla after Mariana left.

'Yeah, holy shit, now I understand what you were talking about before. She's hot,' said Josh.

'I think she really likes you too. She was laughing at all your jokes and was sitting so close to talk to you,' said Ayla.

'Well we have been friends a long time,' I said.

'I heard your meeting her again. The third date man. That's when you have to make your move. Girls like that, nice girls, they wait until the third date before they let you kiss them.'

'Really?' I said

'Hey, I'm a nice girl and I don't always wait for the third date,' said Ayla folding her arms and beginning to scowl.

'You don't wait for the third minute,' Josh said.

'Fuck you, how would you know about my dating life? You don't know anything about me you goddam jerk,' Ayla said as she stood up to her full height of five foot one and scowled up at Josh' wide frame of six foot four.

'It was just a joke, chill out!' Josh said holding his palms out to her and looking around checking the reaction of onlookers.

'Yeah well fuck off, don't talk to me like that,' Ayla said walking away and throwing her limbs around wildly. Half an hour later she had gone off with a couple of other girls too a club. She had not let go of her anger and was still frowning when she said, 'Happy birthday,' to me and marched off into the street.

'That bitch is crazy,' Josh said as he went to the fridge to get another beer. 'People kept telling me she wanted to sleep with me, and she's been crazy to me ever since I told her I wasn't interested.'

'That was very unpleasant,' I said, beginning to feel very lightheaded from the beer and wine. It's a very dangerous combination for me. I'd been trying not to drink since Thailand, but it was my birthday.

'But anyway, back to Mariana. Third date dude, you gotta make your move,' Josh said.

I could think of little else as I lay on my thin squeaky bed that night and looked out the door at the full moon. I thought of getting a job in Rio and building a life with Mariana – that would be amazing. Perhaps things had changed; maybe I was sexier now that I was a man of the world. 'Yes, I was definitely very sexy now and still as charming as ever,' I thought. I would finish my volunteering, then Mariana and I would fall in love and I would get a job and a place for us to live, it was a brilliant plan. I couldn't wait to see her again and I was more in love with her than ever. She was the energy in my universe and after that dull, relentless lifestyle in England, the physical suffering in Nepal and the vulgar gluttony of Thailand, she was my greatest reality – I had to be with her.

In the middle of the night, a noise from outside woke me up. I glanced over to see Josh sleeping soundly, before un-glueing my eyes and looking out of the open door. I could see the shape of a small young woman, it was Ayla, but she was not alone. There were two men with her and they were staggering around and shooshing each other. They came even closer to our door and Ayla started kissing one of them while the other guy gingerly moved behind her and started rubbing himself up against her.

'Shut up, I'm trying to sleep,' I shouted. I hate to shout, but when my sleep gets disturbed I get a bit cross.

'Sorry,' Ayla replied as they all giggled and began walking away from the door and out of sight.

I rolled over and tried to forget this horrible waking nightmare. 'Why was such a lovely girl doing such awful things?' I thought. It took me a long time to get back to sleep because I was so upset by this incident, but who was I to judge such vulgarity. I had more important things to think about.

The Gentleman Tramp

My big date with Mariana came the day after I finished volunteering. I'd moved out of the guesthouse and into an awful hostel.

I woke up nervous and sick. I was to meet Mariana at midday, but at ten in the morning I was sitting on a dirty toilet and experiencing the most vile and uncomfortable evacuation that hurt my stomach and made my head ache. I sat there for so long that I began to wonder if the torture would ever end. Sweat dripped off me and handfuls of wadded toilet paper were required to deal with the horrific explosion. I pulled on the hanging flush but only a trickle of water came out leaving my shameful deposit still staring me in the face. I stood there flushing vigorously for at least twenty minutes wondering how I had been walking around with so much shit in my body.

I temporarily gave up my distressed flushing because I desperately needed to shower and to concoct a better plan to get my self out of this predicament. There was not enough water in the shower either, the nozzle dribbled on to me with scolding heat. I wanted to cool and cleanse my body with fresh cold water. I covered myself in soap and it must have taken at least ten minutes to rid myself of the suds with the boiling squirts. While I was doing this, another traveller entered the bathroom and quickly ran out screaming and whooping about the horrible stench and sight. He returned with the pretty girl on reception as I was drying off with a towel, they knew it was me and they walked straight back out, appalled and in search of further back up. I resolutely stood my ground because it was more important that I be presentable to meet my great love, and I still needed to shave. Having not shaved for a week and a half I had to be aggressive because my blade was not sharp enough. By the time I finished I looked like one of Jack the Ripper's victims. I left the hostel with a lack of self-confidence, determined to be on time for my meeting with the most beautiful woman in the world.

I arrived at the ferry port of Niteroi neatly dressed in my cleanest summer clothes and holding a bunch of flowers when Mariana pulled up in her rusty red vehicle. The door swung open and her gorgeous, brown eyes were covered by mirrored sunglasses. The traffic had apparently been terrible and Mariana was irate. She was very happy about the flowers though – beautiful women should always have flowers.

At the beach, we headed over to a group of sunbathers, some of which were drinking beer under umbrellas and I was introduced to everyone, they were her friends. I had been very good at remembering my student's names, but when it came to these people it was a real struggle. Ana, Uanderson, Rayssa, Fernando, Rafaela, Henrique. I think that was some of them, but I didn't know which was which. They were all very nice and talked about themselves and asked me questions about England and other places I'd been too. I didn't answer the questions very well because out of the corner of my eye I saw Mariana stripping off to her bikini and I suddenly lost the ability to speak or even breathe. I could actually feel my heart going up into my throat. I tried to look away but the funny feeling in my stomach was overwhelming. The other men at the beach seemed to take this in their stride and were no more taken aback with it than by the other girls of the beach, but seeing Mariana in this black bikini drove me crazy. Her bottom was spectacular. I needed a drink. How was I not going to stare?

The other guys actually seemed more concerned with showing off their own bodies than enjoying the amazing female spectacles. I enjoyed all the girls in their bikinis, but only Mariana took my breath away. Looking at her felt like a punch in the stomach, only it felt nice.
Mariana and the other girls lay on the beach sunbathing and listening to music while the guys began kicking a football around. I was invited to join in. They skilfully passed the ball in the air, controlling it with their head, their chest, their shoulders, knees, feet and back before passing it to another member of the circle. When it first came to me I tried to do the same, but it rolled off my foot and onto the floor. When it was passed to me the second time, I gave it an almighty thump and it flew high in the sky and

someone had to run to get it. I said I needed a drink and this guy Fernando began mixing me a Caiprinha – a lemony cocktail with ice and spirits. It was full of sugar but the sweetness didn't put me off as the heat was making me thirsty. I sat down and looked across at the beautiful horizon of blues and yellows wondering how to behave and where this day was going. I was losing my nerve about making a move with Mariana. I couldn't even breathe with her in that bikini.

After a couple more Caiprinhas, Mariana came over and took my hand before leading me into the cold water. It was terribly exciting and I could feel her friend's eyes on us as we rushed off down the beach into another dimension. The water was freezing and Mariana started to get these cute little goose bumps on her smooth bronzed skin. The water at least toughened me up from the breathlessness and it proved I wasn't dreaming.

'I must tell you something,' Mariana said after playfully splashing me with a little water.

'What?' I asked.

'It has happened to me. I have fallen in love,' she said.

'You have?'

This was it, the greatest moment of my life, the greatest moment of anyone's life. Greater than anything that had ever happened before in the history of the universe. I looked into those gorgeous eyes of hers and moved a little closer. 'Well I think that's fantastic Mariana,' I said.

'It feels amazing,' she said.

'It's a wonderful feeling.' The delight in my heart was indescribable. Pure ecstasy!

'I never thought it would happen to me.'

'Me neither,' I said.

'He just makes me feel so special.'

'He?' I said, what did she mean he? 'He makes you feel special?'

'Yes, Fernando, the man in the blue shorts.'

'Fernando. Yes, of course, Fernando.'

'I had to tell you because later I may be with Fernando and I do not want you to be uncomfortable.'

'No, no problem,' I said as I swallowed the vomit that was entering my throat and desperately tried to silence the voice in my head that told me to shout at her. I had to come up with a way of running away from this situation or I was going to do something crazy, I knew it. 'I'm not sure I can come to the film festival now though. I'm meeting Ayla and Josh. You met them at my party.'

'Yes. They are so nice. Ayla is very nice. I think you and her would be good.'

'You never know,' I said.

Back on the beach it went very quiet again, some of Mariana's friends were sleeping and those that weren't, were sunbathing or playing football. I began digging a hole in the sand by rubbing my foot furiously on the ground before complaining of a terrible headache and explaining that I had to leave. Mariana insisted on driving me back to the ferry port.

'Are you OK?' she asked as we drove away.

'Yes,' I replied, 'just a bit too much sun. I don't have the skin or the head for it, I'm afraid.'

'But you are OK. Are you upset?'

'Yes I'm very upset. My heart is aching and I want to throw up all over your car before crying my eyes out,' I thought.

'No, I'm not upset,' I said.

When we got to the ferry, Mariana gave me a kiss on the cheek. This time it didn't feel like happiness. It felt like the end of the world.

Over the next few hours my mind was plagued with luxurious torture. I never wanted to see her again and yet I wanted to spend every second of my life with her. I was infatuated. I knew from before it wasn't healthy to love someone so much and have it unreturned. My only options were to either control these cruel thoughts and be her friend or stay far away. What a fool I had been when I ignored her before. Despite feeling upset that she was not my princess, she had made my life so much better, she was my inspiration. I was going to have to find a way to deal with this.

When you are at your lowest everything can seem to conspire against you. It has happened to me many times, but even on the worst days there will be something good that happens, just as even on the best days there will be something bad. I had gone back to the hostel to find my giant shit still sitting in the toilet, so quickly changed into my Chaplin suit and headed out. I was sitting at an outdoor café and had ordered a fruit salad. My appetite wasn't up to much as the cruel mocking images of Mariana and Fernando danced around my mind and caused a sickness in my belly. I began to play with my food as I watched the happy passers by going about their business without a care in the world as my shoulders slumped with the burden of disappointment and I sighed loudly into the air. I stuck too forks into the large pieces of pineapple left on my plate and moved the plate aside. I began my Chaplin dance pretending the pineapple slices were little feet. The Tramp used potatoes but pineapple would have to do. As a boy I worked on this for hours. Soon I was back in that meditative state where my mind was temporarily free from the heartbreak and I was totally focused on the movements. I don't know how long I did this for, but I was aware of not wanting to stop, for I knew that when I did stop my distraught mind would return to its devilish pranks.

I did finally look up and saw a dark-skinned girl of about eight years old in a blue dress and with a green headband sitting opposite, she was peering around her mother to watch me, while poking her and pointing at me so that her mother could watch too. She was smiling the most wonderful infectious smile, as if she knew I needed reminding the world was a friendly place. I couldn't help but smile back and continued the performance. It's always easier to perform when you have the pressure of an audience, when I finished the girl's big-boned mother had turned around to watch too and she had an even bigger smile. They gave me a little clap and I said thank you. I really needed that moment, as my day was about to get even worse.

My ears were pounded by the thumping music as I tried to dance in amongst the shoves and pushes of aggressive loud-mouthed men and women invading my personal space. They were all dancing in groups and expanding out from their circles to occasionally make contact with another group. I began to see that dark nightclub like a nature documentary. The women were exhibiting their sexual availability with their buttocks and breast as they danced with their friends while other groups of men leered and stuck their chests out.

Alcohol was an important component of this ritual as it lowered inhibitions and the music sent sexual vibrations through the ground and took away the necessity of awkward conversation. Like a Chaplin film, the dance floor was all about body language and The Tramp was never an alpha male. Occasionally a brave male would approach a female from behind, pressing against her buttocks and she would either respond by moving away from him or backing up to him and whispering in his ear, covering him in her scent. The offer and acceptance of a drink or a dance seemed key to the chances of mating.

Those who did not want to mate were there to practice their seduction or weigh up their value as sexual partners and establish themselves in the hierarchy of their social group. The more placid homo sapiens were on the outskirts of the dance-floor, sipping drinks, perhaps having seen enough of all this nonsense. In the centre of the dance floor, fighting for space and recognition, were the more aggressive animals and I was one of them. I didn't want to be a part of their game though, I tried to block it all out and concentrate on my wonderful dancing, but with more and more pushing I began to fear I would have a violent outburst so I left to find Josh. He was sitting with an attractive Brazilian girl and when I went to say hello he said they were leaving.

'I head back to the States tomorrow. It's been great knowing you,' he said. 'You're a hell of a guy.'

I was most touched by this and returned his sentiments.

'I'm sorry your big day didn't work out dude, but it'll be OK. You'll find someone. Maybe back in England,' continued Josh.

'Cheers mate, thanks for your kindness,' I said. 'I think I'm going to stay in Brazil for a while, but I hope to see you again someday.'

'That would be awesome. You should come to New York. I could get you a job, no problem. Would love to see you there.'

'I will try,' I said. 'I will email you.'

'Awesome, take care dude.'

There were a few people in the disco that I knew, but they were all very drunk now, so without Josh I felt even more lost in this awful place. I went to speak to Ayla, she was also leaving Brazil the next day.

'Hey, how was your big date? Did anything happen with Mariana?' asked Ayla.

'It was OK, we're just friends really.'

'Oh I'm sorry. If it makes you feel better, I'm totally off guys. They're a bunch of jerks so we are single together.' Ayla's eyes were glazed over and I didn't feel as if I was talking to her, it was more like I was having a conversation with a bottle of vodka. 'Am I going to see you again?' she asked.

'I was just talking to Josh about visiting New York so I'm sure I will see you again. I will make sure of it.'

'That's so great. You're so lucky to be staying in Brazil. I wish I had more money. I don't want to go home. Can't you take me with you?'

'I can't take you where I'm going I'm afraid.'

'Where are you going?'

'It's hard to say exactly, but I am so glad I met you. You have a beautiful soul.'

'Don't you mean I have a beautiful ass? That's all everyone else says.'

'You're beautiful, but your personality and what is inside you is more beautiful than your looks,' I said.

'That's the nicest thing anyone ever said to me. Wait right here I'm going to get another drink. Don't go anywhere,' Ayla said.

I think I sat there for about ten minutes feeling better than I had all day, before I went to the toilet. When I came out I looked everywhere for Ayla. It wasn't that big of a place. I didn't understand why I couldn't see her. When I eventually found her she was in the corner of the dance floor pressed up against the wall by a skinny, tall man and their faces were stuck together. I waved in her direction, turned around and left.

Back at the hostel the bathrooms were taped off, but I was desperate for the toilet having had a few drinks at the disco. I ducked underneath the tape and into the cubicle to see my old friend, the giant shit, still sitting in the bowl. I quickly peed with deep shame, then went to my room and grabbed all my things before paying the desk and walking off into the night. I walked and walked, looking for a quiet street to bed down in. I found a suburban area with trees and nice looking houses. I pulled out the blanket I had taken from the hostel and placed it on the floor next to a wall. I made a pillow out of some shorts and shirts in my bag. I took off my shoes, hat and jacket, unbuttoned my shirt and waistcoat and lay down.

The awful visions of Mariana with Fernando grew stronger and now I had Ayla and that guy in the club popping into my head too. I still had a little money, I could have stayed in hostels for a couple of weeks longer or maybe even booked a flight home, but another image was popping into my head – the ending from Chaplin's *The Circus*. In the film, the girl he loves chooses another man and he sees no option but to wish them well and even help them overcome their problems. The Tramp is left to go on his way alone. He sighs and then screws up a star that symbolises his dreams, kicks it away before walking off with a jump and a skip into the end of the movie and onto his next adventure. If that's what Chaplin did, then that is what I would do too.

It was time for me to be The Gentleman Tramp and it would begin right there on that street. As I lay there trying to focus on Chaplin and not on Mariana, a few spots of drizzle landed on me, it was quite refreshing, but it got stronger and stronger until I became drenched in violent plummeting rain. It didn't cross my mind to move even when I became squelchy and sodden. I really didn't mind, for the rain at least made my tears invisible.

Scraps

It wasn't long before the streets became my permanent residence.

In the first couple of weeks of homelessness I occasionally treated myself to a bed, but I knew my money was running out and that I couldn't make luxury a habit. Chaplin's Tramp didn't have that option, and after a while neither did I. The option I did have was to call home and ask for money for a flight home, but every time I thought about my boring job and routine in England, I was more certain that it was better to be The Gentleman Tramp. I came close to asking my parents a couple of times, but when I spoke to them on the phone it seemed ludicrous to explain my predicament, so I simply said I was having a wonderful time and that everything was so cheap that I didn't have any problems.

I won't pretend life was easy or nice in any way. It was utter misery for an awful long time. The first few days on the streets taught me that boredom and fear are two of the biggest enemies of the homeless. It was my sixth day as The Gentleman Tramp that was the worst. The previous night I'd stayed in an actual hotel and it had burnt about half my money. After that night of comfort things began to feel very ugly indeed.

It had started out very nicely; I was still booked into my nice hotel on Copacabana beach and had gotten up for an early morning swim. I love an early start to the day – it is so peaceful and rejuvenating. I was nearly at the place that I thought was an ideal spot to take a swim when this brown and white, jig-sawed mutt started shouting at me in a repetitive, songlike chant as he marched in ever decreasing circles. I walked past him and he kept barking into the distance. He was fairly small, not tiny, about the size of a large elephant shit.

'Woof woof woof woof,' he said. There was no one else there but us. He looked clean and healthy and I stifled a chuckle, amused by his posturing and grumpy defence of a territory that he marked out with his cries.

I dived into the icy water and submerged myself in its cold embrace, breast stroking as far as I could before surfacing to greater warmth. When I looked across to check on my bag, I saw the dog was now just metres away from it and had completely changed his behaviour. He now had a blank expression and was still and in total silence – he looked like a Buddhist statue. However, his meditation was short-lived as he soon lifted his back leg and urinated all over the floor right by my things. In a stunned silence, I continued watching him as he circled about my clothes suspiciously. He sniffed my towel and then picked it up in his teeth. I felt forced to react to this insult so I swam to shore as fast as my frenzied Orangutan technique would permit and shouted at him.

'Oy!' I said.

'Woof woof woof,' he said. It was like he was a medieval knight or a cowboy challenging me to a joust or pistols at dawn. He was clearly not a man to be messed with under normal circumstances. 'Woof woof woof,' he continued as I walked closer to him. Part of me really wanted to fight him, to chase him down and give him a good kick in the arse, to teach him a lesson about respect, but I was paranoid about being bitten and going to hospital with rabies and he was barking very loud. You can't trust a man who urinates so openly not to try and bite you.

'Get away from my bag,' I shouted.

I eventually decided to be the bigger man, the better man. I sat down near him and he continued staring off towards the sea and released my towel to continue his monologue of woofs. I inched my bottom closer and closer towards my things, being careful to remember where he had weed. Then without taking his eyes away from the ocean, he stood up before walking round in a circle and settling down closer to me. I moved myself backwards so as to circumnavigate his lazy body and get to my bag. I was outsmarting this fiendish villain, but he stood up again and did another big circular walk before sitting down even closer, this time on my other side so I got up to claim my possessions. I grabbed my towel too and dried off some of the water, then put on some more clothes before heading off. I had won this fierce battle of wills.

The dog started barking again (probably conceding defeat to a superior mind) and I turned around to see him still staring at the sea. He had a way of seeming totally unconcerned by my presence and yet was in total communion with me. I thought it would be interesting to sit down and have some quiet time with this funny old fellow, it was the least I could do after depriving him of a moral victory. It didn't take long before he stood up again and began another one of his slow circles then plonked himself right down next to me. I noticed a warm feeling in my self now that he was closer, and I realised it was the feeling of companionship. It had been days since I'd had anybody to sit with or talk too and those awful nights had left me feeling very alone. I reached my hand out a few times to see what his reaction would be and when he didn't do anything but continue staring blankly I became more courageous and moved my hand closer and closer until I brushed his hair. He still did not react, so this time I put a firm hand on his furry back, he was very muscular, but with soft fur. I stroked him for a few seconds before giving him a pat on the head and he finally turned around and looked at me. It was a very lazy, relaxed look and he was panting a bit from the early morning sun. He didn't look bothered, so I patted his head again and then he lay down for a sleep. I thought this was a good idea so I lay back too and closed my eyes. I must have nodded off for when I opened my eyes he was gone, but I had a feeling I would see this little gentleman again.

I had decided to leave some of my things in the hotel when I departed. I'd gone through my bag and decided what the necessities were – tramp suit, toiletries, shorts, T-shirt, underwear, socks, passport, present from Mon and Chaplin autobiography – and discarded everything else as I was tired of carrying so much around. Like most days, I really didn't know what to do with myself, I wandered around the beach for a while enjoying the sights of the gorgeous bodies of the Brazilians before deciding to visit a tourist attraction.

Black spots appeared in my eyes as I stood in my Chaplin suit queuing for the cable car that ascended to Christ the Redeemer. I could feel the sweat patches forming under my armpits and perspiration dripped down my back as I inched forward through the never-ending line. At the top I was disappointed by the monumental figure of Jesus Christ, who I've always really liked (he's the ultimate gentleman tramp). I like Mohammad, Krishna and Buddha too, they are all so wise and kind, but I had my own idea of what Jesus looked like and the serious and scary looking chap on that mountain wasn't him. It was like when they made the Harry Potter films and the characters didn't match my imagination. The views were incredible though and you could gaze upon the yachts of billionaires and the slums of the poor without having to turn your head. People stood taking identical photographs, copying the pose of Jesus with proud expressions on their faces. Why do people have to photograph everything? I was sick of living life through a screen and wanted to enjoy the moment. I'd been going to tourist attractions most days and they were all very nice. I particularly enjoyed the glistening sunset views from Sugarloaf Mountain, again the obvious disparity was sickeningly apparent, but the hills, towns, sea and people below all meshed together to create a colourful mesmerising beauty, it felt as if my mind was being exposed to a new frequency that transcended the senses, but I couldn't help thinking it would all be better if I was with Mariana. This thought gave me an intense melancholy and lethargy that denied me the enjoyment that other tourists seemed to be experiencing.

I was finished with Jesus Christ by about two in the afternoon and I still had another eight hours before I could go to bed. I had spent previous days wandering around searching for better sleeping locations and had three or four quiet little nooks up my sleeve. I'd struggled to sleep at first, but I ended up so tired that this stopped being a problem after a couple of nights. It was the boredom and sadness of the day that I despised. I went for a walk around Centro, the business district of Rio, from where I used to take my bus, but like the other tramps, I had nothing to do there and after passing all the shops from which I couldn't afford anything and looking with fond memories at the banks that used to dispense cash, I found my self drawn back to the bikinis of the beach.

This time I went to Ipanema beach and the bikinis did not disappoint me – an array of different coloured ones graced the sandy shore. The soft skin of the Brazilian girls made me drool even when I was gasping with thirst. The curves of their boobs and buttocks were a torturous delight, and when a girl in a pink G-string bent down in front of me, it was all I could do not to reach over and bite her bum. I realize how un-gentlemanly this sounds, and I do feel ashamed confessing these awful feelings of depraved lust, but I was dirty and hopeless. I don't suppose that is an excuse, but I thought I'd mention it.

The frustration of seeing these wonderfully tanned bottoms without being able to give any of them a bit of a squeeze made me regret my decision to live like Chaplin and forced me to look for more wholesome interaction. I sat at a café and ordered cold lemonade, a small cake and a fruit salad to do my pineapple dance again. I did it for ages hoping for some attention from somebody, anybody. I just wanted someone to smile at me and remind me I was human and capable of goodness. When that finally happened it was again from a wonderful child.

They looked like the perfect family – mother father and two children, one of each gender. I wondered if the elder child was disappointed that his infant sibling was a girl, and if he wanted to put her in a football shirt and take the pretty bow off her head. The mother shifted the baby girl in her arms, causing the cake she was holding to drop onto the sand. I had watched this happen right next to me so got to my feet and offered my cake to the little baby as a replacement. The mother protested, but the little girl grabbed the cake. Her big brother looked at me with a big smile, the mother apologised for her children, but I waved away her apologies before putting my hand to my heart to express my joy and sincere insistence before taking the flower out of my lapel and presenting it to her.

'She is taken,' said the father with a smile. I lifted my Derbyshire hat and bowed to him, before putting my fists up and doing a little boxer dance, noticing a few people from the beach had approached us to see what was going on. I winked at the man to show I was joking and went to swing for him before spinning around 720 degrees and tumbling to the floor with a backwards roll. I ended up sat on my bottom and holding my head. This lovely family were all laughing but for the bemused infant, and some of the ever growing audience laughed too. Others were unsure what was going on and tried to pick me up so I was able to resume the confrontation, taking the woman's hand and pretending to kiss it before grasping my heart with love. The man repeated that she was taken, so I got ready for another big swing and again tumbled to the floor, this time to the sound of many more laughs.

I stood up and bowed, moving towards my audience warmly shaking hands with all of them and giving them a loving smile. I came back to the family and noticed the baby staring at me holding her cake. The audience watched as I made cute faces at her, getting closer and closer, mimicking the '*coocheecoocheekoo*' people feel possessed to do whenever they are interacting with an infant. I then switched the look on my face to that of a starving animal and took a big bite out of her cake. There were a few gasps but they turned to laughs as I went back to making cutesy expressions at the child, my mouth full of cake. I repeated the same process, making silly faces at the baby and then taking a bite out of her cake before trying to look innocent. This time people laughed hard and a young man put some coins in my hand. I tried to give it back, waving it away, but then the dad gave me some money too, his whole family seemed to be laughing. I thanked them all, not with words but with a wave of the hat before reaching for my fairly small sized bag that I struggled to pick up as the little crowd continued to watch and more people came over to see what was so interesting. I pulled and heaved, but to no effect so I finally gave it an almighty tug and hoisted it onto my shoulder. The momentum of this lift spun me round and the bag went crashing to the floor with me tripping over it and landing flat on my face. When I looked up, my face was caked in sand and I heard massive laughter coming from my intimate audience.

More coins were thrown beside me before I repeated trying to make this Herculean lift with the same slapstick result. I was quickly running out of ideas, so gathered the money that had come my way, struggled my bag onto my shoulder. I waved my hat and held a hand to my heart to express my gratitude and love before walking off with the famous penguin tramp walk, swinging my cane and skipping in genuine delight at what had just happened. Then I remembered my manners and went back to buy another piece of cake to give to the little girl before leaving.

Later that day, I tried to bring my humour to new and different audiences, but sadly they were less responsive. I needed the initial interaction I'd had with the family to spark interest in others. In fact although some people saw me and smiled, I felt most laughter I got wasn't for me, but at me. Some of my spectators had menacing vibes and were shouting what sounded like nasty things as they watched me trip over my bag. But I didn't care, as Chaplin said, 'My pain may be the reason for somebody's laughter. But my laugh must never be the reason for somebody's pain.' At the end of the day, I counted the spare change and I saw I had earned enough to cover my food that day. This plus the memories of all those smiles I had evoked gave me hope that I could live in Rio de Janeiro not just as The Gentleman Tramp but also as an entertainer.

The last few hours before bed were profoundly boring. The adrenaline come down made me understand why rock stars find it hard to relax after a performance. I walked around before stopping for a bite to eat in a fast food restaurant. I would like to eat in these places because it was cheap and I could use the bathrooms to have a good scrub and clean my teeth ready for bedtime (I also love hamburgers). I walked around some more, I daydreamed, I thought of expanding my comedy repertoire and I walked again. Finally bedtime came and I could go and settle down, I never felt comfortable lying down before ten o'clock. On that particular night, I wasn't as tired as usual because I had had a long sleep in the hotel the night before, so I tossed and turned and was more aware of the absurdity of the situation. It all felt far more real and unnecessary than the previous nights.

It came as quite a shock to me when I rolled over in bed to see the dog from the beach sitting right next to me yawning and licking his lips. I jolted up and grabbed my things ready to move somewhere else, but as I was doing this he kept perfectly still and I realized he meant me no harm, so I gave him a nonchalant pat on the head.

'What's your name? Where are your owners?' I asked, but Scraps just kept licking his lips and staring off in a daydream. 'Why are you sleeping on the streets? Don't you have a nice home?' I asked. Scraps stretched and yawned, he looked hungry so I searched through my bag and gave him some cold meat and biscuits I had brought earlier for snacking. He wolfed them down licking his lips and I patted him on the head more.

'I have a nice home, I don't really know what I'm doing here, stupid really. I wanted to help people and I wanted to fall in love, I wanted to feel like a real person, but I feel more of a fake than ever. I did fall in love though you should see her she is so beautiful. She's called Mariana, but she's in love with someone else,' I said as Scraps licked the biscuit packet and lay down.

'Sorry, you don't want to hear about all this, do you? So what's your name? Maybe you don't have a name. Every dog should have a name. I'm going to call you Scraps.'

Scraps stretched one last time and closed his eyes. 'I'm glad you're here Scraps, I don't think I like being on my own.' I rolled over again and closed my eyes before drifting into sleep.

I awoke to a nudge and a strange voice. Scraps had gone and a crazy-eyed, greasy haired man in ripped dirty clothes was kneeling over me, holding a knife to my face and speaking in a muttered gibberish. It was hard to take my eyes away from the shaky blade in his right hand, but I noticed him continually wiping his nose and scratching his face with his left hand. In a state of shock, I could not move and his speech became louder and more manic. I looked left and right, but remembered I'd picked this street as it was so quiet. There would be nobody to help me. His shouts grew even louder and bits of his spit hit me in the face as he hovered over me with foul smelling breath, the knife pressed against my skin.

'Take whatever you want,' I said, 'just take it!' I offered him my bag. He began searching through it until he came across the side pocket with my wallet and spare change. Once he had this he relaxed a little momentarily, but seconds later he became convinced I had more and continued his barrage of slurred

Portuguese questioning. I stared at him blankly and he repeated the same untranslatable words.

'I don't understand,' I said.

He kept going and going with his interrogation and was getting even more worked up, the hate on his screwed up face suggested he was genuinely angry. His eyes looked possessed by demons and he didn't seem of sound mind. I began to fear for my life. He pressed the cold metal to my throat once more and then lifted it up in a threatening motion, but he stopped himself from swinging it back down, perhaps a moment of good conscience befell him, but it didn't last long. The cruel dagger shimmered against the moonlight as he moved it back down and against my throat. I could see fury in his drug-addled eyes as he took deep angry breaths that rattled with disgust through his nostrils. I really thought my time was up. I was about to be murdered on the streets of Brazil. The intent on his face was unmistakeable, so I closed my eyes and tried to picture Mariana's beauty as I prepared for the unimaginable agony of being stabbed.

A low-pitched growl was followed by anguished screams of pain that I was relieved to realize were not my own. I opened my eyes to see my attacker with his mouth wide open, he was reaching back to his leg. Scraps had returned and was biting down on his calf and not letting go. I sat up and grabbed for the man's arm that carried the knife and wrestled him to the ground. I rammed his hand into the concrete floor until he released the weapon and I flung it as far as I could. Scraps still had a ferocious grip, sinking his teeth deeper and deeper into flesh as the man tried to fend him off with punches. I continued to wrestle and got on top of the man, punching him on the nose. This first punch was feeble and timid, so I knew I would have to try again. I caught him much more firmly this time, but I knew if I was to release him he would surely do some harm to either me or Scraps, probably both of us. So I punched him repeatedly, harder and harder as my confidence grew. The final punch sent his head banging into the concrete floor and he seemed to go unconscious and groggy. I waited to see if he was still moving before getting off of him to grab my things and run away from that awful situation. I hoisted my bag on to my shoulders and went to take my first step when the man grabbed a hold of my leg.

He seemed to emerge from the dead like something from a horror movie as he gargled blood out of his mouth and gave me a look similar to the one I'd experienced from the crocodile in Nepal. I kicked and struggled and eventually got free of his grip before running off as fast as I could. I ran and ran until my lungs ached and my heart pumped so hard I thought it might explode. I stopped to catch my breath and then continued at a walk, not a gentle walk but one of those fast walks you see at the Olympics, while I wiped my hands on trees, branches and my coat to rid myself of the horror I had experienced, not to mention the blood. As I motored on, I heard a bark and Scraps had caught up with me, but I kept walking I wanted to get as far away from this hideous incident as I could. I headed for another of my bedtime spots and decided I must stop and sit down. I really preferred to be moving, but I couldn't run all night. Scraps stayed with me, but I didn't try to sleep again. I kept a constant vigil, moving off whenever I felt nervous. I patted Scraps on the head.

'Thanks, thanks. I don't know what would've happened without you. You're a good dog aren't you? Thanks Scraps.' The dog wagged his tail and brushed his head against my leg, he was nursing a few punches from that bastard.

In the morning I got breakfast and treats for Scraps. 'You deserve this Scraps, thanks,' I said. From that moment on we were best friends.

The Police

Scraps stayed with me most nights. Occasionally he would wander off, but when I awoke he was always there yawning and stretching on the floor next to me. It became increasingly tricky to find a good place to sleep because, in the poorer neighbourhoods, I feared a repeat of the drug-fuelled theft, and all of the richer neighbourhoods were patrolled by police officers that would usher me and Scraps away with threats of prison. I began to realize that wherever there are rich people there are police to protect them.

I was reminded of the kids back at school who always had supporters around them to defend their position as being cool and popular. I remembered The Duke (Brian) from work and his giggling little friends who would act as a barrier to protect him from anyone who wanted to shatter the illusion of his power. I began to realise the adult world was just like the school playground, the successful sticking together and watching each other's backs while the weak suffered below them and fought for any kind of respectable position. The police and the kids that protected the popular kids did so because they were terrified of falling further down the ladder into the misery of being poor or despised. They were happy to sit in the middle and hold the line of what had already been established. It made me sick and I prayed for the destruction of these ridiculous social illusions. I had been at the very bottom of the ladder at school. So far down that nobody wanted anything to do with me, and now in the adult world, I had sunk to those depths once again.

Even though I did it for the smiles and not the money, my performances were improving and providing me with more cash than I needed for food. I continued to try my hand at Chaplin's funny business almost every day. I was the clown of the beaches; a wholesome distraction from the beautifully-buttocked women and the muscle men, a contrasting reality in a world of vanity, an alternative interaction and a refreshing view of imperfection.

I expanded the repertoire of my comedy routines; singing silly songs, performing magic tricks that I had been working on for years. Then I found my A material – I would act drunk; give out flowers to women; fall over towels and chairs; raise my hat; do dances; smile at everyone and struggle with a deck chair until it would end up on my head. I got the best performances when I could involve the audience. Pretending to seduce a woman and argue with her boyfriend or husband. I would dance with the women, pretend to fight with the men and lose – rattling good fun it was, but I decided never to take cake from a baby ever again. I just don't have the heart for it. My actions were all done in fun and, people were usually good sports. I realised how almost everyone thrived on the attention just as much as I did.

I wanted to include my best friend, so I would often take Scraps with me. I'd pretend to argue with him or find a young lady to dance with whilst a lead was tied to his neck and my belt. As he would grow distracted and the rope became taught, I would be pulled and fall over, with him seemingly dragging me along the floor (actually I used my feet and bent my knees to push myself along). The cuteness of the mutt really came in handy to my act, and my success doubled when I began to take him with me. He didn't need to perform. He was a natural entertainer.

When I would get a warm reaction with smiles and laughter it would enrich my heart. I really liked to make children laugh , as it felt good for my soul. Asking for money or passing out a collection would have been out of character, so I merely accepted what I was given. I only hoped for enough to keep me fed for the day. I was really taking pride in trying to entertain people and this became my purpose for living.

When I was not at the beach, I would go to Lapa or Centro or the big tourist attractions – Christ the Redeemer and Sugarloaf Mountain. Often there were queues, which was great because people were bored and looking for a distraction. The metro was a great place too. Many viewed me as an annoying little beggar, a bad impersonator, but I knew by the end of my routine they would be happier than before they saw me, and that was all I wanted. I would eat cheaply, either fast food burgers or a plate of rice and beans. Food was always on my mind. It was an obsession.

I daydreamed and fantasised about generously thick slices of meat covered in gravy, roasted potatoes, fresh, multicoloured vegetables, a large beer and a chocolate sponge in custard, but anything to quieten my stomach would do. When deprived of food your stomach becomes your boss. It tells you where to go and what to do. The will of the mind can fight it, but eventually it will lose.

About a week ago, I met a French girl called Charlotte. I was sitting on the brightly coloured steps of Lapa as people walked up and down taking more bloody photographs. I was having a break from my performance and just relaxing.
'Oh God, thank goodness someone who looks like they can speak English. I am so sick of these fucking Brazilians, they are so stupid.'
'Hello,' I said.
'What are you doing here?' she asked.
'Meditating, I didn't think I knew how to meditate, but I think that's what I'm doing,' I said.
'I am trying to get away from the Brazilians. Brazilian men are the worst, they only care about beauty. They think they are so fucking perfect and they are too aggressive. I expect you like the Brazilian girls?'
'I like one yes, but actually they all seem quite lovely.'
'They seem lovely,' she said with an angry laugh, 'but trust me they are not. They will be lovely to you and make you feel special, but ten seconds later they will be saying the same shit to someone else, don't believe them. You are more intelligent than that, I can see.'
'I'm not intelligent,' I said nervously.
'More intelligent than the Brazilians, they have no brain, they think only with their sex organs. I met this Brazilian and I was so stupid that I actually believed what he was saying. I went home with him and now I have caught something. Oh *merde*! Why was I so stupid?'
'We all make mistakes.'

'I emailed him to tell him about this and he sent me this bullshit saying it wasn't him, and that I have a strong character that he doesn't like. What the hell does that mean? I am sick of these Brazilians and their shit,' said Charlotte slapping the steps.

'Oh dear, how terrible for you,' I said trying to sound comforting.

'Do you know this dog?' she said pointing at Scraps who was sitting on a vivid red step and licking his legs.

'Yes, he is my friend.'

'Is it safe to pet him?'

'Yes, he likes to have his ears stroked.'

'*Bonjour, vous n'êtes pas comme les autres chiens au Brésil. Vous êtes beau et frais,*' said Charlotte while stroking Scraps, who was as charming as ever with his dignified stillness and friendly face. 'Shall we go for lunch? I am hungry,' asked Charlotte. I wasn't sure if she was talking to Scraps or me.

'I'd love too, sounds good,' I said.

Over lunch she told me more and more about herself, in a very flirtatious manner. I did pause when she said she studied magic, and when she mentioned that she had done a test that determined she was sixty percent sociopath, but all this got lost in the conversation we were having. Her friendliness and flirtation continued and I considered the possibility that this could be my great romance. We sat at the lunch table talking for hours and hours. She continued to bemoan the Brazilian men and talked about how I was so much better than them. When I told her about Mariana, she said that I could do much better than a Brazilian girl. She talked of her frustration living in Paris, and I really understood. She was getting closer to me and occasionally touched me with a nice look in her eye, so during a pause in the conversation I mustered the courage to lean in and kiss her.

'*Va te faire foutre, trouduc,*' she said recoiling in horror.

'Sorry,' I said.

'Sorry? Sorry is not good enough. You are disgusting.'

'I thought you wanted me to kiss you. Sorry.'

'No, I didn't. Why would you think that? I can't believe you did that,' she said before getting up aggressively and walking off with a quick look round to hiss at me like a cat. We had exchanged numbers so I sent her a text message to apologise again, but she never replied.

I was left with the hefty bill, and as I thought back to the magic and sociopath comments I came to the worrying conclusion that perhaps she was a witch. This was confirmed two days later when I noticed my penis was looking smaller than usual, my back ached and my buttocks were incredibly itchy. I still don't know what magic spells she cast on me, but I hoped that this satisfied her and that nothing else bad would happen. I have started to think of all women as witches. This is not always as a bad thing. Sometimes they are beautiful, kind witches who put good spells on the world – like Mariana. She is the loveliest witch of all.

My night fear was growing stronger. I was scared of drug addicts and criminals and I was scared of the police. I moved to the favelas because I didn't know where else to turn. It was a good move. I had some very peaceful nights there and nobody wanted to bother me. I had heard terrible things of these communities, but I had a wonderful time teaching in a favela and the Cantagalo favela was the safest place I slept. This was very welcome once I hit rock bottom, which happened a couple of days after I met Charlotte and I was scratching my bum at a pizza stand.

I could smell the delicious meat and vegetable pizzas. The man selling them had a big moustache and looked like he took very great pride in his pizza. He was very skilled at cutting them up into slices and made a bit of a performance of it, spinning around and flipping the food in the air before catching it on a paper plate. He was dressed in white and looked so clean. I asked him for a slice and eat it in four greedy mouthfuls.
'Two more please,' I said. This pizza was amazing. I eat one and gave one to Scraps.
'Twenty reals,' said the pizza man as I gobbled. I searched my pockets before realising I had no money. I must have been pickpocketed. The pizza man started to look most concerned and then angry. I offered him my watch but he just repeated '*Vinte, vinte,* Twenty, twenty, twenty, twenty, twenty.'

I dug deep into my pockets, searching my trousers and my jacket before looking though my bag. The pizza man wasn't looking at me like I was a tourist with a problem. He was looking at me like I was a tramp and a thief and he looked infuriated.

There was nothing to do but run, so I ran. Scraps did too. We had a good ten second head start before anyone responded, Scraps flew ahead of me. I went as fast as I possibly could, sensing the presence of my pursuer and focusing on powering away. There were thankfully no cars, just the quiet streets up in the mountains with lots of different routes to take. I got a feeling the pizza man was not alone, and heard other voices shouting at me to stop – the shouts were getting nearer. The ridiculous Chaplin shoes handicapped me, but I was so focused on my running. I think I was pretty fast you know. I wish someone had timed me, in fairness the authorities that pursued me may have been in sandals so it was a fair contest.

I was also hanging on to my hat as I heard the first shouts of *Policia, Policia, Policia*. Turning left and right down streets and lanes, I ran like a wild baboon. I think I was about to be caught by the speedy pizza man when I tripped and piled straight into a set of bins, pounding my head on the concrete.

When I awoke, I was alone. They obviously decided the concussion was punishment enough and that I was just a petty criminal, Scraps was still with me though.

'Woof,' he said.

'Yes I know,' I replied.

So I went to the favela, I slept well. I continued to perform during the day and I continued to feel bored and frustrated until the Rio carnival began and events conspired to put me in this hospital. I never want to sleep on the streets ever again. I want comfort. I want warmth and I want love. Thank God Bruce is coming. Thank God Mariana is coming. I can't wait to see them.

Part 2

'Be the change you want to see in the world.' *Ghandi*

Hospital

When Mariana arrived at my door in a beautiful white dress, like a bride arriving at a church, I was moving myself up and down on the electric bed – it was a great way to meditate. Entering the room awkwardly, tripping on her shoes, she came closer to me with her eyes squished together and her lips pouting, I think she'd had trouble finding the correct room, but I was so pleased to see her. Her face was delicious and when she sat on the chair next to me she finally gave me that wonderful smile that I dream about. In truth, I was feeling much healthier than I had in some time, but for the benefit of visitors I thought it best to assume the role of a sickly individual. Nobody wants to come to hospital to see a healthy person. This was a dress rehearsal for when Bruce arrived, he would be really angry if he flew half way round the world to find me in fine form.

After a little small talk, conversation turned to a very serious subject – food and hunger. I'd described the appalling hospital nourishment and how my stomach never felt satisfied, so Mariana rushed back out of the hospital, returning minutes later with burgers, fries and chocolate milkshakes. We sat and eat together. It was so romantic. I couldn't have been happier.

Inevitably, the initial concern for my wellbeing turned to how the hell I ended up in hospital and what I'd been doing since we last saw each other. I've begun to pride myself on truthfulness, the truth is the truth and my word is all I have, so I explained the whole situation. To her credit Mariana never once interrupted, which is more than can be said for me when she finally got her chance to comment on my lifestyle choice.

'I don't believe you did this, what were you thi…'

'I wanted to be The Gentleman Tramp for real, I wanted to be free.'

'The people who live like this don't have a choice. You are from a rich country and a good family. There is no reason for you to live like this. You could have been killed. I don't understand why you would do this when you could have gone home to warmth and love,' said Mariana.

'I was bored at home, it was miserable I hated it. I may as well have been dead. I wanted to feel something, feel anything. I wanted to understand what it feels like to be free, even if that feeling was horrible,' I replied trying to explain myself while still appearing a little unwell and pathetic.

'You were free. You were free to get a job, you were free to vote, you were free to express yourself. You were free to travel the world for God sake. Many people here do not have these freedoms. Why do you think sleeping on the streets of Rio will make you free? This is not freedom.'

'I hated my job. It was soul destroying. You're not free to think in a job like that. You have to listen to people talking rubbish all day and stare at computers where you read more shit and get bombarded by idiots. Constantly having to listen to people's opinions on things I don't care about. I tried to read and escape, but the people were so loud. They got inside my head and I don't want them in my head.'

'Why don't you just ignore them? There will always be people like that.'

'Because I get lonely, I want to interact, but you can't express yourself unless it's about something everyone else is saying. Like who should be the captain of a football team or who should win a reality TV show. When I try to express myself people make fun of me. I travelled to get away from all of that. People don't make fun of me so much in other countries. Or if they do, I don't understand what they're saying. I wanted to be myself, to be a part of nature so I could think and do what I want and interact with better people and make them smile,' I said. 'I don't want to vote either. The politicians all seem the same to me, I don't like any of them. They don't say anything good. They don't care about people. I don't want those people in my mind either.

'You think your politics is bad. You're lucky with your politics. Here it is a thousand times worse – a joke, but we have to carry on. You have too as well. Or are you going to just stay living like this forever? Even though you don't have too? Are you happy like this? Are you crazy?' Mariana asked.

'No I'm not going to do it anymore, it was really horrible,' I said remembering some of the more unpleasant days I had.

'Then why do it? The people who live like this would give anything for your life. You are so lucky. I really don't understand what you are saying. If you wanted nature then why did you choose to live like this in a giant city? Why did you choose a dangerous city? You told me the Asian countries were more beautiful and cheaper. Why are you here?'

'Because I love you,' I said looking away in shame before suffering through the eternal quiet that always follows these kind of grand statements. It eventually ended when she had thought about her words.

'I am nobody special to love. I am glad that you think this of me, it is very lovely, but this is no reason to live like you have and get sick. It's not fair to say this. You can not blame me,' she said moving over to sit on the edge of my bed and putting her hand on my arm, trying to get me to look at her. 'It is very good to feel love, it is a wonderful thing to have, but you must share your love with the world. Not only for me.'

'I do give my love to the world. I've been trying to make people laugh and smile. I've got a dog now and I don't want to live on the streets anymore. I want to help people and I know I need money to do that. I've been thinking of business ideas while I've been in here,' I said still not daring to look at Mariana.

'That is great. We must help people that are not as lucky as us. It does not mean we should become poor like this. We can't help when we need help ourselves.'

I must say she had amazing bedside manner and smelt like a fresh Papaya that was most welcome after the sterile smell of the hospital.

'I just wanted to be near you and I wanted to be like Chaplin,' I said after another awful lull in the conversation.

'I have wanted to be like movie stars too, but I copy their haircut or buy the same clothes, not this. Then you say you want to be near me, but when you loved your girlfriend you would not even talk to me. This is not love. It hurt me. Even now I have a boyfriend, I will always care for you and talk to you,' Mariana said as I felt her body become tenser through the mattress. I was still too cowardly to look at her fully.

'It is not fair to use me as an excuse for what you have done. I didn't ask you to do this and I don't want you to say this. Have you ever thought about how I feel?'

Yes, I always think about how you feel. I couldn't handle my feelings. I was jealous and sad thinking about you. I love you too much,' I said weakly.

'This is not love. If you love me you will let me be free. If you loved me you would always be my friend. You are living with obsessions. This obsession with Charlie Chaplin, this obsession with me and I imagine you have had other obsessions, like this girl you lived with in England.'

'I do love you and I do love Charlie Chaplin and I didn't love her. I just thought being with her was what I was supposed to do, it's what grown ups do isn't it? Grown up boring stuff, you are doing this grown up stuff with your boyfriend. You give all your love to him and nothing for anyone else,' I said with a slightly stronger voice.

'I give him my heart, but I still have love. He gives me more love. I love my family and friends and everyone. I would not be here if I did not have more love,' said Mariana.

'But why does he get so much of your love?' I asked. 'He's so lucky.'

'We are, in love, it is different. There are different feelings.'

'It's just because of sex?'

'Sex and love are together, yes. Real passionate love encourages sex with the right person. I found this with Fernando.'

'I don't understand,' I said.

'One day you will meet the right woman and you'll understand. She will be very lucky too.'

'I don't want another woman.'

'You think I am something different. I am the same as other women,' she said.

I have always been your friend. Even when I didn't see you or I didn't talk to you. I was always thinking of you,' I said.

Thankfully we were interrupted at this point, as this conversation did not appear to be leading to a pleasant conclusion. The interruption came in the form of a rowdy laugh and the stomp of heavy hiking boots.

'Is he still alive?' asked a dirty and bedraggled Bruce who was completely ignoring me and settling his attentions on Mariana.

'I think he's fine,' replied Mariana.

'What a pity, well if he dies in the next couple of days I want his bag and his Chaplin hat, but you can have his money. Deal?' asked Bruce holding out his hand for Mariana to shake.

'No I want the hat. I don't think he has much money.'

Bruce grabbed my Chaplin stick from the corner of the room and began poking me with it.

'I don't think he has much time left and I really want that hat,' he said as he moved round to the other side of the bed and questioned me as to my health and what had led to this predicament. I explained truthfully again for I could not very well tell lies with Mariana sitting there. I have been a liar on too many occasions.

'What a dick you are,' said Bruce as Mariana excused herself saying she thought we needed some time to catch up. She asked me to call her so we could meet before I left Rio.

'So you've spent all your money?' said Bruce when we were alone before continuing to berate my behaviour and decisions.

'I've got a bit of money, but I've got a real problem here. I think the hospital is going to charge me a lot for my treatment. I don't think I'll be able to afford it,' I said with massive understatement.

'Don't worry, I'll go and take care of it now,' he said.

'Are you sure'?

'Yeah, I've been raking it in, no problem. My expeditions are really taking off and I'm getting paid loads. Next stop is Colombia, so coming to see you is no problem. You were lucky with the timing though. Anyway, check this out'.

Bruce passed his mobile phone to me and showed me the first page of a website. A picture of his cheesy face appeared and underneath it said, *'A real life action man with the friendliness of the boy next door,* says Jean from America.'

'Nice, I always knew you liked the older women,' I said.

'I like all women,' he said.

Bruce disappeared, and when he came back an hour later it was with the doctor who had some papers for me to sign. I was to be released from my prison of treatment immediately.

Bruce organised a hotel for us to stay at –It was large and luxurious with a rooftop that looked out across the city. We spent the whole evening up there. The lights of Rio spread across the beach magnificently and up to the mountain that housed Christ the Redeemer.

'Fantastic,' said Bruce as he sipped on a cold beer, 'what could be better? So you've been living on the streets'? How the hell did you manage that?'

'Well it sounded like a good idea, good for the soul you know.'

'Weren't you scared?'

'An honest man has nothing to fear. Actually I was terrified, but it wasn't all bad. I felt more alive,' I said.

'I know what you mean. Better than doing a boring job and feeling miserable I suppose. You seem much more relaxed now and you look well. Don't do anything so stupid again though. You understand? Never. God knows what could've happened?'

'I look well? Brilliant,' I said.

'Well better than you did; but then you really did look terrible before. Anyway I've been to remote and beautiful places but never lived in a huge city like this. What an experience. What made you pick Rio?'

'Mariana lives in Rio. I've always wanted to come here since I met her. I also wanted to do volunteer work, teaching kids in the favelas. It was fantastic. After I was here for a while I could really imagine Chaplin being here so I thought it was a good place to be.'

'I might have known it was something to do with Charlie Chaplin. When are you going to grow out of that? Anything happening with you and Mariana?'

'Well she has a boyfriend, but we are friends.'

'Don't waste your time with her. She's really nice, but if she's got a boyfriend then what's the point. There are a lot of nice girls out there.'

'So what's Colombia like?'

'I don't know I haven't been yet I've heard it's unbelievable though. I'll let you know and maybe you can come out too, but you need to go home and sort yourself out first. Make some money.'

I slept so well in that hotel, after the streets and the hospital and the loneliness. The companionship of Mariana and then Bruce warmed my soul. In the morning, Bruce went off to see the sights and I went searching for Scraps. I had to help Scraps before I left. I had to find him a home. I had to give him his happy ending.

The Search for a Happy Ending

Amidst a mountain of black refuse sacs on a hot dirty street, a wet black nose protruded. There were a few flies buzzing around, but not as many as you would suspect. I used my Chaplin stick to poke the rubbish bags and there was a bit of rustling before a furry white face with a big, brown spot over the left eye emerged to stick out its long pink tongue and begin panting.

'Scraps, it's me. I've missed you,' I said as he wrestled his way free of the bags and jumped up on to my leg with his low-pitched dispassionate woofs. 'You look starving. Don't worry I'm going to get you a feast.'

And a feast is what he had – chicken drumsticks, biscuits, cold ham, beef jerky and bacon all washed down with a big bowl of water. I'm aware that this is not the best thing to feed a dog, but it's what he likes. It had taken me two days to find Scraps and it's not like I just had a little wander around. I spent all my time walking the city looking in all our old places and asking people if they had seen him using the Portuguese that I had learnt from Bruce's travel Brazil book. Now that I had located my old friend, there was no time to rest. Bruce was adamant that I fly back to England to see Mum and Dad and sort myself out, so I had to find a home for Scraps as soon as possible. My first idea was to visit Mariana, she was a dog lover and very trustworthy so I called her and arranged a visit for that afternoon.

I turned up at her apartment with Scraps and was very excited to be in her home. I had seen where she lived back in England, but her aunt had never let me in. She said boys weren't allowed. Mariana's apartment was tranquil and elegant with white walls supporting some wonderful artwork, some of which Mariana had painted herself. My favourite one was a cartoon drawing of animals on the beach. The colours and the images really got my imagination going.

From the second we entered the apartment complex Scraps was a total gentleman, he didn't bark once, he moved with his head held up high and he kept to his own personal space. He greeted Mariana by walking up to her and sitting himself in front of her and looking at her for a few seconds with a very regal look on his face. She patted his head and then he walked away to sit in the corner of the room. I imagine if he had hands and thumbs he would have been sipping a glass of port and smoking a cigar, and if he had vocal chords he would have commented on what a lovely home it was.

'He is a lovely dog,' Mariana said. 'I like him, he's very polite.'

'Yes, he is very polite such a good dog. It's hard to imagine a better dog.'

'I think you will miss him when you are back in England. The same way I missed you when I came here. I don't think he will write to you either.'

I can't believe she was comparing me to a dog. The cheek!

'I was wondering if you knew anyone who would be interested in looking after him. I want to find him a home before I leave. Do you want him?' I asked.

'I would love him, but dogs are not allowed in these apartments and also Fernando does not like dogs too much,' Mariana said.

I understood about the apartments but I was sick of hearing about bloody Fernando. I'm sure Scraps wouldn't like him anyway.

'Do you know anybody who could take care of him?' I asked.

'I don't think so. I can ask, but my family already have pets and my friends are not in their own homes yet, but I can ask.'

'That would be great. I have another place I can try, but if that doesn't work I don't know what to do.'

'You can take him to an animal shelter,' Mariana said.

I had thought about this, but they sounded very like the Victorian workhouses that Chaplin frequented as a young man. This was not a good ending for a Gentleman Tramp like Scraps. He deserved better. I sat and drank tea with Mariana and I hoped this would not be the last time that I would ever see her. We both promised to stay pen pals forever, but the talk of seeing each other did not feel realistic. She gave me a wonderful hug and a kiss on the cheek when I departed and she patted Scraps head again. I wondered how Fernando must feel to have Mariana's love. How could he ever feel sad or angry or anything other than joy about the blessing he had. I walked away from the apartments knowing that I would miss her for the rest of my life.

I didn't have time for morbid self-attention or indulgent depressed reflection. I needed to find a home for Scraps. I got on the bus headed for the favela where I had been a teacher and after clearing the motorways I was able to see a whole bunch of new characters. A group of women eating bowls of spaghetti and rice while their children ran around; a serious looking man crossing the road while trying to get his spectacles out of his pockets and an old man wearing a yellow Brazil shirt with a football balanced on top of his head. On the bus in England I always felt as if I was passing the same cardboard cut outs of the same people everyday, so much so that I never bothered to look at them.

When I got off the bus there were more new people to see. I saw a woman covering her head with an umbrella berating her husband for something; a young couple kissing and canoodling in a café and a father with his two sons talking to a drink seller with their arms around each other's shoulders. I wasn't sure if Brazil had more interesting and diverse people or if it was me that was different here. My mind was more curious about those around me and I was more capable of seeing the good in them. Everybody was looking at us. It is not everyday in the favela that you would see The Little Tramp walking down the street with his dog Scraps.

When I got to the school, I was mobbed by the students who all came over to hug me. They were reluctant to let go and their friendliness was borderline violent. Scraps began barking because of this avalanche of love. Their new teacher asked them to sit down, and I went round greeting them all individually and letting them pat Scraps, who settled down by Lorena, who he liked the best. The new teacher was very grateful for the distraction as she sat down swigging water and fanning herself with a notebook. It was then that I told the students that I was returning to England and that I wanted someone to look after my dog. I turned to Lorena to translate this message, but as it turned out this was unnecessary as Lorena said her dog had died a year ago and she would love to have Scraps.

'Will it be OK with your family?' I asked.

'My mother will love Scraps. She loves animals. She will be so happy,' Lorena said. I was very pleased to hear this, but wanted to check that Lorena's mother would agree. I gave her my email address and said to contact me by the end of the day, and that I would return the next day if they agreed.

That night, I had to leave Scraps on the streets again which tore my heart to pieces, but Bruce would not allow me to sleep outside and I knew Scraps wouldn't go far.

Bruce wanted me to go to a nightclub with him, but I had already been to one with him two nights earlier and spent most of my time holding my ears in a corner while he danced around with a beautiful Brazilian girl in a red dress that was transparent around the buttocks. She was wearing a purple G-string. I could understand Bruce's eagerness to go back.

I checked my emails at about 10 o'clock and there was a message from Lorena saying that her mother would be at the school at 3pm tomorrow to collect Scraps as she was overjoyed by the idea of having the dog. They really were so happy and Lorena thanked me profusely in the email.

I also had another email from Josh.

Hey man how's things? I hope you're still enjoying yourself. Are you in Brazil or back in England? I've just been promoted at work so working super hard. I hope you're still planning on coming to New York. You would love it here. Would be great to see you if you're passing through, and if you want to come for longer I can definitely get you a job here for really good money. I'm telling you man it's a great life. Let me know what you think. Josh.

I thought this was a great idea. Just like Chaplin, I would head to America to make my fortune. When I told Bruce about it in the morning he agreed to loan me the money to go. This was one of the first ideas I'd ever had that he thought was good and he was very excited and supportive of it.

'What is the job?' he asked.

'I don't know, something to do with stocks and shares,' I said.
'Do you know anything about stocks and shares?'
'I'll figure it out,' I said.

When I went outside Scraps was waiting for me and we spent our last few hours together. We went to the beach and did our final performance for a very lively crowd. We had a spot of lunch and I got all his favourite food. We played and wrestled a bit and I patted his head. I thought back to when he saved me from the drug-crazed mugger and those lonely nights on the streets when he had been my only friend in the world. I would never forget that. I hoped Lorena would stay in touch to let me know how he was doing.

It was scorching hot and the thermometers were bubbling over 40 degrees in Centro as we headed for the bus stop to meet Scraps' new family. We still had quite a bit of walking to do and Scraps hated the heat even more than I did. He scampered around desperately searching for places to hide from the relentless power of the sun. I crossed a road, but Scraps would not budge as he had found some shade and wanted to stay in it. I shouted at him to come, but he wasn't moving, so I just shrugged my shoulders, muttered and carried on walking. He had done this so many times and he would always catch up with me, but a few seconds later my universe collapsed, as I powered on for my destination I was stopped by the noise of a most horrendous bang, followed by a pathetic whelp.

I turned round to see Scraps was crawling out from under a killing machine, a Brazilian bus. He must have begun running after me, the bus had come out of nowhere as the street was clear when I crossed. It must have been just around the corner, speeding towards my friend, speeding its way to devastate my life. I began to walk back fast but with great trepidation. I prayed that my eyes were playing tricks on me as I looked on in terror, encouraging Scraps to get out of the road. The bus screeched to a stop and Scraps was crawling forwards dragging his hindquarters that looked totally destroyed as he smeared dark red blood across the grey street. I reached him at the curb and looked down to see him looking me straight in the eye with an expression that clearly communicated the words help me.

'I don't know what to do,' I said to Scraps. The brutal collision had silenced the world and all I could hear was my heart pumping. I was too terrified to keep my eyes focused on Scraps in case this was real. I stood frozen as he continued trying to crawl closer towards me and up the curb and fully onto the pavement. The driver opened the doors and began speaking rapidly in his foreign dialect.

'*Nao fala Portuguese*,' I said, 'I don't speak Portuguese.' But the driver kept going with his nonsensical words.

He pointed at the now silent and motionless dog lying helplessly on the floor. Scraps eyes were open as he suffered though the tortured and confused pain and panic. His eyes searched desperately for a way out, an escape from this nightmare, but there was nothing there except me, a gathering crowd of voyeuristic scum and the dull business environment of the Rio de Janeiro office district.

The driver continued to speak.

'Just fuck off,' I screamed.

Passengers stared out of the window and the driver began to pull away from this horrific scene with anxiety and guilt in his eyes. The people standing around me were gawping at Scraps and I told them all to fuck off too.

With every passing moment Scraps expression became more calm and sedate as his body relaxed and became free from tension. His eyes stopped darting around and started focusing into the distance as if he was in an art museum sampling great beauty.

I felt totally powerless and confused. I wanted to help and comfort Scraps, but I could do nothing but stare at him. Eventually, I sat on the curb next to him and just shared the moment with him. He gently rested his head on my leg and I put my hand on his back to let him know he was not alone.

His breathing became deeper and slower. His eyes were closing. Tears began to stream down my face as I watched my best friend leave me forever.

'I'm sorry Scraps, I'm sorry. I love you,' I spluttered.

Scraps went into a death rattle, his body twisted and contorted and his eyes bulged. It looked like his soul was trying to escape his body. It looked incomprehensibly painful. Then his body tensed up one final time and he relaxed. My friend was gone. Scraps was dead and I cried like I had never cried before. The floodgates opened and I wept and wept and wept.

Ten minutes after Scraps had died, I wrapped him up in a blanket and went to the park, where we would sit and walk together. I dug a deep grave with my hands; I dug as deep as I could. My fingers and nails became black from the dry soil. My arms and hands ached with the frantic emotional exertion that consumed my afternoon. It was horrible lowering him into the pit and covering him in the waterless soil. I could not stop crying and I repeated how sorry I was and how much I loved him again and again. I wanted to protect him. But he was gone.

That night I slept on the streets, not because I was poor, but because I wanted to stay with Scraps. I curled into a sobbing ball on top of the pile of dirt under which I had buried my friend. Even though I had dug so deep, I was still worried about other animals digging him up.

I prayed for sleep that night, any escape from the mental agony and anguish. I hoped to wake up to find it was all a dream. I texted Bruce, he would've been worried about me otherwise, but I had to lie. Sometimes it feels easier to be a liar than an honest man.

I'm staying out tonight. I want to sleep with a Brazilian prostitute. I can't come here and not enjoy one of those lovely bums. See you in the morning, I texted.

He replied, **What? I hope you're joking. I gave you money to get back on your feet not to sleep with hookers. I don't believe you sometimes. I've come all this way and you do this. Get yourself back here. If you do then use protection, for God's sake.**

When I awoke, I looked for my friend and then remembered what had happened. I went back to the hotel and after getting an earful from Bruce I tried to go back to sleep, but again I broke down crying.

I spent the whole day in this tearful solitude as Bruce continued to make the most of his time in Rio de Janeiro. When he came back in the evening to find me sobbing into a pillow, I found the courage to tell him of my departed friend.

'Shit sorry to hear that mate,' said Bruce giving me a pat on the back.

'Thanks.'

'Are you sure you don't want to go home? It might be good for you. Make you feel better,' he said

'I don't want to go home. I've got the taste of failure in my mouth. I'll go home if you can't lend me the money. Are you sure you can afford it?' I said.

'New York it is then,' said Bruce. I'll book you a ticket and transfer some money to your bank account. Pay me back when you're a rich stockbroker.'

'Thanks Bruce. I really appreciate all of this. I will pay you back soon. You're a good guy.'

'I know,' he said.

Two days later Bruce headed off for Colombia and I got on a plane for New York. It was time to change my fortunes around. I knew my great romance and adventure was out there somewhere and eventually, I would find it. I owed it to Scraps to be a better man.

New York City

Descending into the United States of America my heart filled with fresh optimism and ambition. I was positioned terribly in the aisle of the aeroplane, but when the heads of the other passengers aligned to clear my view of the window, I got the vaguest glimpses of the New York skyline below, which sent my imagination spiralling into visions of epic buildings and colossal landscapes. The excitement was tangible, my outlook indestructible and I had no concerns about the potential hurdles in front of me, as my vision of success was crystal clear. I would bask in the infinite opportunities of America and, just like Chaplin, I would take the country by storm.

I took a taxi from the airport to upper Manhattan where I'd arranged to stay. I felt like a tiny insect among such giant buildings, and hoards of cars surrounded my cab with a strangely enjoyable claustrophobia, the smell of freedom amidst total lockdown. It was a glorious spring day, and outside the car window people were bustling with life.

Dropped off two blocks from Central Park, I was anxious to dispense with my bags and explore the city. I was greeted in the hostel by a sweat-stained man who was preoccupied with watching an American football game on the TV, He nonchalantly took my money and explained the hostel rules before pointing me to my room. I smiled and nodded before heading to the stairs that led me to a hot and humid dormitory with the powerful stench of wet socks.

There were eight beds, six of which had bags on top of them, one had a snoring man on it and above him was my bunk. I threw my bag on it and opened it up to get my Chaplin clothes. The rustle of my backpack was ear-splitting as I tried not to wake this gentleman.

I ventured out into the vast expanse of Central Park, walking briskly along the path I immediately felt that I had come to the right place, it was as if I had set foot into the future and could leave the past behind me. Deeper into the park, people crowded by a friendly game of baseball, others walked with friends and dates, talking loudly and enthusiastically about their lives, some just sat and daydreamed. There were people exercising or running vigorously through the park, listening to state of the art iPods. Then there were those like me, who just watched everyone else like a child enthralled by the diversity of the zoo.

I instinctively wanted to be part of some of the fun activities, and I quickly began to recognise this as perhaps the greatest spot on the planet to work my Chaplinesque funny business. My first idea of how to interact came from the joggers, the fitness fanatics that I had so loathed in the past. I decided to join them for short bursts of running along the pathways, but in a different style. They had a relentless steady pace and carried equipment that measured their calories and heart rate as motivational music blasted in their ears. I ran in the style of Chaplin, with my feet pointing to the sides and holding on to my hat, glancing back frantically to see if anyone was chasing. I could gather enough speed to catch up with the fit people and run alongside them long enough to give them my best beautiful Chaplin smile and raise my hat to them. The first man I did this too was wearing a fluorescent tracksuit and a sweatband around his head, he got mad and shouted at me. The second man was a muscular, athletic, topless fellow with bulging biceps and tight shorts, he glanced over at me, shook his head in disgust and then ran faster to escape my friendliness. But the third person I ran with was a slim chap with a shaved head wearing a white T-shirt, he smiled at first and then laughed as we ran together for a few moments of fun.

I received this spiritual gift about three more times out of the ten other people I ran with. When I became too tired to run anymore, I went over and picked some wild flowers that I began handing out to fair maidens. Many didn't accept, but those who did were greeted by my biggest smile as I grasped my chest with love and happiness before kissing their hand. The final lady of the day was a middle-aged Mexican woman who was with her husband, who had a big thick moustache and a side parting. I approached her with the Chaplin walk and smile and held my heart with love and offered her the flower. She began to laugh and grabbed her husband's New York Giants shirt to introduce me. As she continued to chuckle, I put my arm around her and pointed between us to suggest that we were together. The man looked most upset by this and I offered my fists in comedy Chaplin fashion and I saw the smile crack on his face. I swung my arm around and fell to the floor before holding my heart and smiling for the woman. I closed my eyes while doing this and, when I opened them, we had been joined by a policeman in sunglasses. He was a tall man with big ears and a belly that made me look forward to sampling the various cuisines of the many street vendors in the city. It was obviously good stuff.

'Sir could you get to your feet please,' he said in a strict and professional voice. His automaton tone triggered my good behaviour and I did as he asked. 'What's your name Sir?' he asked. I really didn't want to speak because I was in the middle of being Chaplin. So I didn't answer, I just smiled.

'I've had several complaints about you disturbing the peace Sir, and I'm going to have to ask you to leave the area,' said the policeman.

'How can he be disturbing the peace? This man is not even speaking. Have you nothing better to do?' said the Mexican lady shrugging her arms in disbelief.

'Ma'am I've had several complaints about this man, so if you could kindly take a step back. Sir, I'm asking you to leave the vicinity before I am forced to take you in to custody.'

I really wanted to give this man a joke kick up the bottom, but he seemed more robotic and scary than policemen I'd met in other countries, so I walked off with my tail tucked between my legs, but I wasn't happy about it.

The bad smell and the snoring in the dormitory was very unpleasant, but I slept well and when daylight came I was feeling fresh and ready to see more of New York. I jumped on the confusing subway at the crack of dawn and went south towards Times Square. When I emerged from the dark tunnel of underground trains, my attention was drawn upwards to the gigantic buildings towering above and I had to arch my back and crane my neck to see their tops amidst the flashing adverts and bright colours of flamboyant advertising. Like an ant scurrying around a forest, I traversed the streets of splendour in a trance. At such an early hour the city was virtually deserted. My previously homeless mind was looking for places where I might be able to bed down and I had to force myself to think about what it would be like to live in a massive penthouse. Thinking about sleeping on the streets was not a good idea. It would not lead to anything positive. I was to be a success, not a vagabond. I did not need to think about this.

I eat a hearty breakfast of pancakes dripping in maple syrup with a side of bacon and scrambled eggs, all washed down with coffee and orange juice, in the booth of a pink diner in the gay district of Manhattan. I didn't realise it was for homosexuals until I saw two men in tight T-shirts gazing into each others eyes, and two women giving each other a little kiss on the lips. Any doubts I may have had about the clientele disappeared when I looked in the menu to see the advertised *Big Gay Burger*. I felt very uncomfortable at first, I don't really understand gay people because I've never really met any and I think men look too disgusting to kiss, but I understand the need for romance so I think I could be friends with gay people if they were friendly to me. The male couple were talking about dogs. I would have liked to have told them all about Scraps, but I was shy.

I continued wandering the streets enjoying seeing the colourful shops, hearing the pedestrian chit chat in a wide variety of dialects and smelling the scent of sugary treats from nearby vendors in this crazy, man-made ecosystem. I eventually stumbled upon the Empire State Building and didn't hesitate in going in and ascending to the highest possible point. The view was magical, looking down on the world and imagining all the heartbreak, love and adventure that would be happening, in the lives of those below. Unfortunately the other tourists kept pushing and shoving, and I could not stay in the spot to enjoy the spectacle for more than a few seconds at a time. I would have liked to have meditated for longer.

In the evening, I skipped through the door of a bar on the dark streets of the Bowery into a world of shots being poured and people unwinding after a fun day. The customers were young, but there were mature vibrations rippling through the tavern that made me feel happy to be there. The walls were covered in musical news clippings about famous bands and rock music pumped out of a large stereo system, but not so loud that you couldn't talk. I hate it when I can't hear what people are saying. My happiness took a bit of a dip when I saw the friend I was meeting sitting alone in the corner with a bottle off beer with her head down. Ayla didn't look very well. She greeted me without reciprocating my smile, and ordered more beer and some vodka. Her face looked pale, her white sweater was dirty and her hair unwashed.

'You look well,' said Ayla scratching her arm and wiping her face with her sleeve. I returned the sentiment, but she wasn't convinced I was telling the truth.

'Yeah right I'm on the cover of *Cosmopolitan* next week,' she said looking over my shoulders with eyes like a dead shark, the same eyes that I remembered being so beautiful, sparkly and full of energy. 'I heard from Lorena the other day, she has a job,' Ayla said perking up a little. 'Those kids were amazing.'

'They really were, so how are you doing?'

'Yeah, I'm doing good. I moved out of my family home. I have a job in a restaurant which is good, but I kinda hate it. I live with some other girls, but they are kinda bitchy to me. I'm seeing this guy, but he's an asshole. But yeah I'm good,' she said.

By the time we left the bar, I was very worried about Ayla because she kept mentioning drugs and violence, so I asked if I could help her in any way.

'No you don't have to help me, we're friends I want to help you. I'm going out again later, why don't you come and meet my friends. Well I say friends, Denise and Jane have been making up some bullshit about me, saying I'm never home and I look totally wasted all the time. You know they moved all my things out of the common room and just chucked them in my bedroom.'

'That's not very nice.'

'I know, right? Also Mikey might be there, he's OK really, but he can be a real jerk when he's drinking.'

'You're not really selling it to me,' I said.

'I'll be there too,' said Ayla.

'In that case it sounds amazing.'

I went back to the hostel for a shower and got a little lost before I went to the party. The Ayla I found in this new swankier cleaner bar with chandeliers was totally different to the one I met previously. She was dressed in a red evening dress cut low at the chest so that her voluptuous bosom poured out, her clean dark hair stretched down to beautiful jewellery that brought more attention to her boobs. Her red, high-heeled shoes gave her more stature and confidence as she sipped on an expensive looking cocktail. She greeted me with a big smile and a kiss on the cheek before introducing me to her similarly attractive, but drunk-looking, female friends and a couple of men in jeans and jackets. I was invited to sit down on a long comfy bench adjacent to a huge mirrored wall in the middle of the group. Everyone seemed very friendly and I was enjoying the chatter about clothes, gossip, food and music. As the evening progressed people were standing up a lot more and the music became louder. I felt much more comfortable sitting and I began drifting away from the group as they repositioned themselves to form a stronger nucleus. I might as well have been on another continent once this happened; my frequency was no longer in alignment with theirs. After some whispering with her friend and some fiddling with her phone, Ayla walked off to the door of the bar and out, she was gone for ages. I waited and waited for I thought it would be rude not to leave without saying goodbye, but when she returned she had tears in her eyes and was totally obliterated.

'Mikey is such an asshole,' Ayla said wiping the tears from her face and leaning on me to stop herself collapsing on the couch.

'What's he done?' I asked trying to sit with a stronger posture so that I did not get knocked over by her.

'We just had a fight. He's just such a dick,' Ayla said using her hand to brush the hair away from her face and crossing her legs for greater decency, but swinging her leg so far over that it fell on my lap. 'I feel wasted,' she continued.

'Too much to drink?'

'No drink isn't a problem. I can drink forever. I just did some shards. It was good shit,' Ayla said.

'What are shards?'

'Crystal meth. That's not the problem either, it's that jerk. I need to forget him, I wanna dance. Do you wanna dance?'

'I would love too,' I said (a gentleman never says no to a lady).

'Let's do it,' she said clumsily getting to her feet and pulling me up towards her as I protested meekly. After a few seconds of awkwardness, my hands settled on her warm hips and her hands moved onto my chest and then shoulders. She began grinding her body into me and it felt ever so nice.

'Get your goddam hands off my girlfriend you son of a bitch,' came the cry of a wide-eyed thug with spiky blond hair and a leather jacket. He was early thirties I should imagine, but he was scarred by terrible acne and had ruddy red cheeks, which became more and more noticeable as he marched right up and into my face. He grabbed Ayla by the hand and pulled her away from me.

'Don't talk to my friends like that you asshole,' replied Ayla slapping him round the face. 'I hate you, leave me alone,' she shouted as this man took a deep breath through his nose and pointed his finger at her.

'Me leave you alone? Isn't it you that phones me up constantly? Isn't it you that turns up at my home asking for meth? Isn't it you that said you couldn't live without me? Don't ever, ever slap me again ever.' He replied straightening his jacket and trying to get his composure.

Ayla slapped him again, even harder this time and he responded by shoving her down on the couch.

'You must be Mikey. Look there's no need for violence here, lets all calm down,' I said trying to help Ayla up and standing in the way of the two of them.

'Don't tell me to calm down dude. I don't want to have to kick your ass, but you better step off right fucking now,' said Mikey.

With this statement, I felt a shove from behind that forced my momentum into this angry character who responded by violently pushing me right back across the room and into a crowd of people, I regained my balance and moved back to my original position between him and Ayla, suddenly there was a lot of space around me and Mikey. People had cleared the way to make a circle as if it two Gladiators had entered the Roman coliseum and there was going to be a hell of a battle. I was in a fight and he was coming for me.

He got the first punch in, which jerked me to life. In Chaplin's movies he's often outsized, but he is an opportunist, a vicious attacker, remorseless in his strikes. It turns out that after my recent experiences I'd become the same. I cracked Mikey square on his jaw and got in a flurry of wild strikes as he reeled. One of my shots actually spun him round, and seeing him resting on the bar I kicked him viciously up the bottom and then thumped his ribs, grinding my knuckles in, but I hesitated to finish him off and he grabbed hold of my shirt and threw me to the floor.

We rolled around a few times, I thought I had the advantage but the momentum shifted once more and he pinned me down. That is when the barrage of punches came to my nose and mouth. I saw blood and then not very much.

When I came around, I was being dragged out of the establishment by security and was dumped hard on the cold concrete pavement. A few seconds later they threw my hat after me. When I gathered myself, I searched for Ayla, but realising she was still inside, I decided to go back to my smelly bed.

When I woke up, my sheets were covered in blood. Most of it mine. I tried meditating, but I was preoccupied as to why I was getting off to such a bad start with the authorities in the United States. The only conclusion that I could come too, was that they were idiots.

The Life of Luxury

What would I be like if I were rich? Would I like myself as a rich person? Would I still want more money? I hope I would be a good rich person. I like to believe there are quite a lot of them, but I don't really know.

It was an enchanting warm afternoon with a nice little breeze, flowers were beginning to bloom in gardens and parks and my face was beginning to heal. When I arrived at Madison Square Garden, I had to circle it a couple of times before I found Josh, who had sent an email with instructions on where I should meet him and his girlfriend to go for a family dinner. It was quite an honour to get such an invite. He didn't look as I remembered; the person I met in Rio de Janeiro was dressed scruffily in shorts and T-shirts but this man was in a designer suit. I was wearing my Tramp outfit instead of summer clothes too, so we took some time to acknowledge each other.

'Hey man, good to see you,' he said giving me a warm handshake and placing his hand upon my shoulder. 'You're looking tanned. I bet you have some stories to tell.' He had incredibly confident body language and I thought that I should like to begin greeting people in this manner. 'This is Rachael'.

'Hello Rachael, it's a pleasure to meet you. I've heard so much about you.' I said getting my revenge for the same comment he had made when he met Mariana.

'All good I hope,' she said smiling and looking at Josh. 'I've heard a lot about you too, I love your outfit. You really do look like Charlie Chaplin. My dad is going to love meeting you.'

'Always nice to meet a fan,' I said and Rachael laughed. She was dressed very nicely too in a white hooded jacket that covered up an elegant green dress. Rachael was very beautiful with straight brown hair and luscious lips, her eyes were a hypnotic green and her teeth were as white as snow. Josh was a lucky bastard.

'I hope you're happy to come for dinner,' said Rachael. 'Josh thinks you would prefer a bar, but we don't get a lot of time together because of work and we've been planning this visit to see my family for ages,' said Rachael at an extremely fast and nervous speed.

'No I'm honoured to be invited to a family dinner,' I said

'We will go to some bars another time,' said Josh smiling with a wink. He had told me in his email that this was an opportunity to get work, but I knew he didn't want to mention that now.

We took a taxi over the Brooklyn Bridge and I thought the journey would never end. I was transfixed by the sights and sounds we passed as I tried to join in the small talk. The view from the taxi became less and less crowded as we approached more suburban countryside and then a quiet expanse in which we entered the grounds of the mansion from a country road. The taxi drove over the gravel path and the tyres made wonderful crackly sounds as we slowly pulled up to the front door where I got my first sight of Rachael's mother sitting next to a Labrador and sipping a tall glass of gin and tonic. The night was drawing in and there was a smoky twilight feeling to the evening as she stood up to greet Josh and Rachael before shaking my hand, which I did warmly and with my rehearsed Chaplin smile. She was a slim woman with Greek-brown skin that was tightly stretched over her skull. She appeared to carry no body fat whatsoever and her perfectly groomed bun of hair sat atop of a prim and trim physique. Her eyes were warm but beady and she smiled as she called to her husband.

'Earl, come outside, Rachael and Josh have arrived and you are going to love their friend,' She shouted towards the house before even speaking to me. 'Sorry dear, my husband just adores Chaplin. I do hope I don't sound rude.'

I just smiled, all this talk of her husband was making me nervous as we began to make our way into the grand house.

We were led into the living room where a plump man with a white shirt and cravat stood by a roaring fireplace sipping whiskey and glancing into the distance. He was balding slightly but his hair was neatly trimmed and he was clean-shaven but for short sideburns. Before even greeting his daughter, he looked at me and his jovial eyes widened as he let out a roar of laugher, which he directed up to the ceiling.

'A day without laughter is a day wasted,' he said quoting Chaplin. 'What a pleasure to meet you, my boy. I hear you have come all the way from England,' he said walking over with a slow pace to take in the view of me before shaking my hand. I smiled and nodded, but I was not enjoying his reaction. I imagine it was a similar feeling I was having to how the Thailand prostitutes must feel when they parade for the amusement of old men, but perhaps less intense. Alcoholic beverages were brought for us and I had a Martini because I didn't know what else to say when they asked and James Bond suddenly popped into my head. I didn't like the drink very much – maybe it was stirred and not shaken.

'Tell me boy, have you worn these clothes especially for this evening or do you always dress like this?' asked Earl.

'Earl where are your manners, clearly he has dressed like this for the evening,' said Rachael's mother.

'Actually, I don't always dress like this, but I do a lot of the time. I feel most comfortable in these clothes.'

'Splendid. Do you do anything else like the great man or is it just your clothes?' he asked.

'I perform routines. I was just in Rio de Janeiro and I got a lot of good reaction to my comedy. Not so good here in New York yet. I lived homeless too with a dog like in a *Dogs Life*. That was in Rio too,' I said.

'What? You weren't homeless. That place in Santa Teresa wasn't that bad,' said Josh taking a break from whispering into Rachael's beautiful ear.

'It was after you left. I ran out of money.'

'Yet you chose to stay there and live like The Little Tramp rather than go home. Fascinating,' said Earl. It's nice when somebody gets you.

We sat down and had a most fabulous three-course dinner. For starters it was smoked salmon with a fresh tomato salad. I was utterly starving and perhaps not as polite in my manners as I should have been. I was very unsure of what cutlery to use, but I just watched what Josh was doing and imitated him as best I could while the family had a bit of a catch up. For the main course it was roast beef with potatoes, vegetables and gravy. This is my favourite dinner, but it wasn't as good as the ones my parents do. For dessert it was a Strawberry cheesecake. It was a wonderful meal, and after my initial pig out I tried to savour every taste. The extravagant dining left me feeling extremely bloated, so I began to slump at the table. Rachael's mother gave me a few disapproving looks, but she was lucky I didn't lay my head flat on the table for a snooze such was my lethargy. Eventually, I was invited into the study with Josh and Earl, who offered me an illegal Havana cigar from his secret stash. The end was sliced off for me, and Earl held a light to my face as I puffed away frantically trying to get the thing lit and accidentally inhaled the thick billowing smoke which made me cough and splutter uncontrollably. The two men began talking about work and the current stock situations, none of which I understood. On realising that I was being left out of the conversation, Earl turned and asked me of my plans in New York.

'I hope to find work and modest accommodation,' I said. 'I want to experience living here not just as a tourist, but as a member of society. From there I want to make a success of my self,' I said in my most serious voice as if I were at a job interview.

'What a great plan. Just like Charlie Chaplin, come to America to make your fortunes. I'm not from a rich background myself you know. I had to work and struggle,' he said with tremendous enthusiasm. 'I really understand what you mean and I would love to help you,' he continued with an inebriated look in his eye but a warm glow as if he were talking to a younger version of himself. 'Young man, you are coming to work for me.'

'I'll drink to that,' said Josh as were offered brandies and took a seat in some leather armchairs.

Earl went on to question me about the life and films of Chaplin. At first he wanted to see if my knowledge was as great as his, but when he realised I knew far more, he wanted to learn from me. We discussed his philosophies as Josh sat looking bored. Later in the evening Josh and I had a chance to catch up properly and I explained my life on the streets, which he quite rightly described as 'crazy'. He began to explain the day-to-day running of the stock trading company and the sort of work I would be required to do, but unfortunately I was feeling very tired and it went in one ear and out the other. I was sure I would pick it up in no time. I also got to know Rachael better, a charming girl who listened with care and affection to my hardships. I began to explain my love for Mariana and my friendship with Scraps, and what I had learnt on my travels. Rachael and Josh listened with great kindness and it was a far better therapy session than the ones I'd had with Dr Jove as an adolescent. We talked for so long that we didn't notice how late it grew, so I was invited to stay in a guest bedroom rather than travel all the way back to Manhattan and my smelly dormitory. I was shown the room that had a gigantic and luxurious double bed that bounced firmly when I sat on it. The covers were fresh and smelled lovely and there were flowers on the table beside it. I had my own en-suite bathroom with hot and cold running water emanating from a spacious bath and a powerful shower. The toilet was crisp white marble that had soft smooth toilet paper hanging by its side. When I was left in peace, I took a heavenly relaxing shit followed by a long deep bath before climbing into the crisp warm sheets and turning on my sixty-inch television to watch a late night chat show, before drifting off to sleep. In the morning, I was to buy myself some new clothes and I was to meet Josh on the Monday morning to start work.

'I could get used to this,' I thought to myself as I drifted off to sleep.

The Damsel

Those last days of freedom, knowing I had a job to go too, were tremendous. I finally had some purpose in my life and I brought the loveliest new brown suit ready to start work. I had been given an advance on my wages and had found a modest little basement flat for rent and had moved my belongings from the dirty hostel to my new home. It was unfurnished, but for a bed and a side table. It didn't matter, I didn't really need anything else. I did buy numerous cleaning products and a kettle, so I gave the place a real good dust up.

I spent the rest of my time wandering the vast city seeing tourist attractions, such as the Statue of Liberty, which I viewed from various locations, my favourite being Brooklyn Bridge which was a wonderful walk with great atmosphere. I really got a sense of being on an island and could see the glorious architecture and technology so clearly. I wish I had the kind of genius that could design a city like New York, let alone make it a reality. The city was forged out of the imaginations of dreamers and could never have existed if it weren't for unrealistic thought.

I went to Ground Zero, but there wasn't much there. 'Who could do something so horrible and violent as crash a plane into a building full of people,' I thought. 'Would I do something so atrocious if I thought it was for the good of humanity? Would I do something so awful if I thought I would be rewarded with Mariana in heaven? Probably.' I think I'm lucky to have my brain wired differently. It is the people who pedal the myths that deserve our condemnation, and maybe some of those conspiracy theories are correct. I don't know who to trust anymore. I don't know who is evil and who is good. It's a horrible time to be a human.

Walking around one day I saw a large woman lying on the floor underneath the wheels of a bus, it brought back terrible memories of Scraps and I ran up to help, it was a sickening sensation that came over me. As I got nearer, I ran into a huge crowd of people taking pictures on their phones and I shouted at them.

'What the hell is wrong with you, leave her in peace,' I said as I looked to see her being picked up by two strong men. Everyone thought I was shouting at these men and turned on me.'

'Who the hell are you,' said one man.

'What a jerk,' said a young girl.

I walked off in disgust, what was the world coming too.

I found a little time to return to Central Park and perform, I got a few laughs and it was rattling good fun, but my full attention was on getting a good start to my new career.

Ayla had asked to meet me for dinner in an all-night diner the evening before I began work. This invitation didn't come as a surprise to me as with my new job I was quite the catch for any woman. I decided this would be a good opportunity to try out my new suit. She was terribly impressed and my arrival was greeted by a friendly, lingering hug. The diner was brightly lit and waitresses scampered round the place with robotic politeness as I tried not to focus on the state of Ayla. She was wearing a black Guns N' Roses T-shirt and blue jeans, her skin was ghost white and she was gnawing on a toothpick. Her left eye was swollen shut and darkly bruised, her bottom lip was split in the middle. I did not need to ask why. The conversation grew slowly that evening, but at first there was the most terrible awkward silence, so I decided to be the chatty one and tell her about my evening with Josh and of my excitement about the new job.

'Did Josh mention me? I emailed him, but he never replied. I know he's your friend but I don't like him,' Ayla said sitting up straighter and grabbing another toothpick.

'I like him, but we don't have to like the same people. Of course, all of your friends are an utter delight,' I said emphasising the ALL.

'Sorry about that. Thanks for sticking up for me. That was really sweet. I hate Mikey now. He's not really my boyfriend. I just need him for stuff, especially now that I've lost my job.'

'You lost your job?'

'No-one wants to be served food by someone looking like this, do they? I don't know what I'm going to do. I can't afford to stay where I am. I got home yesterday and those bitches had thrown some of my stuff on the street. I feel really uncomfortable there. The only place left is Mikey's and I don't want to go there.'

'What about your family? Why don't you go back home?'

'I don't know, we had a pretty big argument,' Ayla said staring off into the distance and sighing as if she remembered something.

'You can always stay with me. My place is pretty small, but you're very welcome,' I said nervously fiddling with my tie.

'That's sweet, but I couldn't do that,' she said looking tenderly into my eyes with her one good retina.

'Why not?' I must remember to never ask questions like that.

'Because it wouldn't be fair on you, I'm in a pretty messed up place,' she said grinding her teeth and squeezing her fists together. 'Honestly, right now all I can think about is scoring some more meth. I wish I had more money. I don't know what I'm going to do. I need help. I should probably go back to rehab or something, but I don't have the money for that either. God, I'm so fucked up.'

'Does rehab work?' I asked taking a sip of my coffee.

'I don't know, I guess. At least it would keep me away from Mikey for a while. I need him to get my meth, but you never know what mood he'll be in. He gets aggressive a lot and it's really scary. Then, sometimes, he's so nice. I'm gonna have to call him.'

'There must be some other option,' I said in an attempt to get her to reach her own conclusion.

'I don't know how I got like this. You hear about people dying or going to prison from this shit. I never understood how you could get like that, but fuck I need some fucking glass.'

'I could buy you some from someone else.'

'Seriously? No I can't ask you to do that,' Ayla said with a hint of a smile on her face that she tried to hide.

'I could pay for your rehab. I'm making loads of money now,' I said in a proud voice feeling like the man in the top hat on the monopoly board.

'You're too nice to me. I can't let you do any of those things. Thank you, but I need to sort it out for myself.'

We ordered our meals and eat. I was starving, but Ayla only picked at her food. We shared the bill and I walked her home. On the way we passed my new place and I showed it to her.

'This is so cool,' she said. 'You're so lucky living here and having this great job. I wish I was a normal person with a job and a place to stay.'

'You are a normal person.'

'You think? I don't feel like it. People don't treat me like I'm normal.'

'You are very special, so even better than normal,' I said before we left.

When we got to her place she was lovely and charming, not what I thought people on drugs were like. She was innocent and human.

'Thanks for talking with me. You really stay in my head. I'm really glad I met you,' she said.

'I'm glad I met you too,' I said as I headed off for a good nights sleep, wondering if Ayla was also going to bed as she said or if she would go out looking for drugs.

I glanced at my luminous watch to see that it was 3:30am when I heard the crying and shouting coming from outside. There was a dim glow as the moonlight crept into the room through the pavement level window. The screams of a young woman were mixed with the angry shouts of my neighbours telling her to shut up. An argument was ensuing and the girl's tears were giving way to furious swearing. 'Please don't be Ayla, please don't be Ayla,' I thought pulling my jacket on over my white T-shirt and pulling my socks up to my knobbly knees. As I stepped out of my door the draft went up my baggy boxer shorts and I hesitantly made my way to the buildings front door.

Quickening my pace as the shouts and threats became more violent. I opened the door and stepped out into the cold night air to find Ayla spewing rhetoric at several windows with angry heads leaning out of them.

'Come in Ayla, it's OK,' I said taking her arm.

'Get off me, your neighbours are assholes,' she said recoiling her arm ready to shout some more threatening abuse.

'I haven't had the pleasure of meeting them before. Come inside, I'll make you a drink.'

'You're lucky I don't come up there,' she shouted upwards before following me inside. 'Why do people gotta be such dicks?'

'They think other people are dicks so they are dicks to them. It's a vicious circle,' I said turning on the light to discover that Ayla's face was swollen again and that her clothes were ripped. As I made her a hot drink, I noticed bloody scratches on her arms. She continued to complain about my neighbours and I thought it best not to interrupt her. It's always best to get the upset out of your system.

I'm sorry, you were sleeping, I shouldn't be here,' she said finally, it's amazing how holding on to a hot drink can calm a person.

'That's OK, it's always lovely when we catch up,' I said having a sip from my drink and giving her a genuine smile. 'What happened?'

'Nothing much, just a quiet night in,' she said, her face tightening up as tears began to emerge in the corner of her eyes. Her breathing became shorter and sharper as she began to sob uncontrollably, so I put down my drink and put my arm around her. She moved her head and body into me and cried, so I put my other arm around her too and held her forever. I tried to offer comforting words such as 'it'll be OK', but they were unconvincing. My heart was breaking as I held Ayla. I realized I loved her and seeing her like this was traumatic. Yet there was a tender beauty to the moment that I never wanted to end. It was a cosy misery, I was comforting Ayla but, after my own tribulations, she was also comforting me. It was a beautiful moment.

The sweetness of the cuddle came to an abrupt halt when Ayla lifted her head and kissed me on the lips. She put her icy cold hands on my face and one of her tears dribbled onto my cheek. I didn't pull away until this tender soft kiss became frantic and passionate. In her drug-addled mind, even I was attractive.

'Ayla, we should stop I don't want to be enjoying this,' I said.

'I'm sorry,' she said beginning to cry heavily again.

'You don't have to be sorry. Let me pay for you to have a go at rehab. It'll keep you out of trouble for a bit like you said, and when you get out I'll be waiting for you.'

'But I'm scared,' she said in a nasal weep.

I held her for a little while longer.

'Can you take me to rehab?' Ayla asked a few minutes later as if it hadn't been mentioned previously.

It was surprisingly easy to find the address of a rehabilitation and treatment centre in the area, and we took a taxi there after a little more comforting. I paid and filled out the necessary paperwork posing as Ayla's partner and naming myself as next of kin.

'I'm scared,' Ayla said as she was led away. She had a pleading look of sadness as she departed.

'So am I,' I said.

The Gold Rush

I was at work an hour early for my first day as a businessman having hardly slept. I arrived to find the building closed so I ended up walking round and round the block. I did this so many times that when the doors finally opened I felt tired and dishevelled. I had wrapped a cheese and corned beef sandwich for myself that morning and had to fight my greedy stomach that wanted it as breakfast. I knew I had a long day ahead of me and would need it come lunchtime.

My supervisor was a grumpy, chain-smoking little man with a rough, heavy Bronx accent. He talked fast and without apology and sounded like a real tough guy. I tried to listen carefully for fear of upsetting him. From what I gathered from his explanation, I was there to write numbers on a board. The brokers, on their computers and phones, would call out information about the day's trading, which I was to log on a clearly visible board in the centre of this massive office. It all started out quite pleasantly and my confidence grew. I thought I might be good at this job. I began picturing myself quickly working my way up the ladder, making more and more money until I could invest in stocks too. My stock would rise and I would get fast cars and a penthouse flat. It was so exciting. I also thought longingly of my cheese and corned beef sandwich.

As the morning progressed, people began to shout out more and more numbers and information. Soon I was no longer able to daydream and really had to focus. They began to use acronyms that I didn't understand. It was OK if I could stay on top of it, but on numerous occasions I was trying to remember several numbers at once and my boss would start shouting at me for not getting them written up. I became really confused and people would frequently have to get up and add their information personally. They would do this with a resentful scowl. Once I fell behind it became trickier and trickier. My boss would sometimes come over and help, but he didn't look happy about it. He would help me catch up and I would have a few stress free minutes until I fell behind again.

Despite this, I just about made it to break-time and was looking forward to some food and quiet time. I was just about to unwrap my sandwich when Josh arrived in the office with his buddies; they were all going for a liquid lunch.

'You have to come with us. They do food there,' Josh insisted.

The pub was dark and bawdy, full of office workers. I grabbed a menu and perused the available food, desperate to eat. We sat at a large oval table and a waitress came over. Josh ordered beer for everyone. She put her notepad back in her pocket and I meekly tried to get her attention and order food, but she didn't notice my bird mouth, and when she returned it was with beer only.

'Let's get these down in one go so we can order more,' said Josh to everyone's agreement but mine.

'This time can we get two each? So sixteen beers please,' said one of Josh's pals.

'Sure thing honey,' said the waitress. I really was starving and I didn't want to drink, but I also didn't want to be the odd one out on my first day. As I was finishing my third beer, I made my excuse that I wanted to go to the toilet and I stopped off to order a beef stew and a side of onion rings from the bar. When I returned to the table, I saw two more beers that I was supposed to drink. The other guys seemed to only have one left and I had more than two. I wondered if this was a prank on the new guy. This suspicion was confirmed when I visited the bathrooms for a second time and found another two beers waiting for me, but still no food.

'You got to drink up, it's coming from company money,' said Josh's most irritating friend with his black suit, blond hair and arrogant smile.

As I polished off the seventh drink, my head began to spin and I prayed for my stew. One of the men paid for the whole bill plus tip and announced we had to get back to work. I looked pleadingly towards the kitchens and begrudgingly got to my feet. When we got outside, I glanced through the window to see a different waitress standing around our table looking confused and holding a huge plate of delicious food – it was my order and I wanted to cry.

This was my hazing. Back at work, I felt the taste of vomit in my throat as we staggered to the elevator and I squeezed in with all the other guys who seemed to have regained their composure as I slumped into the corner. Upstairs everyone resumed their positions as I searched for my sandwich, which was no longer in the desk drawer where I left it.

'227.4 up from 226.8,' called some rotten bastard, 'get back to work.' The numbers began to be called out again by what seemed like more people. After an hour of desperate confused hell and misery, people began shouting louder and louder. I wanted to just walk out. I was so confused and couldn't focus. My attention flitted from one thing to another, my body was no longer responding to my brain's instructions. I had to stay, I had to help Ayla and I had to be a success. People were getting mad at me as I was slowing everything down and my writing had become dreadful, the board was now a mess. At some point in that nightmarish, confused and drunken afternoon, I collapsed to the floor and had an epileptic fit. When I awoke I was on a red scratchy couch staring up at a dirty ceiling. I rested there until Rachael's dad came to visit. The jovial look in his eyes from the other night had gone and he now looked scornful as he ran his fingers through his hair and called out to Josh to come and help his goddam friend.

'Shit man what happened?' Josh asked.

'I just had a fit. I'll be fine in a minute. I'll go back to work. What day is it?' I said with my mind jumping around from one idea to the next as I glanced out at the manic workroom behind a glass wall.

'It's Monday,' Josh said after clearing his throat and looking around to see who was in earshot.

'Monday. What month?'

'April dude,' said Josh sitting down beside me and laughing a little at the question.

'Where are we?' I asked trying to expose my eyes to more light by opening them wider. I sat up a little but Josh said I must stay still.

'We're at work. It's a stock trading company. This is your first day. We shouldn't have taken you out drinking.'

'But what country are we in?' I said breathing with fast desperation and making a groggy, desperate noise.

'Are you serious? We're in America. Shall we call you an ambulance?' said Josh beginning to look more concerned.

'No, don't please. I don't want to go to hospital,' I said remembering that this sort of thing had happened before. 'I'll get back to work in a few minutes,' I said trying to stand up. Josh grabbed my shoulders to prevent this and said to stay where I was.

'What day is it?' I asked.

'It's Monday. April dude. Look, do you want to go home? I can call you a taxi.'

'That might be a good idea. Then I can recover and come back to work even harder tomorrow,' I said trying to sound like I could still be a good employee. 'I think I just need to sleep it off.'

'OK just stay there a little longer and I'll go and call you one. Don't worry I'll come with you to make sure you're OK.'

While Josh went off to make the phone call and speak to Earl, I just lay there as people walked back and forth trying not to stare at me. There are few more humiliating things in life than lying down in a comfortable and vulnerable position while people go about their daily duties. You feel as if you're telling them how stupid their daily duties are and, at the same time, that you're private life is being violated. The world of the sick person is undignified, but enlightening.

Josh took me home in the cab and got me inside commenting on what a nice place I'd found.

'I'll call you tonight my friend. Get some sleep,' he said.

When I awoke, Josh was calling.

'There's no easy way to tell you this buddy, but Earl said he doesn't want you coming back. He said what happened was bad for moral and bad for business. He thinks you're a drunk. I'm sorry man.'

'I didn't even want a drink. I don't understand,' I said with my foggy, disoriented mind.

'Look I've spoken to him and he's going to pay you for another month, but he doesn't want you coming to the office again.'

'I thought Earl liked me.'

'He probably did, he's crazy. I have to be nice to him at work and because of Rachael, but he's a son of a bitch. I don't trust him at all. Don't worry about it man. He's an asshole. You're a better man than him,' Josh said.

'OK, well thanks for letting me know.'

'No problem, look I feel bad about all this. Let me know when you're feeling better. We'll catch up properly away from these people. I'm really sorry.'

I stayed in bed for another day feeling groggy and confused. After a seizure it feels as if your brain has been drained of all of its positive energy leaving a contemplative, cotton-wool misery. Hope, joy and ambition goes and reality is all you have left. There is no pleasure for at least five days after a seizure – which is about how long it takes for the swelling of your tongue to go down too.

When I pulled myself together, I began looking for work. I was going to need more money to pay for Ayla's treatment and my other bills. I brought a newspaper and I scoured for jobs. I sent out numerous application forms and updated my old CV in an internet café, but I only had one positive response, it was for a job working as a street cleaner. I had no time to hesitate, so went straight down to the address given and filled out a few forms. I was given the job on the spot.

If it weren't for the low wages this would have been an ideal job. I was very proud to be helping the environment, and I could go to work in my bowler hat and perform for people at the same time as picking up rubbish. It was rattling good fun and would keep me busy from 6am until lunchtime. In the afternoons I would continue looking for something with better pay or I would go to Central Park to perform as Chaplin. Once a week, I would go down to the rehabilitation clinic and pay for Ayla's treatment, but I would never see her. I would always just be given a message from the staff saying 'Ayla is so grateful, but she doesn't want to see you until she feels better and is ready to leave.' I thought this perfectly understandable.

As the weeks went on, money became tighter as my primary funds ran out. I had received no good news from my job applications, so eventually took a second job in the kitchen of a fast food restaurant. I hated the heat and the smell of meat and fat. The employees at the front of the restaurant were like robots with their fake smiles and calling people sir. I was safely tucked away at the back with the other vagabonds where we couldn't be seen by customers and ruin their greedy appetites. I would end each shift feeling greasy and with several burns on my hands and arms. I was an integral cog in the deluxe, double-burger production line. There were three of us for this mighty operation, a young Chinese fellow with a love for computer games, an older Mexican man who talked of his daughter's suicide and broke down crying once a day, and me. We had the overwhelming responsibility of buns, meat and toppings respectively. We would swap around our jobs to stop ourselves going mad, much to the disapproval of the manager Ken. He thought we would be more productive if we each knew our job, but that wasn't acceptable to three go-getters like us. We all wanted to be on toppings all the time as it minimised the risk of burns and was less disgusting. The only risk from the toppings was the repetitive nature of the lettuce, tomato, cheese, sauce and pickle routine. You would go home, but in your mind you would still be shooting the special sauce gun and searching for pickles at the bottom of the barrel. Also, if the ingredients ran out you would have to run off to get more before the buns caught up to you. It was just as stressful as the stock trading company, but for a tenth of the money.

   With the money from Bruce and my pay off from Earl drying up, my wages were not adding up to the bills I had acquired. I'd already received written warnings about my rent, and with five weeks left of Ayla's rehabilitation programme, I had to make a decision to either stop paying for her bills or stop paying for my own. I stayed in my flat without paying for as long as possible, until the owner came around with the police and issued me with eviction.

   'You have not paid to be here Sir, so you have no legal rights. This man is threatening legal action if you do not vacate the premises immediately. He has sent you the final bill and it must be paid in full by the end of the month or the interest will double and you will be taken to court,' said a tall, brunette police officer with a thick Queens' accent. Her body language and tone of voice was polite but menacing, and I felt as if I was being bullied so I packed my things and left. Once again I took to the streets and resumed my life of fear.

The pavements were cold in New York and the evenings bitter and terrifying. I did not have time to wander the streets looking for a great location as I did in Rio. My job at the fast food restaurant became a Godsend as I was given free meals and there was a staff shower room. I also collected cardboard boxes from the disposal room and I took these to Central Park where I made a nest under one of the quieter, more secluded tunnels. In the morning, I would wake up freezing and start picking rubbish. I would try to move energetically to keep my body warm, but my diet was terribly unhealthy and I began to notice this in the way I was feeling. I was taking three toilets a day because the food, with no nutritional value, was going straight through me. I felt heavy and lethargic. When I mustered the courage to perform, people would look appalled by my antics instead of delighted so I stopped doing them and became quiet and reclusive once more. I grew melancholic and fragile, but my resolute determination to help Ayla was as strong as ever. Occasionally, I would come across a fellow gentleman tramp with the same bright idea as me trying to sleep under my bridge. I would start off being polite, but I didn't feel comfortable with them around so I would move on to a different part of the park. Little bridges were the best though. They felt like a little house and I daydreamed about Ayla being there as my wife. I knew we were just friends, but my feelings had grown stronger for her with everyday she was gone. Having failed with everything else, she was now my purpose and dream. She was my romance and adventure. Yet I knew that when Ayla returned to society she would be free from her addictions, and would be the wonderful spirit I met in Brazil that every man would want in his life. I couldn't face seeing her as I was. She had gone in for treatment under the impression that I was a rich man travelling to work everyday in a nice suit and being handsomely paid while living in a nice little flat. The reality was not what she would be expecting.

With one week until she was to get out, I lost my job at the fast food restaurant. They had given me several warnings about my cleanliness and I had tried to wash regularly. A gentleman does his best to be well turned out and hygienic, but it was too challenging, even for me. I used the last of my money to pay for her last week of treatment and set my mind to figuring out how to get home. For so long I thought I had been doing something noble and romantic, but on those cold bitter streets I knew it was all for nothing. Although still hopeful that romance and adventure would find me some day, in America I had failed again.

Romance and Adventure

Huddled up in my tramp clothes pretending to read a discarded newspaper on a bench in Central Park, I dreamed of food. My hair had grown long and unkempt and I was unshaven with dirt under my fingernails. A cold, gentle breeze slapped my face with cruelty and the silence in my mind was deafening. My emotions were void until an irritating sharp pain stole my attention. I had been whacked on the back of a head by something small. I looked around to see people going for walks and two boys playing with a baseball and catchers mitts, but I could not figure out where this projectile had come from, nor could I see anyone who might have thrown it. There was nobody suspicious or vicious looking and it couldn't have fallen from above, so I thought that perhaps I had imagined it. Then I was struck by another object and this time I saw the stone bounce onto the floor. I turned round in a flash and made eye contact with one of the boys, who smiled sweetly at me. He was about ten and he was wearing a baseball cap pulled high on his head to show his whole face, he looked like a friendly lad and his scruffy clothes suggested a day of rattling good fun. His friend was older, early teens I suspect, and he had a sterner expression as if he had learnt more of life's cruel lessons. His hair was darker and longer than his young pal and he was chewing gum as he called for the baseball to be thrown. I pointed at them threateningly before turning around.

I tried to return to my lonesome meditations and daydreams until a larger stone clattered the side of my head. It sent a shiver down my spine.

'Get lost, you little bastards,' I shouted as I turned round faster to catch these lads trying to look innocent once more, but in no doubt this time that they were my attackers.

They looked at each other and shrugged their shoulders. I felt my head and there was a small trickle of blood coming from it. I stood up and began to walk off in the opposite direction from the hormone-fuelled ragamuffins. As I did this, I was hit square on the top of the spine by the boy's baseball.

I turned around to see them laughing cruelly and the red mist descended on my mind. I picked up the ball and began to run after them with the intention of beating them to death with my bare hands. These little shits had made an unwise choice in their attempts to mark this as their territory. I was a lunatic and prepared to hurt them. I threw the baseball at the bigger one, but it missed his head by a half metre and so I gave chase furiously as they ran with desperate, fear-driven adrenaline. Eventually, I calmed as I ran past a family, weak and malnourished I put my hands to my knees panting deeply. I looked up to see that this family of a mum, a dad and three teenage kids was laughing at me; a tramp chasing two young boys who had got the best of him. I looked at the family and raised my hat in apology before walking off with sadness and shame in my heart.

There was nothing for me to do but walk in circles for the rest of the day. I did not trust in humanity to allow me to be still without attacking my vulnerability. I was wounded, and nature is remorseless to the weak. The people I walked past were mostly smiling, jovial and content, so it caught my eye when I saw a sad face staring down at the paved floor and it forced me to do a double take.
'Ayla?'
'Yes, do I know you?' she replied not recognising the filthy man who stood before her as being me. I was no longer the well dressed, up and coming stock broker that had helped her. As she looked up she began to focus on me and her eyes widened and her hand went to her heart, 'You?'
'Yes it's me,' I replied as the biggest grin I have ever experienced slowly spread across my face. I tried to hide my shameful happiness by biting on my thumb and covering my face, but I could not take my eyes away from her beautiful face.
'Did you get sober?'
Ayla stared deep into my eyes, it was as if we were hypnotised by each other.
'Yes I'm sober now,' she said as she moved closer and hugged me. 'I'm sober now,' she repeated as we stood holding each other in the park for the happiest moment of my life.

'Where are you staying?' I asked Ayla after she got me to confess my own story in a coffee shop outside the park.

'One of the women from the clinic is helping me out for a while. She lets me sleep on her sofa. If you want to shower we can go back there. You must feel awful,' Ayla said as I remembered how Sophie had never allowed me anywhere near her until I'd showered back home in England. That Ayla had hugged me on the dirtiest day of my life made me fall deeply in love. On the way back to her sofa, I showed her where I'd been sleeping.

'That's so cool, I want to stay with you,' said Ayla. 'Who needs a stupid house anyway,' she said, her voice echoing in the tunnel under the bridge.

'You can't stay with me, it's horrible. I'm saving up to go back to my family now. You should do the same,' I said forcefully. I hated the idea of Ayla living this awful life I had experienced. She was a princess not a tramp.

'Well can I stay with you tonight at least?' she asked giving me another cuddle despite my filthiness.

'Maybe, but not here I have a better idea,' I said before we headed to her temporary home where I took a long and much needed shower before changing into some of my less disgusting clothes.

Two hours before closing time, I was happy to pay the money for us to go into The Natural History Museum where we headed straight for the dinosaur exhibits. There we stood under the giant Tyrannosaurus Rex fossil feeling small, insignificant and temporary. This is the way I believe we are supposed to feel; with this feeling you can enjoy every second in the warmth of fleeting companionship. The menacing teeth and gaping eye sockets of the Rex were profoundly beautiful and the Sauropods were even more wonderful with their exquisite, gigantic lumbering ways. I imagined the stillness of their minds and the routine of their existences; their battle for survival would have been quite beautiful if only they had the intelligence to appreciate it.

'If you could be any dinosaur what would it be?' I asked as we continued our way around the labyrinth of extinction.

'I don't know. I don't really want to be a dinosaur,' said Ayla scratching her head. 'I think I would prefer to be a sabre-toothed tiger or a monkey. Let's go and look at the monkey exhibit.'

We gazed upon the different primates and wandered around reading the information, holding hands.
'How do you think humans will evolve in the future?' asked Ayla staring at the human face of a chimpanzee.
'I don't know, just more technology until we destroy ourselves maybe. But I don't think that will happen actually. I hope we evolve kindness and understanding,' I said, 'where we can stand to be with our own minds without going crazy.'
'You mean going crazy like taking drugs?'
'Maybe, or like going crazy and shutting yourself off from everyone,' I said, 'or living for money, or getting lost in a fantasy or the internet or television. There are so many ways to go crazy, it's scary. We just need to be nice to each other and nature, I think.'

It was on the way out of the monkey exhibit that we found the Inuit exhibit with its mysterious turns and alcoves. Next to a glass-case enclosure of a small family gathered around an open fire in the snow was a wooden door with a key in it. We turned the key and took it out before opening the door and going inside – it was a cleaning cupboard full of mops and signs and tools. When we closed the door we were left in pitch-black darkness. We locked the door from the inside, and after an hour of giggling and shooshing we were alone in the museum. When we emerged from our cupboard we were children lost in a beautiful world, we ran around with the history of the world to ourselves; that is until the night watchmen found us and led us to the exit threatening to call the police until we ran off into the dark night.

Life was too short to care about money. I gathered what I had saved for my flight home and booked us a hotel. We entered into our little world of luxury. Taking turns to have deep relaxing baths before getting into the hotel's wool dressing gowns, we were a world away from the streets or the treatment centres that had filled our reality for so long. I savoured every moment of getting clean again. I brushed my teeth, clipped my nails, shaved and scrubbed until I felt reborn of my hardship. I emerged from the bathroom and took my place on the bed next to Ayla. Romance soon occurred; it started with a deep, soul-enriching kiss. I closed my eyes and ran my hands up and down her back enjoying the feel of her body beneath the soft material. Her tongue entered my mouth and tasted sweet and delicious. I kissed her neck and her soft face brushed against mine as I moved my hands down to her lovely smooth legs and felt the warmth of her skin. We untied our gowns and our bodies pressed together as I tasted her divine lips again before exploring her body with my mouth. With every kiss she became warmer and more delicious. Before I knew it, her legs were wrapped around me as our bodies embraced; we were entwined in peaceful bliss as if we were a single organism, an evolution of the soul reaching out kindness and understanding to the universe. Her breasts smooshed up against me as we began to make love, we worked our passions up into a wild frenzy before simultaneously reaching ecstasy and collapsing into a blissful sleep. Many people go their entire lives without experiencing real love, but Ayla and me, we got to experience it for a whole day.

In the morning, Ayla insisted on coming with me to work. We were smiling and laughing as I went about collecting garbage from Central Park. She was helping and having a go on the litter picker.

A young man in a suit walked past talking on his cell phone as I put an armful of litter into the rubbish bin. There was nothing distinguishable about him at first glance; he was normal height, normal build, normal accent, normal hair and normal suit. Yet he was talking with unnecessary volume and walked passed as if in a world of his own, ignoring nature and his fellow human beings as he talked to a far away voice. What really distinguished him to me was that as he walked by me he dropped a soda can by my feet.

'You've dropped your can,' I said to him shocked that he would do something so openly disrespectful.

'Hold on a second,' he said to his friend on the phone before turning to me and saying, 'Get it for me, would you buddy?'

I just stared at him. He was also smoking and obviously found my look of shock annoying, as he threw his cigarette butt on the floor too.

'You dropped it, you pick it up,' I said. He stopped walking and turned to confront me. He abruptly ended his telephone conversation saying he would call them back.

'My taxes pay for you to pick shit up, so pick it up. I'm not here to say please and thank you. Who the hell are you to be giving me orders? You're the street cleaner, so you clean the streets. Do you know who I am?' he said as if he actually wanted me to answer his rhetoric.

'I know who you are. You're a machine man with a machine mind and a machine heart. You're a man who thinks too much and feels too little. You're the passing of greed and bitterness. You are an unnatural man,' I said quoting Chaplin before clenching my fist, walking up to this machine man and punching him as hard as I could. He fell over on his backside, holding his chin with his eyes wide open and mouth slightly ajar. I looked at Ayla and she was in a state of shock too, but I'd had enough.

'What the hell do you think you're doing?' shouted a monkey man in a white T-shirt tucked into blue jeans who swaggered over to me like a deranged chimpanzee swinging and thrusting his limbs from the other side of the paved running lane. His hair was dyed black and he chose to hide behind sunglasses. His muscular frame suggested hours wasted in the gym and his skin colour suggested a tanning salon.

When he got close enough to me I punched him just as hard as Machine Man. He did not fall over, but I was pleased to see I'd broken his sunglasses – which he inspected before discarding them. He gathered himself and retaliated with a mighty thump – this was a much better punch than I had ever received before. It took a few moments for my brain to register that I'd been hit really hard, before it sent the message down to my legs which turned to jelly and I lost my balance and equilibrium, falling back on to my own arse and rolling with my legs going over my befuddled head.

'O my God! Are you all right?' Ayla asked kneeling down beside me. I didn't want to answer as the red mist was back.

'I'm sorry, but that's what you get boy,' said Monkey Man.

This wasn't the first time I'd been knocked to the floor and Monkey Man's punch was nothing compared to my seizures. I got back up and took a massive swing at him that connected around his temple. He recoiled in a moment's shock and pain before launching forwards and striking a kick into my thigh and placing his knee fiercely into my abdomen before lashing down blows to my back and neck. I was beaten down to my knees, so I jabbed at his balls repeatedly. This got him really mad and he screamed and dived at me knocking me into the ground with his shoulder before wrapping his arm around my neck.

It took a few moments to realise he was choking me and I was in trouble. I couldn't breathe, I tried too, I really did, but I couldn't. My face started to get red hot and my brain hurt just as Machine Man started to kick me in the guts. It was so difficult to catch a breath that I thought I was going to die. As Machine Man bent over to shout abuse in my face, I saw Ayla run up behind him and kick him hard in the ass before jumping on his back and scratching at his face.

I was mightily relieved when I finally got a breath and I rolled over on to my stomach to rest and take some long swigs of oxygen. I felt Ayla's soothing hand on my back and I realised more people were now on the scene. She had been pulled away from me and a police officer was yanking my arms behind my back and putting me in handcuffs and reading me my rights.

'I forgive you,' I said to the police officer and everyone listening. 'I forgive you.' I had not meant to say this, but I did.

'You dirty son of a bitch,' I heard Monkey Man shout. 'Lock him up, he doesn't even sound like an American.'

'Lock up that crazy bitch too,' said Machine Man.

When they dragged me to my feet I noticed that quite a crowd had formed – actually the audience was even bigger than some of my best performances at Central Park. I was put into a police car and the door was slammed, the other door opened and Ayla was shoved in next to me.

'Fancy seeing you here,' I said. As we drove off I saw another police car arrive and I assumed it was for Monkey Man and Machine Man, they were in the middle of a crowd of spectators and police. As we drove away, I looked out at a more tranquil part of Central Park and wished I could stop getting in trouble.

We were taken to the cells where we stayed for a couple of hours before being given an almighty telling off and getting the news that Machine Man wanted to press charges. Why were the police taking the other people's side? I was provoked and Ayla was defending me. They interviewed us separately and took our statements. I told the truth and nearly broke down in tears when confessing that I was living on the streets and that I wanted to go home. With my one phone call, I spoke to my parents in England, who agreed to put some money in my bank account so that I could return. They said other things too, that I shan't repeat. The police spoke to Machine Man and Monkey Man explaining mine and Ayla's situation and they struck a deal. The police told me we would be a free if I would simply apologize to the gentlemen in the fight. I swallowed my pride and met them outside, escorted by the police. Ayla was waiting there too with a female guard.

'I'm sorry for my attack,' I said.

'I'm sorry too,' said Ayla.

'You bet your ass you're sorry. Nobody hits me,' said Machine Man with scratches and a bruise on his face as he pointed and darted a vicious look between Ayla and me.

'You can't just go around hitting people here in America,' said Monkey Man trying to look wise and in control.

'I know. I was overcome by rage as I tried to keep this city clean. It's not an excuse for violence. I'll never be fighting ever again for the rest of my life.'

'Because you'll get your ass kicked again,' said Machine Man.

'Shut your mouth,' said Ayla.

'It's OK,' I said

'Hey come on now,' said Monkey Man. 'They said they're sorry and look the guy was trying to do his job and you threw your crap everywhere. He was wrong to hit you and that's why I stepped in, but you kind of asked for it,' said Monkey Man.

'Hey fuck you, I helped you when this guy had you pinned down,' said Machine Man turning to Monkey Man and invading his personal space.

'Pinned down? I was choking him to stop him handing you your ass son, and you jumped in for a cheap shot until the girl started kicking your butt,' said Monkey Man.

'Anytime you want to go, then you just say the word. I was trying to help you, but if you disrespect me you'll be in a world of trouble just like these two,' said Machine Man taking a step back and moving a little closer to the police officers.

'This is a police station and there will be no fighting Sir. You need to calm down right now,' said the lead police officer. 'We don't want to have to put you in a cell.'

'Gentlemen, lets not give in to hate,' I said getting ready to speak some more of Chaplin's great words. 'We don't want to hate and despise one another, only the unloved and unnatural hate. We have the love of humanity in our hearts. In this world there is room for everyone and the good earth is rich and can provide for everyone. The way of life can be free and beautiful if we can unite to free the world of hate and intolerance, if we can fight only to stop indecency. In the name of happiness, let us shake hands in peace. Gentlemen unite for we hate for no one,' I said offering my hand for all to shake.

'Great speech son,' said Monkey Man shaking my hand.

'That was awesome,' said Ayla.

'Well said,' added the policeman as I shook his hand too.

'You're crazy,' said Machine Man.

Within half an hour I was released and back on the streets. I went to book the next available flight home before going to the bus station with Ayla. She had decided she should go home too.

'Can I visit you in England sometime?' she asked giving me a farewell hug.

'I insist you do,' I replied kissing her on the cheek. 'I hope to visit you again some day.'

I felt sadness when Ayla had gone, but I knew she was headed for a better and happier life, so I smiled. I had travelled so far, but it was time to go home. It was time to forgive myself and forgive everyone.

'I am The Gentleman Tramp and it is time to share my love with everyone,' I thought as we flew above the clouds of the Atlantic Ocean. 'I want to make this world a better place.'

Home Sweet Home

When I arrived home I felt a sense of unimaginable warmth emanating from my family. I am, and always have been, a truly blessed individual. I spent the first few nights sitting in the living room with my parents soaking in what it meant to be back. I was so lucky to have this home. I saw so many that didn't know of this luxurious state. So many that did not have a sense of being cared about.

As the days passed, this warm glow began to dim and be replaced by brute ambition and I received emails that made me wish I was still out in the big beautiful world.

Hey brother how's it going?
Dad emailed saying you were on your way home. Did you get back safely? Enjoy it and don't worry about anything. This is a fresh start and you can do whatever you want and be anyone you want (even Charlie Chaplin if you must). Also don't stress about the money I loaned you; I know you're good for it. Colombia is fantastic. I spent two weeks living with a tribe on one of my tours. They took me hunting in the Amazon rainforest and I was part of a Shamanic ritual, fantastic! I'm back in the city now to meet another group for an expedition, but after that I'm going back to the tribe by myself. I want to really live as they do and try to understand their culture. I want to see how their lives are impacted by the modern world and become one of them, for a while anyway. If you ever want to join me let me know.
Bruce

I replied
Hi Bruce,
       Fantastic! What could be better? I bet the tribe will love you and good luck on your next expedition. I would love to visit you somewhere again, yes. But it may be a while, as I want to make a little money. It is great back at home. New York is incredible and it was an interesting trip. But Colombia sounds

better. *I will be in touch very soon to tell you of my plans and I will make the money for you in no time.*

Speak soon

The other email was from Mariana, it read.

Hello,

So where in the world are you now? I cannot keep up with your adventures. I am sorry I did not make more time to see you in Rio. I was kind of depressed a little. I start to fight with my boyfriend a lot. Love is full of such happiness and such sadness. But I think it's worth it, so it's OK. I like my job too, but I really just want to travel like you. What a dream this is. I would love to know how you are. I hope you are feeling well.

Mariana xx

I replied

Hello Mariana,

My adventures have come to an end and I am at home in England to make some more money. I still would love to travel, but I just really want to give people a smile. This is my ambition. Too bad about the fighting, but if it is worth it as you say then that is good. Sorry, I'm afraid I don't know about these things. You deserve to be happy and you can do anything you wish. If you want to travel, then you can travel. I'm so glad I came to Brazil and that now we can stay friends forever. You're very important to me. I avoided you because I was jealous, but I feel I have outgrown these awful emotions and I love you very much and you are in my heart since we met in the café. Keep in touch with these emails for I most definitely will.

I have continued to email Mariana and we have chatted back and forth ever since. I have my best friend back. But Bruce, I guess is in the jungle away from the madness of the internet.

Within days of arriving home the clouds descended over England and the heavens opened. As I write this I can barely remember a day in which it has not rained, but London is still beautiful, a multicultural festival of diversity. I love it here.

A week after my homecoming, while staring out of the window of my childhood bedroom, I crashed to the floor and began convulsing wildly (again). I didn't tell anybody about it because I want to forget this part of me, and discussing it makes it real. The discomfort is only temporary, but the humiliation is permanent, so it's best I keep it to myself. The days that followed the fit were an atrocity of groggy, confusion and darkness that I had to fight with enthusiastic meditation.

I searched for a job relentlessly with few promising leads. I thought a lot about the teaching I'd done in Brazil and wanted to meet and help more people, so took a temporary position as a hospital porter until I could find something to fulfil my great ambition. The hospital management were very keen for me to join the team and it wasn't until my first day that I realised why. It was because my colleagues were a collection of maladjusted and melodramatic manic-depressives. On my first day, I took a cancer patient down for an X-ray, tried to resolve a quarrel between two drunkards in accident and emergency, cleared out countless bins full of medical waste and transferred two corpses down to the mortuary. By the time I got home late in the evening, I felt none too chipper.

I spent that first week in a state of regretful denial. Despite all my tribulations, my view of myself had always been that of The Gentleman Tramp and an entertainer. I could not mesh this vision of myself with the depressing surroundings of the hospital, the inactivity of the workload or the uniform I was forced to wear, so I ignored what I was doing and daydreamed through the experiences. However, while taking an old man for an operation I noticed him making jokes and I realised this was the perfect environment for The Gentleman Tramp. 'Life is a tragedy when seen in close-up, but a comedy in long-shot' said Chaplin. I began to perform.

After another week, I was told by the head porter to stop acting like a clown around the hospital, but I ignored him; I knew I was a hit with the patients. The five minutes it took to transport a sickly person to a different part of the hospital was the perfect amount of time to work my Chaplin routines. For patients who got to know me and saw me regularly, I wouldn't even have to call out their name. I would simply approach them with the beautiful Chaplin smile and walk over and do them a little dance. The elderly people especially loved this; I guess Chaplin must have been the same age as many of their parents. I could entertain any ethnic group, as Chaplin's silent humour was universal.

Sometimes it was difficult to maintain this positive act. One day, a few weeks ago, I had to take a small boy into the morgue. He had been a lively chap who I'd been taking for X-rays. He had his own bed spread with a cartoon mouse. He always looked so cosy in his bed and he would tell me about his books as I pushed his bed along like a chauffeur. It came as a terrible shock when I was asked to go up to the children's ward with the blue trolley. I thought it must have been some sort of mistake. I went to the ward with a middle-aged African man, named Junior, who was my favourite of my fellow porters. Junior spoke often of his own two young children, they were both boys and he'd said they were the reason he went to work everyday. Junior had a gigantic bright, white smile and an infectious laugh that always cheered me up, but as we approached the small child shaped bundle in a bedroom of the children's ward his smile had gone. The kid was lying in the familiar spot, but covered with unfamiliar sheets. As we moved the trolley into the room and got closer and closer to the body, I could hear my own heart thump violently in my chest and I looked to see Junior had a tragic thousand-yard stare.

Neither of us spoke as we uncovered the trolley and moved the boy across, before encasing him with the tarpaulin that stretched across the metal bars. We wheeled him to the elevator in a silent agony. I had to clear my throat and choke back tears.

Inside the dark, sterile caverns of the morgue, Junior broke down into a fit of sobbing and began to curse the unfairness of life. I felt obliged to make sure the proper thing was done with the boy. I moved him to a separate tray and slid him into his refrigerated chamber while Junior wept a lifetime of injustice. As I closed the door to the fridge, I closed the door to my belief in reason. I became more confused about life and my heart ached for the child. When my break time arrived, I went outside and cried, sniffling into my shirt.

Outside of work I do not dress fully as the tramp, but I always have something of his with me; the hat, the coat. I love to feel connected to this character as much as I can. I can't wear the outfit to work of course because of the uniform, but sometimes the hat and cane come out there too. I try to start conversations with the other porters, but only Junior is always friendly, the others block me out with crossword puzzles, reading or the small TV in the corner of the room. But sometimes I get them to talk, and sometimes I even get them to smile. I count how many people I can make smile each day. Then I try and break my record. It is my purpose for getting up. My record is now twenty-seven. I've started exercising too. I try to walk to and from the hospital each day even though it takes a full hour. I have also started going for swims and want to find someone I can play tennis with. I ask most people I meet but no luck yet.

The hospital is a great place to be The Gentleman Tramp because I know a lot of people feel sad. I greet patients with a smile on my face and I do my funny dances, tricks, drunken impressions and occasionally my falling over routines. I am regularly shouted at by real drunkards, who call me names but I am familiar to all this sort of abuse by now and I've begun to think of taunting as a sign that I'm doing the right thing. I only become really annoyed at work when it is my turn to clear the bins, which is often. Pushing the dirty, smelly things through a well-populated building is humiliating, especially when you pass a pretty nurse. Apart from money for food and some movies, I have been saving my wages away for Bruce. I have been volunteering for all the overtime so it is quickly adding up.

Patients often try and give me tips. I refused this money until a couple of families became insistent. 'My granddad he just loves you,' said one woman. Some of the other porters have picked up on this and have tried to emulate my happy style. They come back kicking things and saying it's not fair. Unfortunately a lot of my time is just wasted at the hospital, waiting for a call from other departments and I hate the slow quiet days. Life is too short and precious for this. On these days I read. I love to improve my mind. I have also been concocting business plans and my favourite idea is to open my own circus. I want to acquire exotic and amazing animals from around the world and employ experienced vets and animal experts to look after them. I want modern-day clowns that aren't dressed in colourful costumes, but just ordinary men performing funny business. I want to have magicians and performers with daring and cunning to bewilder the audiences. I want enticing, bewitching, sexy women luring customers into the world of wonder. The *piece de resistance* will be a choreographed stunt show starring me as The Gentleman Tramp. I don't need to search for romance and adventure anymore. I have both those things inside of me, I always have, and I simply need to share them with the world.

However, Mariana's emails have been filling me with joy and fresh travel ambition. She has so much hope and enthusiasm for life and the world. She has talked about how she is going to Tokyo soon for a new experience. She thinks her and her boyfriend need some time apart. I have begun to casually mention my own interest in seeing Japan. I daydream about us being together in this mysterious country. I know, she has a boyfriend, but there is nothing wrong with a good old daydream.

Two weeks ago I borrowed Dad's car for the day, I was feeling funny all morning so for my break I thought I might try and escape the hospital for a while and get some decent food. I had another patient to take from accident and emergency to the intensive care unit, but Junior offered to do it for me. Actually, he looked glad of the job as he'd been getting dirty looks from the lifeless drones in the porter's room because he'd started trying to play some bongos he'd brought in from home.
'Enjoy your lunch,' said Junior.
'Thanks'. I said.
Half an hour later, I was back in the hospital as a patient, being wheeled along on a trolley by Junior who was asking me what happened. I didn't know, but the police later informed me I was

fitting at the wheel and had driven up a curb and into a building. The car was a wreck. Nobody else was hurt, thank God. I shouldn't really be driving with epilepsy of course and I never will again. My parents were not pleased, but they seemed to be more worried about me than cross. God knows what could have happened. I began to feel all those old awful feelings return; the shame, humiliation, embarrassment and guilt and the desire to apologise for being alive. I've been trying to fight them ever since, as I don't want to live like that anymore. I lived like that for too long.

Bad things are always going to happen to me. It's no big deal; pain, rejection and even death are just temporary moments that are gone in no time. They're nothing to be afraid of. It is cowardice and suffering that lasts for eternity and that is what I want to avoid. So, I won't be scared anymore and I will battle on with romance and adventure in my heart, ready to share my love with everyone. No matter what happens life will always be good if I just remember to smile.

Just heard Mum crying and Dad telling her everything would be OK. I ran downstairs to find out what the problem was. They had received an email from a stranger, who said he were a friend of Bruce's. The gist of the message was that Bruce has contracted dengue fever and they're trying to get him to a hospital, but they're in the rainforest. They also said that he was struggling with the side effects of a hallucinogenic substance he had taken in the jungle that had made him 'behave out of character'.

There is not time to waste. I have booked a flight to Colombia and I leave tonight. It's my turn to help Bruce. I'm sure he'll be fine, he always is. I can't imagine Bruce being in any real trouble. Actually, I can't ever remember him being sick. He'll be fine, but I want to go and help anyway. Perhaps I'll go to Japan afterwards and see Mariana.

If you are to meet me on your own travels, please be nice to me. For The Gentleman Tramp will surely love you.

Made in the USA
Charleston, SC
05 May 2014